Fielded DREAMS

Content Warnings

This book has the following content warnings that may not be suitable for all readers:

- mentions of alcohol and food

- sexual content

- mental illness (anxiety and depression)

Dicktionary

The following chapters include on-page sexual content:

This book is dedicated to all my baseball lovers who are showing up and sticking through nine innings of America's pastime.

And to my grandpa, whose love of baseball transcends after all these years.
And to the Oakland Ballers, thank you for keeping baseball rooted in Oakland.

A Note From Brittany

Dear reader,

I was born and raised in the San Francisco Bay Area. Beyond that, I still live in the Bay Area, and I love it. When I was younger, I was exposed to the world of baseball thanks to my family. It all started with my grandpa (who has since passed), when he established my town's Little League in the late seventies. My dad played baseball until his teens (wrestling and football were more his thing) but my grandpa was still involved in baseball until his passing in 2003. Then my brother played Little League from eight until twelve and I was involved again in that world, doing things like scorekeeping and working the snack bar.

All that's to say, baseball is a big part of my life.

If you follow baseball closely, you may be aware of a team called the Oakland Athletics. The A's for short. They had a movie made based on the A's! It has Brad Pitt!

In recent years, the A's have been under arguably greedy ownership, who do not care about improving the well-being of the A's and essentially, letting it rot in a stadium that yes, isn't in a great area to begin with. And what do they do instead of trying to work hard to keep the A's rooted in Oakland? They petition to move. To Las Vegas. (Actually before that, they decide to play in Sacramento until their stadium is done being built.)

It is, arguably, a shitty situation. And as someone who actually is more of a Giants fan than an A's fan (sorry, still love the A's but I'm wearing Black and Orange when we're at a Bay Bridge Series game...well not anymore technically, RIP) I feel for the strong A's fans. I may not be a strong A's fan, but I am a strong Oakland fan. And I want to scream at all the negative things people talk about Oakland (things like good thing they're leaving, Oakland's a shithole, and I KNOW, but can't we focus on the good things Oakland has?)

So, when the Oakland Ballers announced they were going to bring baseball back to Oakland and make it stay, I was delighted. I've been to a game before, and have really enjoyed it. It's intimate, it's fun, their mascot is named Scrappy the Rally Possum, it's all around, a fun time. And as I sat on the bleachers in Raimondi Park, I thought to myself: let's make this the backdrop of a romance novel.

And thus, Fielded Dreams was born. Out of my desire to finally write a baseball romance, and the city who's been through a lot. I hope while you read Fielded Dreams, you think about the Oakland fans who have rallied behind the Ballers, behind "Sell the Team" and keeping baseball rooted in Oakland.

And most importantly, I hope you enjoy this book, with some knowledge of the reason why I wrote it.

For more resources on #RootedinOakland, you can check out the Oakland Ballers or @lastdivebar.

Love,

Chapter 1
Corey

Peering up at the posters hanging in my childhood bedroom of professional baseball players I looked up to, literally, before I went to bed every night, I ask myself, "What the fuck happened?"

When I was younger, I would shut my eyes and go to sleep, whispering phrases of motivation, I told myself I was going to be on a poster someday. I'd be famous in the major leagues, hitting home runs to the cheers of tens of thousands of people. Hell, maybe even become talented enough to get on a billboard that says, "Vote for Me!" when it came time to make selections for the All-Star Game.

But no.

Instead, I'm back at the last place I want to be: my childhood bedroom at the age of thirty, and no major league team poster or billboard showcasing my likeness on it.

I slump against my pillow, still the same striped navy blue and white pattern from my youth. Ironically, I was never a hardcore New York fan. My mom just bought it because it was on sale.

If there's something I should tell myself to prevent myself from moping as much, it's that I'm still a baseball player. Just not in the major leagues, not even the minor leagues, really. The Pacific league, they call it. A bunch of unaffiliated partner leagues spread throughout the West Coast. A select few are lucky enough to be called up to a team during the season.

I thought last season, I had it— my chance to be called up. I was playing in a Triple A team in Albuquerque, and each game I played, I tried to be patient. Wait for the moment someone would reach out to me. One game down, and another, and another, but no call. I guess my dreams were too lofty, because my record wasn't all that great anyway. I wasn't leading the league in home runs, just had a few decent good hits and an above average RBI. I wasn't wowing anyone, I was just doing my job helping the team advance a runner.

When the team let me go last season, I felt a pang of hopelessness vibrate throughout my body. I wanted to argue against my coaches. I wanted to scream "You don't know what you're doing!" but I couldn't let those be my parting words. I did ask why and they told me there was a stretch of time where I was just not performing to the potential they wanted out of me. To get us wins and all that. So, we parted with them saying there may be a chance that we might meet each other again. That I might get to a point where I could be major league ready. Their recommendation was to play in the Pacific league and they'd "keep their eyes on me."

"They've got a new team out in your hometown," Coach Ed tells me. "Neptune Beach Seals. After they approved the move from Oakland. Said there's that old abandoned plot of land where the amusement park used to be that will make for a great field."

Fuck. Anywhere but there, please.

"Yeah, I'm aware," I mutter.

It's the talk of the mid-sized town I grew up in. Neighboring city Oakland loses their major league baseball team and everyone's upset, rightfully so. The town has seen some shit when it comes to sports teams abandoning it. The first time, it was okay because they were moving across the Bay. This time, it stings. The owners basically said "fuck it" and are moving yet another team to Las Vegas. Don't get me wrong, I love some Sin City, but these are teams that I grew up with. My family had season tickets. Even though I live states away from them, I know that my parents still indulge in a few baseball games. They even got those fan-made "Sell" T-shirts to wear in protest.

Then, a few of those fans, after scouring locations for a park, decided to build it right along the bay in Neptune Beach. It's not Oakland; we are its smaller, bay side neighbor, but people are ecstatic that there's a potential now to watch baseball along the water. Really feels like they're inching closer to being just as cool as San Francisco. Maybe with the splash hit counter and everything.

"I talked to their coach. He said he's keenly aware of you and your recent performance in the minors. He'd be happy to give you a spot, doubly so because you're born and raised."

"Amazing." I will myself not to sound so despondent. I'm grateful to even be given the chance to still play baseball when apparently, I'm not good enough to even stay in the minors. Could it just be with any other team? I would actually love to play in other cities that have Pacific League teams: Ventura, San Luis Obispo, even in the hot Arizona desert. I already accustomed myself to the heat living in New Mexico. But, the one team that needs players is the one who's brand spanking new. The one team that's located ten minutes away from my family's home.

"Corey? Are you awake? I made breakfast!" my mom calls up from the first floor.

I roll over to my side and sit up straight in bed. I step onto the carpet and take a few steps to open the door.

"Yeah, I'll be down in a second!" I shout back.

I shut the door and hastily throw on a shirt from my closet. Most of my T-shirts are all from my former team, and anytime I wear them, I feel remorse about my life and the course it's taken, so I instead put on an "LGU Baseball" shirt I've had since college. My alma mater hasn't rubbed me wrong, yet.

I race down the stairs and walk into my parent's kitchen. As much as I want to frown that my life isn't all going to plan, my smile turns upward when the scent of cooked bacon and eggs fills my nostrils. If there's one thing Kim Ramirez can do, it's cook food that puts a grin on your face.

"Smells good in here," I note.

My mom turns away from the stove and smiles at me. "Well, good morning to you too! How'd you sleep last night?"

"Fine." My tone comes out monotone. I'm not great. I'm lamenting about the stiffness of a mattress that is a decade old. Past me is regretting selling my high end mattress I bought after moving because I took a pay cut and needed to set aside money in savings. I can tell my parents are picking up on my distant behavior, which turns my thoughts into more mush. Toying between feeling appreciative of my parents and yet feeling like I'm stuck with no light at the end of the tunnel in sight.

"Are you ready for your first day of practice with the Seals?"

"Yeah." I take a bite of the bacon and stand up to grab some hot sauce to sprinkle on the eggs.

"Nervous at all?"

I take a deep breath in the fridge, letting the cool air infiltrate my nose. I should try and be more responsive, for my parents, who love this town with all their hearts.

"Not really," I shrug. "I'm there to play baseball and that's what I'm going to do. I'm going to give it my all as I work toward getting drafted for a major league team."

"It'll come." My mom says it with a slight elevation. "I know one day you'll be in the outfield of a major stadium. You'll get the call."

"Yeah. I hope so." I swallow back some of my breakfast. I know it won't be tomorrow, next week, probably not even next month. All I can tell myself is that it will happen.

I push the chair back, wincing when I realize I scraped the legs against the floor and it sounds like nails on a chalkboard.

"Sorry. I'm just...I realized I should start getting ready. Get my stuff together for practice. You're still free to drop me off?"

"Yes of course, hon. Is it still at nine?"

"Yeah." I nod. "I'll be down here around eight forty-five. Thanks, Mom."

I take my plate and scurry back up the stairs toward the bedroom. It's a strange feeling: standing at the top of the steps while the house is so quiet you can hear the wood boards under the carpet creak with each step. My dad is out working, doing the same job he's been doing since I was in elementary school, fixing power lines. He's out of the house by six every morning. My brother's room is kept the same, but he barely visits home. Makes sense when you're the general manager of a five star resort in Ko Olina. The last time the Ramirez family was together was for Bryce's wedding two years ago.

I set the plate down on my desk and set my duffel on top of the bed. I'm as prepared as I can be. I have my arsenal of bats and gloves that I rotate through, clean baseball pants and shirts, and cleats. Oh, don't forget the cup. I'll get branded attire when I arrive to the park, received as part of a sponsorship deal from a local merchandise business.

For now though, I just wear a black athletic shirt and my old team's shorts. I sling my duffel over my shoulder and quickly step downstairs, right on schedule.

My mom grins at me once I hit the wood floor.

"What are you smiling at?" I ask with a slight grin back.

"You look just like you did when you'd go to Little League practice. I mean, yes, you are taller, but your face still is just as excited as you were going to the park all those years ago."

"You think so?" I don't want to tell my mom that her vision may be slightly deteriorating. I'm not wearing any sort of expression right now. If anything I might be excited to just get out of the house and experience the Bay Area weather I missed so much. The summers that aren't so dry and stuck in the nineties.

My mom tilts her head up to me. "I do. I don't know, you kind of have some glow to you. A Neptune Beach glow. Call it mother's intuition."

I chuckle. "Sure thing."

She drops me off at the field, and I give her a wave and tell her I'll text her when I'm finished.

The site of the former Neptune Beach amusement park is now just a lot of grass, a field, and some bleachers they they are working to build to house fans during games. Volunteers are putting together a small snack bar and they've set up some portable bathrooms until they fundraise enough to get plumbing built in. One lofty goal at a time.

There are already players warming up on the field. They're stretching on the grass and a few are talking amongst one another. I walk toward the dugout and drop my bag along the fence.

One of my teammates looks to his right at me once I set the bag down.

"Hey." He tilts his head up at me.

"Hey." I make eye contact for a brief second before returning to set my phone in my pocket.

"Kyle Berhow." He reaches his hand out. I grab onto it and shake it once firmly.

"Corey Ramirez."

"Ah, the Neptune Beach native." He nods slowly. Should I be excited that word is getting around about the irony of my origin? Right now, feelings lean more toward creeped out and slightly worrisome that being born and raised here is not something I should be boasting like it's tattooed down my arm.

"That's me." I shrug nonchalantly. "Hometown hero or whatever you want to call it."

"Sure, man." He laughs awkwardly. "I just thought it was cool they were able to get someone on the team that knows the town so well."

"Yeah, I guess it's pretty cool." And even with not living here for the past seven years, it truly does feel like things have changed and yet, stay the same. There are new homes being built, new restaurants replacing ones I'd frequent, but weirdly, the charm has yet to disappear.

A whistle is blown and everyone looks up to see that the group of coaches huddled in the outfield are calling for us to circle them. We jog over and I decide to stop short and give some distance between myself and the coaching staff.

"Welcome everyone to the Beach!" the head coach, Darrell Tucker, exclaims, propelling his assistant coaches to start clapping. The rest of the team clap and whoop after them and I fight myself to try not to barf. Couldn't tell you how many times I've heard that phrase uttered. Little League All-Stars. High school. Thankfully, our travel baseball team wasn't affiliated with the city so we called ourselves the Raging Water—not to be confused with the water park.

"We are so excited to welcome each and every one of you to this team. We are making history right now, being the first independent professional baseball league Neptune Beach has ever had."

That gets a few more whoops and I unknowingly start to grin myself. What? I can be upset that I'm not where I want to be and still be happy for everyone who rallied together to make this a reality.

"You all have traveled near and far to be a part of this momentous occasion. And we are so excited as well to have a player who was born and raised here in Neptune Beach." Coach shifts his gaze to me and raises his arm up in direction of where I'm standing. "Corey Ramirez here has been rooted in Neptune Beach baseball history since he was four years old, playing T-Ball with Neptune Beach Little League."

Everyone starts to turn their bodies a bit to get a look at me trying so hard not to shrink away and hide. Too bad there's not a hedge I can lean into and disappear. Instead, I just have to grin and bear it, like I'm so excited to be singled out in a crowd of thirty people for returning back to my hometown. If only they knew I'd rather be anywhere else.

***

We wrap up practice and I feel good afterward, rejuvenated. That's what baseball has the ability to do. It gets my heart beating faster and adrenaline coursing through my veins. I don't want to sit still. I could easily do another hour of drills fielding dingers in the outfield.

You can make an argument for each position on the field and why it's difficult. Being an outfielder requires you to run. When I was a kid, the first time I started playing baseball around four to six years old, if you got stuck in an outfielder position, it was because the coach thought that you were going to just pick up weeds whilst everyone else was still learning the fundamentals of swinging a bat. It was, at the time, the position that no one paid attention to.

It wasn't until I was older and players had more powerful hits that I started honing in on my position. I was a fast runner. If baseball and track weren't in the same season, I would've tried to do both. I was blessed with long legs and quick reflexes to run and catch any ball that dared to make its way to the outfield. I've even hit my chest a couple of times into the fence to ensure that the ball didn't land on the other side of it. Being centerfielder is exhilarating, and the rush of the outfield fans yelling when I make a leap for a ball makes me want to leap out of my clothes.

Everyone packs up their bags and begin walking to the parking lot, but I stop short at the curb and set my bag down.

The *thunk* sound it makes causes one of the players, Scott Eversole, to turn around and eye me standing near the curb with my arms crossed.

"You didn't drive?" he asks.

"No. My mom dropped me off."

He starts chuckling. "Aw, how sweet."

I narrow my eyes at him. You don't have to make snarky comments about my modes of transportation. We're not in high school, no one's trying to get street cred because they have a car anymore. Or shouldn't be. Well, I suppose except Scott, who exaggerates the motion of getting his key fob out of his bag and presses unlock on a black Audi sedan.

You play for a small town independent baseball league, Scott. No need to assert yourself as king of the parking lot with your basic European car.

"See you tomorrow, hometown hero."

I don't signal with anything in response back. I just lift my eyebrows and watch as everyone gets into their vehicles and speeds out of the lot. This snide remark with another teammate shouldn't have an effect on me. I don't need to be making friends when I'm trying to get the fuck out.

I feel a twinge of jealousy when I see him speed out of the parking lot. Something I miss a lot is my car. I remember saving enough to put a down payment on it six months after I moved to New Mexico. It was the first big purchase I made. I'd always wanted a Type R, and I bought one. Black with red trim. I'd take it out on rides on the open road when I wasn't playing baseball. It was the method I used to escape the stress from pressuring myself to be perfect so much. When I'm on the road, I don't think about it. I just admire the landscape in front of me. Saying goodbye to it was the hardest thing I've ever had to do. I know I could've kept it, but it wasn't paid off yet and I couldn't risk not being able to make the monthly payment.

Coach slides up next to me, looking straight into the abyss and nudges me in the arm. "Hey, good job today. You've got speedy legs. I know you're going to give us a strong outfield."

"Thanks, that's very nice of you." I don't turn to look at him and see if he's smiling or not.

"Waiting for a ride?"

"Yeah." I sigh. "My parents live ten minutes away. Shouldn't be much longer."

"All good. I'm not trying to kick you out."

Silence looms between us before he speaks up again. "So, how do you feel being back home?"

"It's fine." I shrug. "My parents are happy I'm home."

"But are you?"

I slowly angle my neck toward him. It's one thing to air out my frustrations to my parents, who despite their enthusiasm for me being home, also share in my commiseration that I'm destined for big things.

They tell me they'll fly whatever distance to see me take a major league field. Do I share that same sentiment with my coach yet? It feels wrong when he might already be picturing me as a rising star of this team.

"I'm just here to play baseball." That's enough out of me. We don't need to get into feelings on the first day of practice.

He pats his hand on my upper arm. "Yeah, keep doing that." In perfect timing, my mom drives up to the curb.

She waves to Coach and I nod to him before picking up my bag to put in the trunk. "I'll see you tomorrow, Coach."

"Yup. See you tomorrow, Ramirez."

My mom peers over from the window and excitedly waves at him. She starts to roll the window down and the moment my butt hits the seat, she shouts to Coach.

"Hi!"

Coach waves back and walks closer to the driver's window. "Hi, Mrs. Ramirez. Darrell Tucker, manager for the Neptune Beach Seals."

She shakes his hand. "Kim. Nice to meet you. How was practice?"

"Great." He smiles. "Corey here did a great job out there. He's a good outfielder."

"That is lovely to hear. Corey's been playing baseball his whole life."
And he'd very much like to go home now, thank you.

"He's a good addition to the Seals. I'm excited to see his progress."

My mom's grin grows. "We're so excited to be watching him in Neptune Beach. I'll be like going to his games as a kid again."

"That's great. Well," Coach swallows, "I'd better let you two head home. Corey seems beat over here. I'm sure he'd love to rest up before practice tomorrow. Good to meet you, Kim."

"You as well!"

My mom begins to drive off and once she turns onto the road with the bay alongside us, I rest my face on the window, looking out at the water, wondering how much time will pass before I can get myself out of Neptune Beach again.

Chapter 2
Corey

There is little that can cure my ache for being "stuck" where I'm at, but a trip to the town's local dive bar might at least help.

I'm sitting at the table, just recently finished dinner with my parents. Slow cooked chile verde with tortillas is always a go-to comfort meal. I clear my dishes and let my parents know I've decided to do something about my moping and traverse outside of my home, knowing that I will risk bumping into people that I may not want to.

"I am going to head to Jolly Oyster," I announce to my parents, who are still talking amongst themselves at the dining table. "Just for a quick drink to...celebrate getting through the first day of practice."

"Are you asking if you can take the car?" my dad asks.

"Yes," I confirm. "If that's okay."

"I know the Jolly Oyster isn't far, Corey, but I don't know if I would like if you drove."

I sigh. "That's fine. I should be safe. I'll just order a ride then."

"No, mijo." My dad begins to stand up and grips the table. While he spends much of his time moving around for his job, he's lost some strength to stand up as easily. "Let me drive you. You can call me when you are done and I'll pick you up."

"Dad." It is a kind gesture, but my parents are going to be in bed at nine. It does me no good to fight with my parents though, because they will argue that raising me and giving me a home, even now when I'd rather be on my own, trumps any argument that I should be making.

"Okay." I relent. "Thank you. I'll be in the living room."

Not long after, we get into my dad's truck and head to the small "downtown" area of Neptune Beach, which is mostly just three blocks of small restaurants, shops, and the Jolly Oyster. I have stepped foot in the Jolly Oyster once. My parents took me out for drinks at the longtime Neptune Beach institution to celebrate my twenty-first.

"Fancying yourself a drink tonight?" my dad asks once we he turns out of the little suburb my parents live in where all the houses are a different shade of "neutral".

"Just felt an itch I guess." I would call myself a social drinker, only engaging with it when I've been invited to partake. I don't want to fall into a rhythm where my lows lead to resorting to coping mechanisms, but I needed to get out of my house and of the funk that being borderline mocked as a "hometown hero" has led to.

"That it?"

My dad wouldn't ask that unless he had an inclination it was in fact, not it. While I hide things from my mom so I can best appease her mood, I always felt like I could confide in my dad about the struggles I've been dealt. Not to say that my dad is my unofficial "punching bag," but I've had my fair share of shouting fights with him growing up. That'll happen when your father was too busy to coach you during Little League but tried to critique your playing style on the sidelines anyway.

"I...I needed something to cope with after practice." Instead of getting into a spat with my teammate on the first day, I was going to drink the emotion away instead.

"Had a bad first day of practice?"

I lift my head up and look at the uncovered sun roof on my dad's truck.

"It wasn't a bad practice," I counter. "It just had its moments."

He starts laughing. "Okay...are you going to tell me what moments those were?"

I let out a breath. I should be honest and transparent about what I'm feeling, instead of letting these emotions bottle up inside me until I combust.

"Everyone wanted to comment about how I'm like a 'hometown hero', playing baseball in a city that knows me and I know it, but...I don't know. It's great that I'm a part of something that's so historic for the town but, I'm also trying to move on to do bigger things and move on quickly."

"Yeah, mijo. I understand." My dad's eyes remain fixated on the road in front of him. "But, your mom and I have been enjoying you home. That hasn't really happened since you were in high school, but I also want you to be able to spread your wings and live out your dream of being in the majors. And now with Oakland leaving, well, maybe you'll be lucky getting drafted by San Francisco."

But there are thirty two teams in the majors and being chosen to be in one nearby has what? Some low percentage I can't calculate off the top of my head.

"Maybe. I'll take what comes my way."

He flashes me a smile while still keeping his eyes on the road. "We'll go wherever you go. I haven't visited the East Coast much."

"There's some cool locations to explore. New York and Boston, Philly. Chicago."

"They're all so cold in the winter." My dad pretends to shiver when it's very much a comfortable seventy degrees outside. "I'll need to buy a jacket to wear in the snow."

"I'll make sure to get you and Mom one." I laugh. "If it happens to be that I move somewhere where it snows a lot. I won't really be playing during that time though, you know, because of how the schedule's laid out."

"Yeah you're right. Something that we're spoiled with here."

"You know you will probably run into people you know," my dad chimes in. "I don't know where else kids your age like to go in Neptune Beach other than the oyster."

"I know." I also know that while there are people from my small graduating class who have fled the nest and live all throughout the world, a good handful of them have stayed to build their lives in the only city they've ever known. And that's exactly what they had planned. Why go anywhere else when you know there's something for you here?

"Okay. In case you were fed up enough about being asked about baseball. You're never going to escape it."

"Yeah." I nod. "It's a part of my life, now and forever." But maybe if I have a glass to drink and let the alcohol warm me and lift me up to another level, for a moment, maybe I just won't mind.

"I just...need to be somewhere to feel like I can get away."

My dad pulls up to the outside of the building that houses the Jolly Oyster, which has a run-down beach shack vibe to it. Dark wooden panels that bring the building together and a painted wooden sign perched atop the slanted roof that says "The Jolly Oyster: A Neptune Beach Institution Since 1968" complete with a smiling oyster mascot next to it. There are some people milling about outside smoking and laughing amongst one another.

"You are welcome to stay as long as you like, but I'm letting you know that I also like to be in bed by a certain time, and your mom also doesn't want me to be out past a certain time, so..."

"I will get a ride if I stay out too late." And cross my fingers that hopefully there are rideshares available who will drive around town that late on a weekday if I do need to request one.

"Okay." The car makes a click sound when the doors unlock and I pull on the door handle to open it. "I'll see you later."

My dad nods. "Okay, have a good time mijo. Stay safe, please."

"I will." I close the door and wave to my dad before he drives away.

The doors to the bar are open already, so I walk in and take a place at the bar top. For a Thursday night, the bar is decently busy. Not full; no one is making a crowd just to order drinks, but there are people sitting on the bar stools, chatting with one another and a few of the dining tables are occupied with bigger groups. As I sit down, I hear the clanking of pool balls hitting one another and laughter at the back of the bar where there's the pool table that the bar's regular's enjoy congregating.

Once I sit down, it doesn't take long for the bartender working tonight to slide up across from me and begin making small talk before asking what I'd like. I don't recognize her. She's dressed in a black v-neck and black pants, and has curly false eyelashes and long, jet black wavy hair. Tattoos peek out from her sleeves and down her arms.

She lifts her head up. "How's it going?"

I tell her my go-to short response I've seemed to give a lot of people who I've met for the first time. "Fine."

She tilts her head slightly. This is a very "locals driven" bar, and she must be surprised I'm not a regular. "You from around here?"

I chuckle. "Believe it or not, I am. Just been a while."

She nods slowly. "Yeah, surprised we have a new guy come in on a Thursday. What can I get you?"

"Rum and coke to start."

She nods and starts building the drink. "So, are you visiting family?"

I shake my head. "Just moved back for work."

"What do you do?"

"I, uh," am starting to feel like I don't want to divulge that. "I'm in athletics."

She looks up for a beat and leans in to get a better look at me. I wonder if she'd call bullshit or maybe she recognizes me. I don't want to assume based on looks what kind of things she might be into, but sports doesn't seem like it is one of them.

"Athletics? What does that even mean?"

I sigh. At this point, I should've just said I'm in tech and then people wouldn't bat an eye.

"I..."

Before I can even get the sentence out, someone latches onto my shoulders and starts furiously shaking my body.

"Corey?" the familiar voice asks excitedly.

I turn around and let out an authentic gasp when I see a familiar face. "Oh my god, Lance?"

We shake hands and wrap our arms around each other. I guess I shouldn't be surprised Lance Fairbanks is here. My best friend when I was eight up until high school. Lance and I met because we were both drafted to the same little league team and instantly we became a dynamic duo. We were both stellar in our division, and people tried to separate us to have their fair share of the pot, but my dad did his fair share of convincing Lance's dad, who was our coach, to keep us together until we graduated from the league at twelve.

Lance was a good baseball player up until we graduated, and he even got a scholarship to play baseball for Cal Poly, but as he started going through the motions of school, practice, and games, he got overwhelmed quickly. When it came time near graduation, he decided to go on co-op since he was a Civil Engineering major, and said goodbye to baseball. He didn't think he was going to be drafted by any team and he'd rather go on a path of something more stable. Now, he works for the county water district. We haven't really spoken since college. Not that we spoke much then, we were both so occupied with everything we were involved in. But, if there's anyone besides my parents who I'm happy to see in Neptune Beach, it's him.

"Hey, congrats on joining the Seals, man. I would've called to ask if you wanted to hang out once you moved back but life's been busy. I wasn't even going to come out tonight because I was so tired from work, but I'm glad I did!"

"Yeah, now I'm starting to be glad that I came out too." Maybe I should've also tried to be the better person and reach out, but, with Lance and I going on a solid four year now of no contact, would he even have wanted me to touch base?

"Sorry I didn't reach out either," I say, reaching to take a sip of the beverage that was starting to grow condensation around the cup and wet my fingers once I pick it up. Boy, that is a lot of rum and not a lot of coke. "Still trying to get used to being back home I guess."

"All good." Lance grins. "Being an adult sucks. But hey, you're here now! And you got a drink in your hands. Time to get the party started. I've actually been playing pool in the back with some friends. Wanna hang out with us?"

I swallow back another sip. I might need a couple more of these rum and cokes to get through the act of socializing with strangers.

"Anyone I know?" There are a few more people from our class who also live here, but I'm a little selective about who I spent all my time with. Lance was at the top and a few baseball players who I was forced to see all the time followed after on my friendship pyramid. But a lot of them have since moved out of state or to Southern California.

"No." Lance shakes his head. "These are a bunch of beach transplants who work across the bay and live here. We all met from a running group and when we don't run, we drink."

"That sounds like a good way to spend your time."

We walk to the infamous back of the bar and a group of guys who now look like they're closer to my age once I step closer to them are milling about the table while there are still pool balls scattered about.

"It's your turn, Lancelot!" one of the guys chimes in. "We've been waiting for you."

Lance reaches up to scratch behind his ear. "Sorry guys, I bumped into an old friend."

"Lancelot?" I whisper to him. "Did you grow up and tell people you want to go by your legal name?"

Lance chuckles. "No, these guys just like how my legal name sounds. I go by whatever you want to call me."

I laugh, remembering what we used to call Lance in high school. "Should I bring back Glove Guru?"

He playfully rolls his eyes at me. "I haven't played catcher in almost a decade, I doubt I'd even be able to catch like I used to." Lance played catcher and he was very good at catching, obviously, but he also figured out strike zones well and had an arm enough to stop stolen bases.

"Hey!" Another friend waves at us to get us out of our nostalgic stupor. "Are you going to introduce us to your friend, Lancelot?" I still don't know if I'm used to hearing that. Even his parents only called him Lancelot if he was in trouble.

"Oh, yes! My bad. Guys, this is my friend Corey. We used to play baseball together."

One of the guys around the pool table perks up. "Wait, Corey? Are you Corey Ramirez? I think I saw you on some Neptune Beach social media page. You're playing for the new baseball team right?"

"Yeah." I nod. "I am."

"Corey used to also play for a few minor league teams too." Lance chimes in. "He was like, one of the best players growing up."

I elbow Lance in the arm. "Hey, you weren't so bad yourself."

"Yeah, but you actually got drafted by a team. I doubt I had what a team needed to get picked."

I don't want to argue against Lance and tell him he absolutely could have if he put effort into it, but that would insinuate I thought that he should have left giving up on being an engineer and the heavy commitment that came with it in hopes he would actually get the call. That's also why I kind of just stopped talking to him all the time, because at one point, I didn't know if me talking about baseball would make him upset he gave all that up to be in a career he dreamt of.

"Well, I'm still waiting for that call to start in a major league game, so I guess you can argue that I don't have what a team needs either."

He gives me a little forceful pat on the shoulder. "You will. Hit a few home runs, work some magic on the field, and you'll get there."

I smile a bit. "Thanks, man."

I decide to stick around, watching the guys take turns playing pool against one another. I don't engage in the act myself; I don't even know if there was a moment in time where I touched a pool cue, so I don't think I'd be very good at it if I tried. Lance tried to convince me that anyone who drinks a little bit is automatically good at pool, but I was actually content for once just people watching and occasionally talking to Lance's friends about growing up in Neptune Beach, leaving, playing baseball in different cities, and my weird funk I'm in finding my place back home.

After a few drinks and almost four hours of socializing, I realized it's almost midnight.

"Shit." I look at my phone. "Time flew. It's almost midnight."

"Yeah, I need to be up for work in six hours," Lance chimes in. "Did you drive?"

"No. My dad dropped me off. He offered to pick me up too, but he's probably asleep. I don't think he's going to like it very much if I called at midnight when he has to wake up early for work."

"I can drive you home." Lance walks over to close out his tab.

"Are you sure?" I trust that Lance wouldn't have offered if he didn't feel sure himself. I don't think I even saw him with a drink in his hand for a while. Once we started talking and playing pool, we kind of really forgot that there were drinks that we could order at the bar.

He nods. "It's fine. Your parents don't live far from me anyway. They're still on Bayport?"

"Yep, still there. How about your parents?"

"Still on Aragon. But I don't live there anymore."

"Ah, well you do have to escape living under your parent's roof at some point." Although Lance's parents lived in a five-bedroom Victorian mansion nestled in the wealthiest part of Neptune Beach. When we were kids, it felt like we could be as loud as we wanted upstairs and no one could hear us down the hall, or on a lower floor. That's how large it was, with all the nooks and crannies that made it the best home to play hide and seek. And, cherry on top, there's a pool.

We walk outside to the quiet, empty street. A block away from the Oyster is Lance's car, or truck I should clarify. It's a nice maroon color, and looks almost brand new.

"Sweet ride," I quip.

"Thanks." The doors unlock and we sit down on the plush leathery seats. "Bought it last year. My mom insisted I should keep driving the Mercedes because they wanted to just buy the newest model, but I needed to get a car that I finally wanted."

"Makes sense. So, where are you living if you're not at your parents?"

"I rent an apartment near Freeport Shopping Center. God, trying to convince my parents to do that was like pulling teeth. I swear, my siblings are never escaping that house. They're all like 'Save money! Live at home!' Leon's still in college so that makes sense. Leanne, well, she's still practically glued to my parents so I guess it makes sense she wants to stay too."

I shake my head. "Don't know what that feels like."

"What?"

"You know, actually wanting to stay at home. Not being sick of eating dinner with your parents even as an adult."

Lance tsks. "Leanne's different. She's...she's like Neptune Beach's biggest fan. Everyone knows her."

"Yeah." I chuckle. "Hey, that's good for building community." I don't know too much about the goings on of Lance's siblings beyond what I follow them quietly on social media. Leon, the youngest, is wrapping up undergrad and got accepted to law school at Stanford. The one child following in the family law practice. The one firm in Neptune Beach. Leanne graduated with a degree in Business and somehow, well thanks to her parent's actually, got enough money to start a food truck that is now one of the most beloved businesses in the entire town. Hell, the entire East Bay Area. She's got the biggest social presence out of all the Fairbanks.

"She is. She's going to go places. Or, she should. But she doesn't want to."

I scoff. We couldn't be more opposite.

Lance pulls up to the driveway of my house and puts the truck in park. "It was good seeing you man," he notes. "Seeing you kind of made me miss when we didn't have to partake in adult responsibilities and just goof off like we used to."

"Yeah, those were the good ol' days."

Suddenly, an idea comes to Lance. "Hey, if you're not doing anything tomorrow, you want to have dinner with us? Leanne usually cooks a dinner once a week for the family and Leon drives home for the weekend. I'm sure my parents would be really excited to see you again."

I tug on the hem of my shirt. On one hand I'd be thrilled to see the Fairbanks family again, as they've all grown. But on the other hand, am I entering into a realm where I shouldn't be, getting too attached to a family I know will forever be rooted in this town? Put my best face forward for those who want to sing the town's praises with everything they do?

Sure, I can swing a night.

"Yeah." I nod. "That sounds great. I'd be happy to see your family again."

"Great!" Lance beams. "Be there at six?"

I shoot him a grin before going back inside and contemplating my decision. "I'll be there."

Chapter 3
Leanne

There is no better feeling than being aroused by the smell of your own cooked food.

Maybe being aroused during sexual intercourse evokes some better feelings, but I haven't felt that in a long time.

When I went to college, a part of me knew I'd always find my way back. I just never thought I would be doing something completely different than what I studied.

My mom saddles up to me while I'm stirring a pot of corn chowder I made as our starter for dinner tonight.

"Looks delicious, Lele. I don't think I've ever seen you make a chowder before."

"I went to get lobster this past weekend and they had this delicious corn chowder. I knew I just needed to make it again for myself." I don't think I could've splurged for the lobster to add in, though. I love my family but I'm going to need to sell a lot more meals to afford "lobster dreams."

"Well," my mom starts to gently pat my back, "we're always happy to try anything that you want to feed us." I lean into her and she plants a kiss on my cheek.

Being a chef was never on my dream career list. When I was younger, it was a basketball player. Then, it became a Broadway performer. Then, it was to be in sports. Becoming a chef was merely a happy accident.

It all started one day when I was cooking in my college apartment, trying to conjure up any dish I could with my low college student's budget. I wanted to replicate as much of a home-cooked meal as I possibly could. So, I'd drive to the nearest Asian grocery store, stock up on assortment of noodles, sauce, and meat, and just make, in a sense, oodles of noodle dishes.

Once I had the recipe perfected, I brought them to potlucks with my friends. Then, I'd start making potstickers and other Chinese dishes. I politely asked my Po Po how to make a doong, or sticky rice wrapped in banana leaves. I took a class in entrepreneurship to fulfill my degree requirement and was hit by the inspiration to make my cooking hustle into a small business, and it blew up. It helped a lot that the student population was heavily skewed toward Asian, Chinese specifically. I just didn't think I'd go viral to the point where, after I graduated, people wondered what was going to be next for "The Dragon's Belly."

I have to be thankful my parents believed in my dream as much as I did, so they helped me out when I wanted to buy my own food truck to take my business on the road.

Now, I get to be the only food vendor that will be at every single Neptune Beach Seals game to serve my Chinese comfort food for thousands of people who want to flock to the park to watch some baseball players play.

"Even if I want to try making something with pork blood?" I grin. It's not going to happen, because I don't think that I could stomach it myself, but it's fun to see my mom's eyes almost bulge out of their sockets in shock.

"Um." She gulps. "Sure, honey. If that's what you're interested in making."

"Don't worry," I reassure her. "I've never even tried pork blood. And I'm actually kind of scared to."

She sighs. "Good. While I do think that you can make anything turn out a masterpiece, there are some ingredients that are harder to cook with than others."

"Trust me, I know." I think about experimenting with different ingredients all the time, attempting to conjure up some special limited-edition menu items that might fare well with my audience, but I've never pulled the trigger. I'm stuck in my ways. Maybe that's why I've decided to stay in the Bay Area my entire life. I was born and raised in Neptune Beach, then when I was accepted to a number of colleges, I could have gone anywhere in California. But I decided to go to a school that was less than half an hour away from my parent's house. I came back to Neptune Beach to grow my own business in a town I know and love like it was tattooed on my sleeve.

Change is scary and I'm terrified of taking the plunge.

I continue making the rest of the courses I have planned out: home-made pesto pasta, and grilled lemon pepper salmon. Lance emailed the family group chat this morning, asking us to make an extra serving for someone he was planning to bring over. He didn't disclose who, but my first inclination was to think that Lance was bringing a date. Weird that he's yet to tell us that he's dating, and he thinks the first thing they should be exposed to is a dinner with his arguably loud and energetic family? That seems logical.

"Hello!" Leon's voice echoes throughout the first floor.

"We're in the kitchen!" I call out to him. Leon's a fourth-year Econ major at Stanford. He comes home every weekend for home-cooked meals and grocery trips with Mom and Dad. Looks like he might be repeating the pattern for the next few years as he also got accepted to Stanford's prestigious law school and submitted his intent to attend.

"How's it going?" he asks, reaching to wrap his arms around Mom. "Smells good in here."

"Thanks." I beam. "Corn chowder, pasta, and salmon. More of a homestyle meal this time around, but still will do its job of hitting the spot."

"I'm sure whatever you make is going to be delicious, Leanne."

"D'aw." I swipe my hand away. "Look at you trying to win best brother."

"Speaking of brother, Lance here yet?"

I shake my head. "No, and what's up with this 'I'm bringing a plus one' text? Who is he bringing to infiltrate family dinner?"

"No idea. Do you know, Mom?"

We both eye her, waiting for her response, but she simply just shrugs her shoulders, clueless like we are.

"I don't know. Lance just said it was a friend."

I tilt my head back. "God, that could mean anyone."

"Do you think it's a date?" Leon asks.

"No." Maybe? I don't know. It doesn't seem like Lance to be so secretive if it was. "And why would he bring a date to family dinner? Unless he liked the person to think they were good enough to meet the family."

"You're right." Leon nods. "They need to earn that right."

Suddenly, we hear footsteps entering through the doorway and murmurs of two people talking amongst each other.

"Hey, I'm here!" Lance shouts.

"In the kitchen!" Leon responds.

Lance walks in, grinning at all of us as he steps into our now-crowded kitchen. I know that everyone is eager to get their grub on, but I still need to plate everything and set the table.

"Hey, guys." Lance waves to us.

"Who's the friend you brought?" Leon asks immediately.

"Woah." Lance holds his hands up. "Hello to you too. He's coming in a second, just needed to use the bathroom once we got inside."

Behind Lance walks in a man about the same height as him, with a sturdy build. He's wearing a black Neptune Beach Seals hoodie and shorts and I gasp once I realize who the curly, short-haired, light brown skinned man standing next to my brother is.

"Oh my god, Corey Ramirez?" my mom squeals. She rushes over in a snap to envelop her arms around him. "Well, this is a huge surprise!"

Corey stumbles back a little bit and lightly pats his hands on my mom's back. "It's great to see you, Mrs. Fairbanks."

My mom scoffs. "You know that you don't need to call me that as an adult. It's Lisa to you."

"Okay, Lisa."

Leon slides up next to them and is beaming whilst looking at Corey Ramirez in the flesh. It has been a long time since I've seen Corey. Since he was in high school. Him and Lance were inseparable from the moment they got put on the same Little League team together. It felt like every week Corey was over at our house, but I'd only see them for a minute. Once he came over, him and Lance immediately retreated to Lance's room and they'd only leave to get a snack or something to drink.

When I was younger, I got actual FOMO when Lance and Corey would be playing games and I was never included. It sucks to be a middle child and it sucks big time to be a female middle child in between two men.

"Dude, it's been what? Six years? And you're a pro baseball player now? That's awesome, man."

"Hey, thanks." Corey nods at Leon. "And I heard you're going to Stanford Law School next year. That's awesome."

"Eh." Leon blushes. "It just means I've signed my life away to the legal system. At least I'm familiar with the campus."

"Hey." My mom gives him a stink eye. "We are very proud that you have decided to pursue law. We're very proud of all our children and their accomplishments."

"But we all know Leon's going to be the one who is bringing home the moolah," I quip. Whereas I decided to be the one child who took a chaotic route and spend her savings to start a business that has a small following. Boy, do I hope these Seals fans have a craving for some stir fry.

Corey lets out a slow chuckle and my gut reaction is to just blink profusely.

Did I mention teenage me had a monumental-sized crush on Corey Ramirez? And now, looking at him again, some other new feelings come into view. Like how he's not the teenager I thought was cute. He's got full arms, and his hair grows over his forehead a little bit, as opposed to the short cut he had in high school. It's like a glow radiates around him every second I fixate on him.

"Hey, Leanne," he says, stepping closer to me. Oh no. I probably smell like sweat and cooked salmon. He steps to the side and gives me a one-armed hug around my shoulder. "It's good to see you."

And that, my friends, is why I can't be ogling at Corey Ramirez. Because to him, I'm still just the little sister.

"It's good to see you too, Corey." I smile. "I'm excited to see you play for the Seals. I'll be at all the games. Not because I'm a huge Seals fan, which I am, but I won't really be watching any games."

God, why is it now that I'm becoming such a worder?

"Yeah." Corey nods. "Lance told me you're catering the games with your food truck?"

I nod with a little more vigor than deemed necessary when it comes to talking about me and my job.

"Yes!" my mom juts in. "Leanne secured a deal with the Seals to be at every single game with her food truck! And she's catering the Meet the Team Donor event next week at the Boathouse."

Oh yeah, that event. Where I'll also be seeing Corey, likely in full uniform. But more frightening, that event will be the chance where I can hopefully schmooze people in Neptune Beach who I know have large sums of money because they had to have donated at least a thousand dollars, if not more, to make the Seals team possible. If I can schmooze them, they may eventually use me to cater their corporate events or lavish anniversary parties at their beachside mansions.

"Yep." I nod. I need to figure out what my menu is, whenever I can focus on anything else that's not Corey's face. Corey's...everything.

"Oh yeah, I'm supposed to be at that. Tell all the people who have donated to the team we really appreciate you and stuff."

"My parents will be there," Lance chimes in. "Because the firm helped donate enough to help the team put a big LED screen in the outfield to project who's at bat and the score."

My mom's cheeks start to turn a hint of pink. "We are just doing what we can to help because we love baseball and we love Neptune Beach."

I am very proud of being the daughter of two people who have worked hard to be successful and are able to afford to donate thousands of dollars to help a small, brand-new baseball team install a scoreboard. As much as I want to boast that I worked really hard to build my business and gain the following I have, my parents helped me buy most of my equipment to start out. I can still be proud I'm a woman of color owned business, but I'm in the same crowd of the rich and elite of the beach just by being born to a white lawyer dad and a Chinese-American mom who had to work two jobs to provide for her immigrant parents and get herself through college.

"Well, I am very thankful for you. For helping out the team and also being so welcoming to me when Lance and I were younger. I...appreciate that I had a place to escape to."

I blink at him. Did Corey just admit to having a tough time growing up? I've met his parents. I've even bumped into them at the store after Corey moved out. His parents are super sweet. I guess they don't need to be to blamed. Maybe it's not because of his parents. Maybe he's battling monsters in his head that I never questioned growing up and I only want to ask about now.

"Oh, don't make me cry before dinner," my mom says. She sniffles once before reaching to wrap her arms around him again. "You are always welcome here. Even if none of the kids are home. Julian and I only go into the office three times a week now. We're always free to grab lunch, go for a run. But, I am not very fast. I may just walk. These joints don't work as well as they used to."

"Walks are always fun. That's one thing I've been looking forward to since coming home. There weren't really beaches to walk along in New Mexico."

Everyone mills about in the kitchen some more, talking amongst one other while I put on the final touches for dinner. My mom's poured everyone a glass of wine and the table is set, complete with gold bead chargers my mom insisted we bring out for this special occasion. Eventually, everyone leaves to take a seat because they know that I will be bringing the food soon. Everyone, except one person who wants to wander around the kitchen aimlessly looking for something. Who made the guest of honor look for something in a house he hasn't stepped foot in almost a decade?

I set the pot of soup down on the kitchen island in front of me. "Looking for something?"

"Um, yeah," Corey says, looking to his left toward the sink. "Just a glass for water."

"In the cabinet to the right of the sink."

He turns in that direction and opens it up. He peers in and sees that, lo and behold, there are tiers of water glasses, each from a different fundraising event we've participated in over the years.

"Cool, thanks." He grabs a glass and walks over to the refrigerator to dispense ice and water into it.

Do I let the silence loom over us? Do I ask him questions like "How's it been?" and "What's it like to be home?"

When both Corey and Lance both received athletic scholarships to play baseball in college, everyone was ecstatic. Obviously, with baseball being such a major facet of our lives for so long, I manifested a draft pick for both of them. Lance ultimately got burned out, had a big case of imposter syndrome, and decided not to pursue the draft. It was disappointing, but I understood the desire to pursue something more secure. And he had a job lined up with the county water district.

Corey getting selected was an amazing moment. He was like an unofficial brother in our family. He called Lance to tell him the good news and then his parents put on a small celebration at their house.

That was the last time I ever saw him.

I won't say that Corey being drafted to the major leagues was a bad thing to happen, but I wonder if things would have been better if he accepted a fate that included coming back home and building a life here.

I guess now's the time to find out.

"Smells good in here. I'm excited to try some of your cooking," Corey states before I can get any of my thoughts out.

"Oh!" I raise my eyebrows. "Thank you. I hope it tastes good then."

"I don't doubt it will, Leanne."

My breath hitches. This is just him being nice, right? This is not something I should be reading deeper into?

"Um." I clear my throat. "I'm going to go and bring the food out to the table." I start to slide my hands into pot holders and grab onto either side of the platter where I've set the salmon.

"Do you want help?"

I shake my head. "No, no. You're our guest. I'll bring everything out. Keep everyone eagerly waiting at the same time."

He nods. "Alright. Looking forward to it."

"Yeah, good." I croak. I'm also looking forward to seeing how long he'll stay around, but something tells me I shouldn't be holding my breath.

Chapter 4
Leanne

"Does my chef's shirt look okay?" I ask my mom while she puts some finishing touches to my table scape.

We're in the event space where the Neptune Beach Seals are hosting their donor appreciation event. It's an old Navy airplane hanger they've spruced up and decorated with lounge furniture, cocktail tables, and lights in different shades of blue.

There's a lot of differences from running a food truck to catering a private event. I thought that I could just make food and people would come. But my mom, with all the insight she has about events where people of wealth are in attendance, advises to me that you need to dress up the table. Put the food into little cute containers so it's memorable. God, the amount of work that I had to put in to order these small Chinese takeout containers and put stickers of my logo on them was time I could have spent doing other shit like perfecting recipes. When I work the food truck, I normally wear an apron and t-shirt, but my parents surprised me with a black chef's shirt, embroidered with my name on it and "The Dragon's Belly," so I couldn't opt to wear something else.

"You look beautiful," my mom grins, stepping closer to me. "You always look beautiful, but you are rocking that shirt." She leans forward and picks up a part of my collar. "Leanne Fairbanks, Chef. The Dragon's Belly."

At least I feel official.

"Now hopefully, people will see my amazing table and taste my amazing food and I'll start to get inquiries about catering large-scale private events!"

"I think you're going to get a good crowd. Your dad and I will even send our friends to come and try your food."

That's very nice of her to offer. Let's just hope I don't disappoint. "Thanks, mom."

She rubs my arm, picking up on the heightened nerves I contain. "You're going to do amazing. I can't wait for everyone to experience your amazing dishes."

"Me too," I whisper. The "what ifs" keep rattling around in my mind and many of them lean negative.

The event starts and I'm surprised how many people are dressed to the nines for this event. My parents dress the same as they usually do: a good ol' blazer and pants combo. My mom's is a satin, ocean blue color, and my dad dawns a gray suit and navy blue tie.

But some of these attendees are in dresses, heels, and luxury branded suits that scream, "I have money to buy something that has the Gucci logo patterned on it."

This is very different from my typical crowd of people who see me at the food truck fairs. Or if they are the same people, they are much more mellow tonight.

I smile as a few people begin to take the small takeout boxes filled with various dim sum sampler dumplings. I try and get an initial read on what their thoughts are. I don't know why I'm hoping someone is going to react like a kid in a candy store and start jumping for joy. If it's going to give me some affirmation that my food is good, it should be like how I react when I'm going to a dim sum restaurant, seeing the carts of food pass by and picking bounties of what dishes I want. It's hard to perfect the art of dumpling making, and go on to steaming it and hope it doesn't stick to the point where it falls apart, but I love a good challenge. And I'm fueled by the desire for it to be just as good as what I've tasted in restaurants.

I make sure that the table's fully stocked and then I waltz over to the buffet area where my team has been hard at work preparing the stir fry noodle dishes and shrimp.

"Hey, Leanne," Jackson, one half of the Seals leadership team comes up next to me. "Thank you again for catering our event. The food looks amazing."

"Oh, you're welcome! I hope everyone likes the food."

"That's why we picked you to cater it. Because we really like the food and we want our guests to also know that too. Plus you're going to be at the games. People won't be able to escape you."

Well that's one way to coerce people into trying your food. Just force them to because there's no other choice. Well, there will be other food trucks rotating every game, and the typical hot dogs, chicken tenders, and garlic fries.

Maybe in comparison, no one would want to eat my food when they can have chicken tenders. I know chicken tenders are comforting, but I want people to have the mindset they can try something else too. Something you might not always find in a ballpark.

"Good point," I nod. "Well, I still appreciate you making all this food for the event. You came up with quite the menu. I'm very impressed."

I start grinning. "Thank you. This is kind of a new thing that I'm experimenting with. I have the food truck and do pop ups at the farmer's markets, but I've taken off so much that I think I could have a real shot at doing private event catering, so I'm hoping to let people know that tonight."

"Well, I will definitely send some people your way," he tells me. "I know your parents are here too doing the same thing, but we'll shout you out during the program too. This food could be yours if you just walk up and try some." Jackson does that sentence in a little Price is Right voice and it takes some of the nerves off from what I was feeling earlier.

"Thank you Jackson. And thanks for allowing me the chance to work with something so important to the community."

"Anytime," Jackson smiles. "Don't forget to have fun tonight! We have an LED dance floor that I want to see you tearing up later."

"Hah." I tilt my head back. I think I'm going to need a little bit of motivation and a lot of wine to get me to get freaky on the dance floor. And to get me to point where I can do that with the potential of Corey seeing.

"I'll try to have fun. Promise." I don't know in what capacity that looks like, but I will try to not be focused on trying to make tonight perfect.

I turn around and see my hired staff for the night: my best friend from high school, Emma, who doubles of my sous chef, and Vic, who is Leon's age but reached out to me to help out with events because he's interested in learning to be a chef as well.

"How's it going, team?"

Emma and Vic are beaming when I meet their gaze. Glad I chose a team of people who are happy to be here and who share a level of passion almost on par with mine. Who can be excited for me, even if I'm struggling to let loose myself.

"We're great!" Emma says. "Everything is in chafing dishes. People have told us it smells amazing and they can't wait to try."

"Great," I nod. I hold up little promotional cards and show them my attempt at making something pretty.

"Make sure that while you're keeping an eye out for people taking the food, that you also let people know that we're branching out beyond our pop ups and the food truck. We're trying out private events and catering and we're available to take inquires. We have to sell ourselves, and even though you all shine in the kitchen and serving to guests, we have to sometimes put an extra smiling face on to make sure that people remember us."

Vic holds out a thumbs up and points it towards me. "You got it, boss!"

Moments later, Jackson welcomes everyone to the event and tells them that the food is ready for them to grab food, keeping his promise to shout out me, The Dragon's Belly, and every exciting thing we're trying to do. He speaks very fond of me and the business, stating things like, "We're so happy that we have the pleasure of welcoming a local, woman of color owned and operated business during our home games." People claps and let out a couple of whoops while I try and contain the flush spread across my face. I know that all of those accolades Jackson listed off are supposed to give me a little bump too, but a part of it makes me also feel like I have a lot of responsibility as someone who may not have it as easy as some other businesses. I want to make sure that the food I serve still touches someone, even if its a cuisine they may not be accustomed to.

Once everyone sits down and begins nibbling at their meal. I take a quick scan through if I can see a read on people's reactions. Everyone just looks...focused. Some are chatting in between bites. No one looks to detest their food which is a plus. I peer over to take a look at Corey. It's still so surreal that he's back in Neptune Beach. Him sitting at the dinner table last night like he's a part of the family. He used to join us for dinners at least once a month when him and Lance were in high school. Back then, he was a bit of a chatterbox. He used to not be so timid. He just wanted to talk about baseball, constantly. My parents loved to listen, because they supported baseball since Lance began playing. I was too fixated on his pretty face light up as he talked to focus on anything else.

Right now, he's keeping his eyes trained on the food that's in front of him and he's like an outlier against the other baseball players that are surrounding him, who are happily chatting and eating the food on their plates.

Does he get along well with the team?

Is he just not happy to be here?

What is going on in that mind of his?

Why am I so eager to know?

I'm taken out of the trance I'm in once a couple comes up to put some more food on their plate. When I take a second glance at them, I realize that their not just any couple.

I make eye contact with Greta and Tony McDonnell, own the Cardinal Point Winery. Besides having a wine that is delicious and costs a hundred dollars a bottle, they also have a beautiful venue space that hosts a bounty of elegant and luxurious weddings, with large budgets. If I can be on their preferred catering list so that couples can choose me to cater their wedding, I will be over the moon. It will add so much business and be the next thing I need to grow into what I dreamt The Dragon's Belly of being. Especially because I know from their social media and people I've known since high school who are Asian like me, get married there and have beautiful Chinese banquet weddings.

Hell, I was almost going to have one there myself.

I stop the weird staring contest that I'm having with her and make conversation. "Enjoying the food?"

"Yes," she nods. "It's very delicious. I need to give my regards to the chef. And lucky for me, she's right here."

I start to blush. "Well, thank you. I, um, know that you have a wedding venue just up the hill and this is kind of my catering business, so I wanted to see if there was a way I can look into being a preferred caterer? If you have an opening?"

She jumps a little bit, like she might have been surprised that I asked here. Am I even important and relevant enough to be asking her for such a thing? They tell you to shoot your shot, but I'm asking to be in the likeness of huge catering companies, some that bring in millions of dollars a year in revenue, which I can't compete with yet.

"Miss Fairbanks." Oh no. She proper named me. This can't be a good sign. "I think that the food you've prepared is delicious, and I wish you great success in your endeavors. I just think this cuisine is...niche. It tastes amazing and you're a very talented chef, but events want to see a robust menu."

I nod. "I understand." I didn't understand. All I was fixating on was how the first thing she said about my food was that it was niche. We have a strong Asian population in and near Neptune Beach. I can be what they need as a Chinese woman chef.

She elaborates. "And you can have variety while still having a majority Asian menu. I don't want you to think that I'm telling you no now because we don't want an Asian-owned catering company. We just think that you need to bring more that we can offer it to guests. Any prospective guests."

"That makes sense." I try and not sound too disappointed. "I appreciate your feedback. I hope that I'll soon be able to come back with something to continue the conversation."

"And I hope so too."

"Thank you," I whisper. I take a deep breath and exhale through my mouth when they walk back to their seats. I need to step away for a moment, so I scurry over and pretend to be busy clearing off the table where we put out the appetizers.

I don't want to start crying. I want to tell myself that Greta McDonnell is right. I'm still so new and I don't have a fleshed out menu. I don't have a lot of experience in events. And I'm...

I don't want to agree that I'm niche. I don't want to be excluded because I'm highlighting a menu that showcases another country's cuisine. It's the food that my family and ancestors eat, and there are so many other people out there who are like me that love our culture's food too.

"Hey," a voice comes up next to me. I turn my body and see that Corey's standing right next to me. Shit. I feel tears spilling out from my eyes from the thought of putting myself as a "niche."

"Oh," I whisper. "Hi Corey."

His face softens. "Hold on, are you crying? What happened? Is everything okay, Leanne?"

I sniff. "Yeah. I'll be fine."

My fists are balled up on the table as I try to stop crying. My eyes trained on the tablecloth and I see a hand close around mine. Without thinking, I interlace my fingers with his because I just needed to feel secure about something, and he gives it a light squeeze back.

"Wanna talk about it?"

I shake my head. If I talk about it, I'm never going to get over this headspace that I'm in. But I also shouldn't keep feelings bottled up, and if there's someone who's here to listen to what I have to say, a friend who actually might care?

I take in a ragged breath and deflect from my sadness. "I'll be okay, I promise. Did you like the food?"

"Yeah, yeah of course I did Leanne. The food was delicious. Why, did someone say it wasn't good?"

"No, it wasn't that. Do you know about Cardinal Point Winery? Like...I don't know if you've been there."

"No, I've never been. But...name rings a bell, maybe because my parents brought it up. I might've went to a wedding there when I was younger. Why?"

"So, the owners of the winery are here tonight and I thought, I was given the best chance to talk about The Dragon's Belly and sell my services and maybe I was a little too confident, but I got told that my food is...too niche for what they want to show their clientele." I try and not choke as I replay the events to Corey out loud.

"My dream is to take *The Dragon's Belly* and make it into something that is more than just a food truck that I have to drive around from place to place, and I thought this would be a perfect thing. It would take my business to the next level. It's a beautiful venue located in the mountains and so many people host events there, and I think that I have the opportunity to do something to expand my reach with the community and create some amazing food that doesn't limit me to just a truck, and...it just kind of is hard to get told no. I mean, I get where she's coming from..."

"Do you?" Corey butts in.

I blink. "Yeah. I'm not as established as the other catering businesses on their preferred lists." I'm new. I didn't have a proposal built up to show her. There are little things that I didn't do to be more prepared.

"Is it rude of me to say that I don't agree with her?"

I shake my head. "Um, no. I guess not. Why do you not agree with her?"

"I think that she's asking that you're supposed to be like every other caterer in their book. But you're not like every other caterer. You make food that's an ode to your heritage and your family and so what if it's niche? It's not like this place isn't teeming with Asians. They should be happy that an Asian caterer is reaching out to them."

I fumble on what I should respond with. This is the longest conversation Corey and I have had since he's been back to Neptune Beach. After thinking he has nothing to say to anyone, he's pouring out his thoughts to me. And gripping onto my hand to show he care's or something, to top it all off.

"I...I know. And I'm going to show that to them." I don't bitch and moan about how I think they're also making a mistake. And I definitely don't look like I'm about to melt from Corey Ramirez actually showing some consideration for how I feel.

"You will." He nods. "If there's anything I know about a Fairbanks, it's that they're going to keep at it until it gets done. I'm going to get back to my table now. I'll see you later."

"Okay," I gulp. "See you. And thank you, for the little pep talk."

He tilts his head up. "Anytime. Just doing what any friend would do."

Friend. What a word. That makes me feel good I have someone in my corner, and yet, simultaneously, that I've been trapped in a box in Corey's mind, and how I have this wild desire to be something more.

Chapter 5
Corey

Today's the day.

The Neptune Beach Seals opening home game.

I slide my hands down my ocean blue colored jersey, moving to trace the embroidered "Seals" across my chest.

We're sitting in the dugout when Kyle comes up next to me and asks me if I'm ready for the game today.

"Yeah." I nod. "Well, I'm just going to get out there and play. It is my first time playing against this team so I don't know how good they are."

"They won the championships last year," he quips. "But every season's different. Our best case scenario is that they are suddenly not good and we'll win. We have some good players this year."

"We do." And it was something I genuinely believed in. After weeks of practice and understanding how everyone's play style fits in with one another, we have a pretty decent team. So far, we've only done scrimmages with one another so it's hard to gauge how we'll fare against the competition. All I'm hoping is I can get a few hits this game.

"I'm hoping I'll get a home run this season," Kyle says.

I raise an eyebrow at him. "Have you never hit a home run before?" I think he said he just graduated from college, so this is his first time being on a professional team. And I know I'm only six years older than him, but I feel ages older just because of how many games I've played with people who have later gone on to play in the major leagues.

"No," he says. "I've had plenty of hits in college, but never a home run. The closest I got was the ball hit the fence but bounced back into the outfield."

"Damn, those are the worst. Not for the person that hits it, obviously. For outfielders like me who try and run as fast as they can to keep the runner at second."

Plus, it makes me worried I might throw it with enough power but it might not get to the infield fast enough to make any plays. Or turn into a really sloppy one.

"You've got a good arm. You're amazing to watch in the outfield. I know that I'm one of the younger players on the team, but I think that I can learn a lot from you."

Wow. I'm starting to feel slightly emotional over this. Not enough to show it, but to think, someone eager to continue their baseball career is telling me they can learn something from me?

"Well, thanks man. Yeah, if you want to take some time after practice or on an off day to do some drills or something, let me know. I have lots of free time."

I've thought about taking on an extra job because I could use some extra money, but I need to figure out something that can work in my schedule. Maybe Leanne needs help with some events she is taking on.

I've never thought about Leanne Fairbanks as anything more than just Lance's annoying younger sister. When we were kids, she'd always try and insert herself to play whatever video game Lance and I were playing, but had no idea how the game even works. Their parents forced us to give her a chance to learn, but it always slowed me down.

But she's not the same person anymore. She's mature, grown up. Shit, she has her own business. And last night, I talked to her more than I ever did growing up. When we were kids, I'd tell her to go away because Lance and I were trying to defeat some bad guy in a video game, but now, I'm thinking about asking her questions about what she's been up to and getting to know her, because I realize that there's something worth getting to know when it comes to Leanne Fairbanks.

I look at my phone. There's still more than half an hour before we need to be ready for the opening ceremony. I think I can take a peek at Leanne's food truck before the game starts. Lance is helping her out today as well. If anyone asks, then I'll say I needed to go to the bathroom for some pregame alone time.

I step out to the front of the park and see so many people dressed in blue in support of the Seals. Of us. Of me. I'm assuming they know that I'm on the team, or maybe for a few people, this is their first day of finding out who's who on the team.

Some people shoot glares at me as my cleats make contact with the floor, walking closer and closer to Leanne's food truck. No one comes up to say hi or ask for an autograph. Good. I think that I will be in a better headspace after the game. That is, if we win.

Leanne's food truck is a bright, eye-catching shade of red with gold cursive lettering that spells out "The Dragon's Belly" with the tagline "Fiery and Steamy Goodies" and a cute, animated dragon slurping up a bowl of noodles.

There's a crowd of people who are waiting in line to order their food and an equally sized one who are waiting for their food to be ready. I feel a little bad that the other food trucks aren't seeing the same kind of love, but I'm rooting the most for Leanne.

The food I tasted at the Meet the Team event was some of the best Chinese food I've had, and Lance used to take me to dim sum once a month with his family. Leanne's food may not be the same kind of food that you find at a traditional Chinese restaurant, but hers is packed with so much good flavor, I wanted it to tingle on my tongue forever. It transcended me to somewhere I haven't been in a long time. A place where I finally felt like I was home. And it's all from a woman who years ago, would annoy teenage me with her desire to try and play first-person shooters for the first time.

"Oh, hey, Corey!" Lance waves once he gets a free moment after giving someone their food. "What are you doing out here? Aren't you supposed to be in the dugout?"

"Yeah, soon." No one's worried about my whereabouts, I hope. "Just wanted to come out and see how the truck was doing."

"Man, we have been going nonstop essentially since the gates opened. Someone told me they bought a ticket to the game just because they wanted to grab some food. Dude had never watched a baseball game in his life, but we've somehow convinced him."

"Hey, I'm not going to complain about that. Whatever Leanne puts in her food is like kryptonite."

"Right? We actually might sell out."

My eyebrows perk up. Already? The game hasn't even started yet. At least everyone's stomachs will be satisfied when we're throwing the first pitch.

"Damn. Well, I'm glad to hear it. I should get back to the dugout. Tell Leanne she's killing it today."

"Here. Let me call her over so you can tell her yourself. Leanne!" Lance shouts and disappears from the pickup window for a second.

Next thing I know, Leanne steps out from the back of the food truck and walks over to me.

"Corey!" She perks up. "Hi. Lance said you wanted to tell me something?"

I did, but I was perfectly content with just having Lance be messenger pigeon and tell Leanne that I think she's doing a good job. Now that I'm talking face to face to Leanne, I'm suddenly feeling a strange sensation. My hands start to clam up and I feel nervous.

Why? I think to myself. It's just Leanne.

But Leanne isn't the same as when we were kids. Her features have matured out. She's got beautiful curves. For the first time, she's making me wonder what's under that apron.

Why the fuck did I start thinking my childhood best friend's little sister was attractive?

Since the moment I saw her cooking in the kitchen when I went over to their house for dinner, if I'm being honest. Leanne in her element, exuding this joy over making dinner for her family. And at Meet the Team, when I caught her crying over being thought of as a niche caterer. I didn't think the next words that would come out of my mouth would be words of comfort, of saying that whoever told her that was wrong, but my heart shattered, seeing her so sad.

Seeing her turn that frown upside down at how many people are enjoying her food, wiping the sweat off her forehead is doing something to me.

Something that I hope isn't going to deter me from doing as best as I can on my first home game of the season.

"Y-yeah," I croak. "I just wanted to wish you good luck on your sales today. But I don't even think I need to. These crowds are speaking for themselves."

She shakes her head. "It's wild. I thought that people didn't usually come to the games an hour and a half before, but we had a line even before we opened."

"See?" I shrug. "There are people that like this 'niche' food that you're making."

She blushes. "I'm glad. It's been a busy day so far, but I love it. I love the rush of cooking and talking to people who want to eat my food. How about you? It's your first home game, literally at home."

"Yeah." I nod. "Isn't it ironic?"

She pinches her fingers to the point where they're almost touching. "A little too ironic." She laughs and rolls her eyes. "Okay, I'm done quoting Alanis."

"I guess I did start it with saying the word ironic." I laugh. "But, I'm feeling good. Excited. I'm also feeling nervous. Some of these players are from another state and have never interacted with someone from Neptune Beach before. They don't have this burden on their shoulders to do well. Maybe there may not be someone that knows me in the stands, but I'm sure that most of the fans do. And that is slightly terrifying."

It feels like I'm back in high school when we'd play baseball on our home field. We were good, top of the division. That led to fans being filled up every night of people eager to see Neptune Beach High try and keep their first place standing. If I struck out, the groans I'd hear from the fans crushed teenage me. I felt like I let people down. I felt like I failed, and now that I'm having this full circle moment again of performing in front of people who know my name and my family and want me to do well, to make Neptune Beach proud.

"You're going to crush it," Leanne tells me. "I think you're going to get a hit on your first at bat. And when people are cheering, I'm going to cross my fingers that they're going to be cheering because of you."

"Thanks." I smile down to her. "When you get a chance, sneak away for a bit. Just to see some of the team in action." See me, specifically.

"I'll try." She turns back to look at the truck, whose lines are beginning to look less chaotic now that people are walking to take their seats. "Good luck."

She scurries to get back into the truck and as I'm walking back to the dugout, I take off my ballcap and rifle a hand through my hair.

I can't be thinking about Leanne in this way. Taking my breath away, she's at the front of my thoughts, I want to spend my free time trying to get to know her.

I'm trying to do my damn best so I can be on my way out, and I know for damn sure if I did something about my feelings and confess it to Leanne, that she isn't going to leave Neptune Beach to try and be with me.

Chapter 6
Corey

"Now batting, Centerfielder, from right here in Neptune Beach, California, Corey Ramirez!"

The fans erupt in loud cheers when I step out from the dugout and take my first at bat as a Seal. Before I take my stance at home plate, I close my eyes, inhaling through my nose and exhaling through my mouth. The one breath where I can drown out the cheers and focus on what I need to do.

There's already one guy on base. He got walked, but I don't want my first time on base to be a walk. I was a little surprised Coach wanted me to bat third. Third is a spot reserved for players who can hit in hopes of advancing as many players potentially left on base. Third means Coach thinks I can bat. Third means I can potentially hit a home run and score two for our team.

I peer up at the stands of people who are eagerly waiting for me to take my at bat. "Let's go Corey!" a familiar voice pushes its way out of the cheers. I take a brief look up and standing along first base is Leanne and Lance, banging against the fence.

"Woo! Go Corey!" Leanne claps. I turn my face down so no one can see how giddy Leanne's cheers are making me feel, and to hopefully not fixate on her too much to distract me from getting a hit.

I walk up to home plate and pull my bat back, training my eyes on the pitcher trying to wind up his pitch. He throws it at me.

Ball.

I wind up again, gripping onto the bat. This pitcher has a thing for staying as close to the bottom of the strike zone as possible, but I know that I can make contact with the ball. I just need to time it correctly.

Next pitch, I attempt a swing but I'm too late. The ball ends up in foul ball territory and hits against the fence along third. I heave out a sigh. It means I get a strike, but I'm still feeling confident that I can make a hit.

The next pitch is a ball, and now I'm beginning to lose hope this guy is going to throw me something that I can hit. I know how difficult it is to throw a ball. Lance's dad asked if I wanted to pitch once in Little League AA, the time where most kids learn to pitch for the first time in their life in hopes that another kid will hit the ball off them. I attempted pitching once, and it was not fun. My arm is way too wild to throw inside of an imaginary box. And then I hit a kid in the arm. That sealed my fate and started my trauma on ever wanting to pitch.

On the next pitch, I watch the ball come toward me and something registers that I can make contact with the ball, so I swing.

And sure enough.

When the ball goes flying, I start to run. I keep running until I see the ball get caught. When I fixate on the ball touching the grass in right field, rolling all the way until it hits against the wall, I pick up the pace. I make it to second and Scott, who was on base already when I got up to bat, makes it home.

RBI on my first at bat as a Seal? I'll take it with pride. I vigorously clap and turn to look at my teammates who are jumping gleefully in the dugout that I've scored our first run of the game.

We're able to keep a strong lead for the entire game and come out strong in the end and win with a score of seven to three. I scored one run and got on base once more during the game. While I'm not proud that I hit two outs this game, I'm happy I was at least able to make contact with the ball each time I was at bat.

Coach gives us a post-game pep talk, telling us that we did a good job for our home opener. There were also mistakes that we made: we let in a run because our fielding was sloppy and someone dropped the ball in error. Benny, who was the pitcher for the game, sat in shame at how many players he walked. Sometimes I forget this is some of my teammates' first time being on a professional team. The range of skill level for players in this league are wide, and I think that I'm more on the skilled side.

"This is our first game though. We have many more games to go. And next week, we will be the road for our first away series. Stay focused, work hard, and keep the same energy for tomorrow. We play six games in a row, which is a big difference than what many of you are used to. Rest up, but celebrate. Good job tonight."

We clean up and Coach lets us know that we stay after the game to sign autographs for the kids who attend. I'm feeling slightly more energetic than I have in a long time. Maybe even a little giddy. I didn't let any balls past me, I got two hits, and even though the last couple of weeks have had me feeling like I'm going backward in time, I'm better about putting on a happy face to people who may come up to me and ask about how I feel being back at home. My skills are good, but that just means I'm on an upward trajectory of getting out faster.

I walk out onto the promenade area where the food trucks were set up and a line of kids are holding out pads of paper and balls for us to sign.

"Look, Carson," a mom says to her son. "It's Corey Ramirez!"

Does this kid know who I am? This is probably the first time he's ever heard of me in his life.

"Hi there." I sheepishly wave.

"Hi," the kid says back. He must be no older than eight.

"Would you like to ask Corey to sign your ball?"

"Can you sign my ball, please?" the kid asks in a cute whisper.

"Sure thing, kid." I take the marker the mom passes me and sign my name. "Are you playing baseball right now?"

The kid nods. "I just finished up Single A."

"That's awesome. What position did you play?"

"First base."

"Wow!" I raise my brows at him. "You're catching the ball a lot then."

"Yeah, my dad has been helping me practice catching balls. I've been getting a lot of the other team out."

"Hey, good job!" I hold up my hand for a high five and he eagerly slaps his hand against it. "Keep practicing. That's how you're going to be a good baseball player."

"Thanks!" He beams with excitement. "I will. So I can be a pro baseball player like you when I grow up too!"

Yeah, me too kid. I haven't gotten there yet.

"There you go." I chuckle. His mom mouths a "thank you" and nudges her son to keep making his way down to get other members of the team to sign his ball.

I keep smiling and signing autographs for more fans who are all eager to talk to me, telling me they thought I did well during this game, when someone slides up next to me and brushes against my arm.

I pause signing for a moment and turn my head over to who's trying to get my attention.

"Hey!" I grin when it's Leanne who's decided to catch my attention.

"Hi." She smiles back. "I just came to say good job on the game."

"You did? Thank you." I extend my arm and pull her in for a side hug. My fingers tingle when I touch her bare arm. I don't try and let my hand linger on her, even though I think her skin is silk smooth, even with it being lined with beads of sweat from the slight heat that visited us this weekend.

"How'd food sales go?"

"Amazing. We sold out of all our food. I thought that I planned appropriately for a big turnout, but even still, I ran out of food. Good problem to have though, right?"

"It's great." I grin. "It means people like your food."

"Yeah." She shifts her gaze to the floor. "I just wish that everyone can share that excitement."

"They will." I look directly at her when I'm telling her that, to make sure she believes what I'm telling her and that I believe in her.

Our gazes fixate on each other for what feels like a minute before she clears her throat and turns to face the truck.

"I should go help Lance and the team clean up."

But as Leanne starts to move, Lance steps out of the truck and runs toward us.

"Hey, good job man! I only got to see you for the first at bat but you guys won! Great way to start off the season."

"Thanks, Lance." I hope he doesn't think anything of that weird time stop where it feels like Leanne and I were the only two people in the world.

"Hey, some friends are thinking of celebrating after at the Jolly Oyster. Down to join?"

"Um."

Tell yourself that you want to be better about being at home. And you won, that deserves to be celebrated.

"Yeah, that sounds fun. I'm down."

"Great. We have to drop off the truck and I think Leanne and I both want to shower and we'll head over."

"Yeah." I'm definitely in need of a shower. A long, scalding shower. Where I hopefully don't think about Leanne while water drips down my body. "Text me when you're ready to leave and I'll get dropped off."

"You got it, bud." He flashes me a thumbs up. "Congrats on the win again. Can't wait to celebrate."

"Same."

"Well, I guess I'll see you later," Leanne quips.

I give her a wave. "See you later."

***

The Jolly Oyster is nothing short of bustling. A good amount of people are still in their Seals t-shirts and fan jerseys, beers in hand and milling about the bar.

I step in, wearing a navy embroidered Seals polo and khakis. If someone recognizes me, then I guess I have no other choice but to accept I'm a popular figure again in this town. I'd rather be a fly on the wall.

I tilt my head up and scan the room to see if Lance or Leanne are making themselves comfortable. When I see Lance standing near, to no one's surprise, the pool table, I walk over. As I step closer, I see a better view of Leanne's wavy hair that cascades down her back. I begin to step closer, and I can't keep my mouth from going agape.

Leanne is dressed in a floral camisole and denim shorts. I can better see her curvy body shape that she typically hides behind her apron or chef's shirt.

"Hey." She smiles up at me.

"Hi."

She holds up a glass of something red-colored to take a sip from.

"Vodka cran, I assume?"

Her eyes widen. "How'd you know?"

I burst out laughing. "Leanne. I would be surprised if that was anything other than a vodka cranberry. Unless you were drinking a Shirley Temple."

She sighs. "Okay, you got me. I'm a basic bitch. And I needed something alcoholic after how chaotic today's game was."

"You are not a basic bitch. Okay, maybe just a little." I nudge her playfully. It's okay to be basic.

She rolls her eyes. "Well..." She eyes what drink I've chosen. "No one wants a...is that just bourbon on the rocks?"

"Yes it is." It is more of an easy sipping drink as compared to the beers that the rest of the people standing around the pool table are using, but I needed something to keep my body warm and my mind a little more at ease.

Leanne sticks out her tongue. "Bleh. I cannot do dark liquor."

"It's an acquired taste for sure."

"How are you feeling after the game?" she asks. "I don't know if your body feels sore afterwards, like it does after a workout."

"Well, it is kind of like one big workout, playing baseball, but I feel good. Stretching helps."

"Good." She takes another sip of her drink. I am trying so hard not to fixate on this has been the most skin that I've seen on her in years. I don't want to tell myself I might have an attraction to Leanne, but I'm not going to deny she's good looking.

Is she dating anyone? She still lives with her parents, so I don't believe she's married or engaged. She doesn't wear a ring, but maybe she doesn't wear a ring because she's constantly handling food.

After mingling and somehow being roped in to play a game of pool with Lance as my partner, I walk over to the bar to get myself another drink. I'll figure out a way to get home.

Sitting up at the bar is someone I didn't think I would see back at Neptune Beach.

We lock eyes and he tilts his drink to me.

"Hey, Ramirez," Greg Nguyen greets me. "Good seeing you, man."

"Hey. Yeah," I awkwardly respond. "You too, Greg."

Greg Nguyen was a close friend of mine. Hell, he was probably second on my list under Lance if I had to rank friends. Greg wasn't in baseball, but we were in other after school activities together. We did Robotics together and had SAT prep classes on Saturdays, a brief opening in time where baseball didn't consume my life. I wish I could be spending a weekend not grasping standardized test questions that didn't really help me get into college anyway, but life was full of what-ifs and never guarantees. My parents wanted me to be prepared for anything.

Greg was always hailed as the smartest person in the class. He was a "nose stuck in a book" student, didn't participate in any sports, but still very involved in community service and robotics. He graduated as the class's valedictorian and went to Berkeley to study Architecture.

I feel bad that it sometimes felt like I kicked Greg to the side, metaphorically, because we were good friends and we did share good memories together, but when I was making baseball my entire life and Greg wasn't a part of that, he kind of just became a second thought.

Seeing him back now ignites something in me to try and make up for lost time.

"Heard you're back to play for the new pro team. That's cool."

"Thank you. Yeah, it's been good. Won our first game earlier today. What about you? Are you living back in Neptune Beach?"

"Yeah. I am. I moved back after college to work with my dad's architecture firm."

Another example of someone from Neptune Beach finding their way back. "Cool dude."

"Um," he swallows, "we should try and hang out sometime, since you're back."

"We should." I nod. "Yeah, let me get your number..."

I reach to pull out my phone from my back pocket and my arm accidentally hits someone as they walk behind me.

"Oh shit, sorry." I turn around and see who I bumped. I sigh when it's at least someone I know. "Oh my bad, Leanne."

She starts to speak but her face goes pale when she looks at Greg and sharply turns back at me. "Don't worry about it," she rushes out. "Greg. You're here, how...funny."

Greg just gives Leanne a slight wave back and I am starting to realize I may have found myself in between two people who have some history.

Leanne breaks her silence. "I...I'm going to get some air."

I quizzically eye her briskly walk out of the bar. I look over to Greg, who's got his lips glued to his glass and eyes trained on the major league game happening on the television.

"I'm...just going to see what's wrong..." I whisper to myself, and maybe Greg, if he hears me. All of a sudden, it seems like he's kind of shut himself off.

I walk outside and try looking around for a moment for Leanne until I find her standing up against the bar's wall with her arms crossed. She's pursing her lips and staring out onto the quiet street, where a few cars pass every couple of seconds.

"Hey." I step closer to her. "Are you okay?"

She peers over to me for a moment, but turns her head sharply away. "Yeah, I'll be find." She brushes her hand away. "You should go back inside. Don't worry about me."

I shift my stance so that I'm standing inches in front of her. "I don't think I can do that. Not when you're visibly upset," I tell her, my voice strained.

I am trying to piece the events that happened throughout the night that might have led her to be upset. She was fine up until I accidentally bumped into her and she shoots glances between me and Greg. Do her and Greg know each other?

"Is it Greg? Do you know him?" Leanne and Greg weren't really friends in high school, and I don't think that Greg and Lance really hang out with one other.

"Please, Corey, I said I don't want to talk about it." Tears start streaming down her face, and without thinking, I reach my hand out and wipe them off her cheek with my thumb. I can't help it. Wanting to comfort her when she's upset. Being some kind of protector to her when she's standing here all alone. It's only been days since I've seen Leanne, but all I want to do is be around her and find little ways to make her smile.

She leans into my touch and start opening her mouth, but she's not saying anything.

"Please, Leanne. Will you tell me?" I know Greg and I were close, but if he might have done something bad to Leanne or if she has a bad image of him, I would like to know if there's something I could do to help.

Leanne takes a deep breath. "Okay. Yes, I do know Greg. He's my ex-fiancé."

Chapter 7
Leanne

I wait for Corey to do anything else except blink back at me after I've dropped this bombshell confession to him.

"Corey?" I'm genuinely curious if I've given him a stroke.

"You and Greg were engaged?"

"Yes. We got engaged on the day I graduated from Berkeley."

Greg and Corey were in the same graduating class together, and from what I remember, they were kind of close because they were both on the robotics team. I know this because I'd try and sneak glances of Corey while he was on campus or try and accidentally bump into him when he'd be walking down the halls after school hours.

"When'd you guys meet? Maybe I would have noticed if you two had something together in high school, or if you guys talked...Neptune Beach High wasn't tiny but it wasn't huge..."

"We met in Berkeley," I interrupted him. "Well, we got to know each other in Berkeley. I knew of him because he was your class' valedictorian. I saw him give this really inspirational speech on your graduation day, but we'd never talked prior to that.

"Greg and I met through badminton club. I went because my room-mate played badminton, but I didn't have any intention of playing. I was going to a badminton club at a Bay Area based school, of course I was going to get creamed if I never swung a racquet for the first time. Greg told me he didn't really play either, that he started when he came to Berkeley and he'd been really enjoying it.

"As we were casually talking, he said I looked familiar, but that he'd never met me before. That's when we realized we were both from Neptune Beach. He knew Lance just by having some of the same classes as him, and then he said he was closer with you. Knowing that you and Lance were best friends throughout high school.

"I won't bore you with the details. They don't get much more interesting after that. We talked, sometimes until the sun came back up, and I was genuinely smitten. I thought he checked off all the boxes: smart, funny, compassionate. He'd offer to keep me company studying so I wouldn't get distracted, and told me some best practices for retaining information because I was kind of struggling my first year. We started dating once the spring semester started back up in January and even though he was my first boyfriend, at the time, I didn't want to spend my life being with anyone else."

It had been a long time since I had told someone in that much detail about a life that I once considered a fairytale. That someone also just happened to be my brother's best friend, who also was close with my ex.

"And you're no longer together."

I shake my head.

"Are you still in love with him?"

I shake my head again.

"I'm not." I'll "Bible" swear if he wants me to. "I also broke off the engagement. Not like that needs to be extra proof, but I do not have feelings for him anymore."

But since Corey's been back, there definitely isn't just friendly feelings roaming around in my head either when I see or talk to him now.

"Why did you break it off?"

I haven't talked about the breakup in a while. Sometimes, I still think it's hard to articulate why I decided to break something off that on the outside looked perfectly fine, like we could've tried harder to make it work instead of me saying I had enough.

Corey reaches his arm out and strokes his fingers along mine. "You don't have to tell me if you're not comfortable."

"No. It's not that. It happened over a year ago, and it's not like I'm trying to keep face to please anyone anymore. My parents are supportive of what happened, even though it cost them more than they want to admit in venue fees. I broke it off because I came to the realization that I was more in love with the idea of being in love instead of the man itself. Greg and I...we thought we were in love, but I think it was more infatuation and attraction than genuine love. The kind of love you're supposed to have when you dive into something like marriage."

Corey pauses for a second, before I watch his brows furrow into a V, his neck beginning to show some shade of red.

"Did he ever hurt you?"

"No," I respond quickly. I don't want Corey to immediately walk back inside and start a ruckus if he gets the wrong idea planted in his head. "Not physically. He said some things that stung a little emotionally. He thought he was being helpful, and maybe I didn't want to hear it but..."

"Was it about your business?"

I nod. "In his defense, he wasn't the only one."

"That doesn't make it any better," Corey says, with a more stern tone all of a sudden. "No one should be telling you that you're not allowed to follow your dreams."

Easy for him to say. He worked his ass off in baseball to be recruited by a good university and do well enough that he eventually got drafted by a major league team. His path may be full of more turns than what he was hoping, but it doesn't negate any of the amazing accomplishments he has made thus far. Everyone had their idea of what I wanted to do and when I told them I was going to quit and start my own business, they wanted to drop me in a snap because they didn't think I was gutsy enough to make it successfully.

I scoff. "Yeah, you get to say that because you were born and bred to be a baseball player all your life. While you were out there, playing in the minor leagues for thousands of fans, I was here trying to convince everyone that I could start and manage my own business. My mom tried to discourage me because she didn't want to waste money on something that wasn't going to work. And then Greg only piled onto that instead of trying to back me up and tell them I deserved to do what I wanted."

I remember the day I told my parents that I was quitting my job and wanted help to pursue this new business. Looking back, I understood that they were trying to come from a place of love. My mom is the daughter of two immigrants who couldn't afford to drop everything to "pursue their dreams." Escaping Hong Kong was their dream, and they had to endure long days and laborious jobs to make barely any money to raise four kids. My mom took on a lot as the oldest, picking up my uncles from school while everyone else was working. So, when she had the heart to heart conversation with me that she just wanted me to be successful, even if that meant being in a stable job, I wanted to just do what made them happy, even if it meant I'd be stuck doing something I wasn't happy with.

"But, I also want to see you happy," she had explained to me. "And if that means you're going to try out this food truck business, then, we will support that. Just know that you are going to figure out a way to raise most of the money you need to get there. We're not here to be your bank when you run out of funds."

"I know," I told her. I was ready to do two jobs until I felt comfortable enough to make it a full time thing. She said she would be okay with that. Both of my parents would. Maybe it was because they knew I was a talented chef and deep down, if I could prove to them I could do this, they'd admit they were wrong in letting me pursue my dreams.

Greg was still ambivalent about the whole thing, which after time passed, leaned more toward anger that my free time went to promoting The Dragon's Belly. I was fighting to get into every pop up, farmer's market, guest spot at a brewery I could find to sell and market my products. Which meant I was gone weekends when Greg wanted us to spend that time planning a wedding or going out on dates. He never once told me he was proud of me for following my dreams. He wanted to be critical, indirectly reminding me I was potentially setting myself up for failure, and then he told me he was doing this "out of love for me and my mental well being."

Bull-fucking-shit.

I exhale a broken sob, more so relieved I got all that off my chest. It took a lot of therapy and blocking out negative thoughts to be in a place where I am now. A good place. And I still have those thoughts of giving up because I don't think I can do it.

"Hey, come here." Corey takes one of his arms and wraps it around my shoulder, pulling me into him so I can rest my head on his rock-hard chest. I sheepishly wrap my arms around his back and when he pulls me in tighter, I grasp onto the back of his soft T-shirt.

"Thank you for telling me." he says, resting his chin on top of my head. "I'm sorry you went through that."

I pull back and try to wipe my eyes with the back of my hand. "It's okay. I'm a lot better now. But, yeah. Greg and I...I knew that I had to break things off with him if he wasn't going to support what I wanted to do and continuously make resentful comments when I was putting him on the back burner. I do feel bad I decided I didn't want to be with him anymore, because he tried to apologize and fight for our relationship, telling me that he still loved me, but I wasn't in love with him anymore. Ultimately he let me go because he wanted what was best for me when it was evident I wasn't budging on my decision."

"Do you think he is he still in love with you?" Corey asks.

I shrug. "I think he was for a bit, but it's been over a year now. We've both moved on. I don't think he's dating anyone, but he doesn't bother me anymore. We kind of just make eye contact for a moment and walk away if we run into each other like we did just now."

"Shit." Corey laughs. "I didn't think that when I'd be away from town, that I'd be missing like...all this tea. The Neptune Beach equivalent of Pandora's box has been opened. I shucked an oyster and this is what came out!"

I roll my eyes, but can't help but shoot a grin his way. Corey being here and talking to me is making me happier than I thought. I guess it's good that Corey knows about me and Greg. I was starting to feel worried that him and Greg were also going to get chummy when Corey moved back to Neptune Beach. I'm not going to gatekeep who Corey is friends with, but I think he should have heard it from me because I had a feeling Greg was going to walk back in my life at some point. It just had to be because he's hanging out with the guy I might now be attracted to.

"Wow, how punny. Because we're at the..."

"Jolly Oyster." He nods. "Yeah, I thought so."

Corey takes a step back. "So, wait. You and Greg are no longer together and you're trying to avoid Greg but you both live in Neptune Beach. Have you ever thought about...moving? So you didn't need to see him? And to try and start anew too?"

"Why do I have to be the one who moves? We're both adults, if he has a problem seeing me around, he needs to be mature about it too." Somehow I have been successful enough to maneuver away from bumping into Greg. I know he lives on the east side of town and I live on the west side, so I can go to another grocery store I know that he doesn't frequent. What would shock me is if he suddenly takes an interest in baseball and go to the Seals games, but now that Corey's suddenly disappeared from their conversation to check up on me, then he knows we're talking. As friends at least.

"This is my home. It's been my home for the past twenty six years. I've successfully maneuvered away from speaking to Greg so far, that isn't going to change."

"Yeah, but...even after you were starting out your business, breaking off your engagement, did you ever wonder about just leaving Neptune Beach and starting fresh? Put the negative memories behind and explore a whole new world?"

I purse my lips. I've wondered. There's a big, bright beautiful world out there, and I've only explored a fraction of it. I've never even left the country. Growing up, we'd go on road trips down California, and I enjoyed playing tourist in Hollywood and going to Disneyland, but I'd never imagine living anywhere but Neptune Beach. As small as it is, it's what I've grown accustomed to.

Corey...he's trying his best, but I can see he's only here for a short while before he gets the call to do the next thing in his life. Even though it was what he grew up with too, he's seen parts of the world, and he's ready to see more. His dream of being in the Major Leagues is still alive.

"I think I'd rather just not get my heart broken again. I want try and fixate my mind on other things, in the comfort of my own home, to add."

I gesture to Corey. "And here you are, just itching to get out of Neptune Beach the moment a team calls you up." It makes me realize that any feelings I have for Corey will need to dissipate, because I can't be with someone who is going to tell me they love me and make it a point to leave me when they're given the chance.

"I just know there's more to fall in love with than Neptune Beach," he tells me, looking straight into my eyes. I know he's not saying that to me, that he's just referencing a place, not a person. Not me.

"I feel like I can convince you not to be so up and eager to leave," I tell him. "I just need to show you."

His eyebrow perks up. "What do you mean?"

"You're so fixated on leaving that you're not living in the moment of being in Neptune Beach. Come on, grumpy pants. You can have so much more fun if you went out and did things around here that are just as fun instead of moping around that you're not out of here yet."

He chuckles. "And you're determined to find that for me?"

"Of course I am." I smile. "Call it a challenge of sorts, if you will. And who knows? Maybe you'll find a way to stay in Neptune Beach even longer."

Chapter 8
Leanne

good morning! hope you're excited about today! meet @ my house at 10. bring a jacket.

why? it's june.

where we're going, you're going to need to protect yourself from the wind. doesn't matter what temperature it is.

you got it boss

I finish getting ready for the day, trying to whip up some kind of cute outfit without screaming, "I dressed to impress!" for this date that isn't a date.

I scurry downstairs, seeing that I have some time left before Corey arrives at my house. As I race down and hurry into the kitchen to quickly make a cup of to-go coffee, I almost slip on the wood floor when I make eye contact with Lance, who is quietly sipping on coffee out of a mug that reads "Smut Slut."

"You're dressed nicely." Lance eyes me suspiciously.

"Thanks. You're using my mug," I retort.

"It's in the cabinet, it's free game. And what, maybe I am a smut slut." He turns to examine the mug, which is also covered in chili peppers. "I can appreciate smut."

"Oh yea?" I lift an eyebrow. "What's the last 'smutty' book you read?"

Lance goes quiet for a moment. Yup, that's what I thought. The man likes to read, which I appreciate, but I know the books Lance checks out from the library are all sci-fi-fantasy books. I'd try and slide him a romantasy, to add some central romance plot to his reading habits, but he'd complain it was too much at the forefront of what he's reading.

"I'll have you know, I did have my eye on the deluxe collection of Hunger Games, which has romance."

I scoff. Yeah, I guess it does. And I was also eyeing those books myself. Those sprayed edges ignite something in me.

"Sure, so I guess you can keep drinking out of the mug." Even though I wouldn't say Hunger Games is smut, and honestly, I'd rather it not.

"Answer the question, Leanne. Why are you so dressed up to go somewhere at ten in the morning?"

I sigh. "Am I not allowed to go out on the weekend?"

"No, you are. I'm just curious where you might be going."

"Out." I'm not lying when I answer him.

He rolls his eyes. "Do I get to know where? And with whom?"

"I'm just hanging out with a friend. We're going to drive somewhere, and eat some lunch."

"Alright." He shrugs. "I will let you be secretive, but just know I'm suspicious, and I am assuming that you're going on a date."

I groan. "It's not a date."

When Lance goes back to sipping on coffee and scrolling through his phone, I send a quick text to Corey to see if I can catch him before he knocks on the doorbell and Lance bolts up, trying to figure out who is the person I'm trying to keep under wraps.

Lance narrows his eyes. "Well, you don't really have a lot of friends, so I don't understand why you have to keep who you're seeing under wraps like this."

For some reason, that stings a little. I'm not saying Lance is wrong. I don't have a lot of friends, by choice. I've become selective of who I've let into my corner, and trust with confiding in. That doesn't meanI can't go out and meet new friends either.

"I need to get going. I'll be back by tonight." I sharply hoist my purse up on my shoulder and swiftly walk to the foyer to put my shoes on.

"Wait, Leanne! I'm sorry, I didn't mean it like you're someone who people don't want to be friends with." Lance finally starts to show some concern.

"Don't worry." I plaster on a smile. "You're right. I don't really have a lot of friends. But I should be able to go out and do what I want without anyone asking where I'm going. I'm an adult, Lance."

He sighs. "You're right. I'm sorry that I worded it that way. I just...if you're going through something, you'd tell me right? I don't want you getting hurt. Again. I...saw Greg was at the bar last week after the Seals game. I didn't talk to him or anything, but...yeah. If something's bothering you, you know how to reach me."

I relax my shoulders a bit. "Yeah, I'd tell you. Don't worry." The breakup was awful and I am happy I was able to grieve my relationship with my family, but I don't have my eyes set on being in a relationship again any time soon. The potential of being hurt again is not something that I want to endure for...well, forever, as wistful as that sounds.

"Okay." Lance nods. "Have fun today. I'll see you when you get home."

I shoot him a soft smile. "Thanks. See you when I get home."

I hop in the car and slowly drive around the corner to Corey, standing against the fence. I throw on my hazards and press the unlock button so he can sit down.

"Hey," I say over the sound of my latest pop hits playlist blasting in the car. "Sorry if I made you wait. Lance was interrogating me more than I wished about my whereabouts and who I'm hanging out with because I wouldn't disclose any information to him."

"Ah. I take it he didn't want to hear no for an answer."

I nod. "I love Lance, but he exudes protective big brother energy to the extreme sometimes, and I need to remind him that I'm an adult and I'm capable of making my own decisions and that includes not telling him where I am at all times."

"What did you tell him?"

"I told him I'm hanging out with a friend. We're going to get lunch and I'll be home in the afternoon. No names or locations were disclosed."

Corey leans back in the chair. "Okay, good."

Today's adventure takes us to a place that's a little out of Neptune Beach, but boasts a great view, with some amazing cuisine to compliment. As much as I want to be secretive to him about where we're going today, I realize I can't. I have to put in directions on how to get where I want to go, or we might just keep driving endlessly until we reach Oregon.

"Starting route to Tomales Bay," the automated directional voice begins.

"Tomales Bay?" Corey looks at the map. From here, we should get there in about an hour and a half.

"Yeah," I tell him, following the directions to hop on the freeway. "This is my first city on my 'local is better' tour!"

"Ah." Corey nods. "You know, I don't know if I've ever been up there."

"What?" I turn to look at him quickly before focusing my gaze back on the road. "Really? But oysters!"

"I have never had an oyster."

I gasp. "Corey Andres Ramirez!"

He sits up straighter. "Wow, it's that serious huh? I am kind of surprised you remember my middle name."

I don't admit why I have that so vivid in the back of my head. "I have good memory. I bet you know my middle name, too."

He tsks like it's easy for him to remember too. "Yeah, it's Elizabeth."

"Oh. So you do remember." That definitely does not qualm the feelings I've worked so hard to subside in my journey to keep this strictly platonic.

"It's a pretty generic middle name, no offense. It's not hard to forget."

"Yeah, whatever. Anyway, stop deflecting from the problem at hand which is you've never had an oyster before."

"No." Corey shakes his head. "I haven't. And to be honest, I haven't really had much of a desire to? They're kind of slimy. And I like seafood, but something about oysters screams 'too much seafood taste' for me."

I will admit, oysters aren't a crowd favorite. Most people aren't a fan of seafood in general, but I enjoy a good sea creature. It's one of my favorite cuisines, if you could lump seafood into one big group. There's something oddly satisfying about slurping up an oyster with the sound of the ocean splashing against the cliffs. And, even though there are many places along the state where you can hear the ocean and enjoy some good seafood, this one happens to be an hour away from Neptune Beach, and in my opinion, has some of the best oysters I've ever tried. The only oysters I have yet to try are those from the East Coast.

"Well, I think they're tasty," I say as we leave the East Bay and cross over the bridge into Marin County. "And looks like now I'm going to take your oyster virginity. I'm honored."

I slump back in my seat. Taking his oyster virginity? Why the hell did I just say that? By uttering that single word, I've entered unchartered territory with Corey. Where I start saying sexually charged words that can be construed in different ways. I try and not slump down in my driver's seat too much.

This is going to be a long day.

"Sorry." I shake my head out of the funk. "I didn't mean to use that kind of phrasing. Just..."

"You're really excited about taking my oyster virginity," Corey jokes. "I get it."

This man is going to ruin me. "Nooooo, forget I said the V-word!"

"Can't." He smirks. "It's burned in my mind now. Might as well get it on a shirt. 'Oyster virgin.' We still have time right? Here, postpone the date until next week so you can make me a shirt."

Date? Did he mean to say that or is he just spewing words from his ass too?

"Sorry." He clears his throat. "I didn't mean to call it a date. I just...I didn't know what else to call it. I'm just thinking of it as a friend date."

"Yeah, no worries," I reassure him. "I got what you mean. People have friend dates all the time."

"Yeah." Corey nods to agree. "Exactly."

After our weird exchange of words, the rest of the drive remains quiet. It was just me, Corey, and the music on my 90s chill rock daylist until we pull up to the outdoor oyster bar overlooking the bay. Even as it approaches noon, the fog is still making its presence known. That's the wild thing about summers here in the Bay Area. One week, we'll be cooking in the heat and the next, it'll be overcast and barely cross seventy degrees Fahrenheit.

I tell the host my name and reservation time, and he ushers us to our picnic bench. Reservations here are definitely a requirement, especially during the summer. This particular restaurant has other locations in the area, but this is one next to the oyster farm. I wanted to a farm tour, but we would have had to be here at nine thirty. I don't know if Corey's a morning person. And this is a little bit out of the way so we did have to drive a distance to get here.

"So," Corey says immediately once our butts hit the seats, "why is your first place to convince me that it's worth staying at home is to a place that has a food item I've never even tried? I thought the whole point is that you're trying to convince me to stay."

"Honestly? Well, one the view." I gesture out to the calm water beside us. "Which is so peaceful and makes this experience ten times better. But after that night we talked at Jolly Oyster, when this whole thing started, I thought 'What a shame that this dive bar, the only dive bar in Neptune Beach, doesn't sell oysters.'"

Corey raises a brow. "Do you think anyone would even trust to eat an oyster if it came from The Jolly Oyster?"

Well, I guess it's not very jolly if it's been shucked open for someone's enjoyment, for starters. "No. And if they did, then kudos for them for trusting that they can provide good oysters at a decent price. A little fun fact about me: a restaurant can advertise dollar oyster happy hour all they want, but I'm kind of sketched out that it may not be that good. No matter how much I like oysters."

"Noted. Anyway, so you were there at Jolly Oyster, wishing they lived up to their namesake."

"Yeah, and then I thought, well, if the Jolly Oyster can't give me what I want, then I'll go somewhere that I know will. And boom! Here we are. The Jolly Oyster feels like such a staple in our lives in Neptune Beach, I figured we should live up to its namesake and be jolly while having an oyster."

Corey grins, a wide-toothy grin that's making my heart want to leap out and go splat all over him. I'm never going to get over how mesmerizing he continues to look after all these years.

"But what if I don't like how an oyster tastes?"

I sigh. Besides me having all a bunch of oysters to consume on my own, which is not a bad problem to have, I would feel bad that I set up this whole cute idea for it to crumble when Corey takes a bite of an oyster and shudders if he thinks it's gross. I blame the Jolly Oyster for having the name it does that spawned this idea in the first place.

"Then this idea would have been for nothing," I mope.

"Hey," he reaches out to touch my arm. "No, it isn't. I'm still thankful that you took me here. I kind of forget that this side of the Bay Area is here. It's nice, to kind of go somewhere that can feel even smaller than Neptune Beach. It's kind of relaxing."

I smile. "Good. I'm happy for that, at least."

Corey decides to let me do all the food ordering, because I have a plan of what I want to order already: a plate of fresh oysters, grilled ones, and maybe some sourdough and butter for starch. I also decide to throw in a charcuterie board in case Corey isn't a fan of the oysters. Corey suggests that we share a bottle of wine to go with our meal to top things off.

"Are you sure?" I ask. The wine I was looking at runs a whopping forty eight dollars per bottle. I guess I'm okay with adding that to the total bill, but it wasn't something I initially planned for.

"Yeah." He nods. "I can take care of the bill."

The person taking our order repeats it back to us before shuffling away from our table, like he can sense we're about to engage in some heated argument about who's paying.

"Corey!" I lean in over the table. "You can't front the bill. I'm the one that picked the restaurant and invited you. I didn't choose somewhere cheap."

"So? You didn't call dibs. By the way, I call dibs."

I didn't know dibs still needed to be called to front a bill. Throw in a bottle of wine to share and this is becoming the most expensive friend date I've ever been on. And Emma and I like going to all you can eat hot pot at least twice a month.

"Fine." I pout. My mom would be disappointed with me that I didn't try and argue further. "Thank you, I guess."

"You're welcome." He grins. A staff member brings the chilled bottle of white wine and two glasses for us. Corey grabs a hold of the bottle and pours a glass for me and then himself. He gently slides the glass my way and lifts his up slightly.

"Cheers." He smiles. "To losing my oyster virginity."

I blush. I'm honored to be the person taking Corey Ramirez's oyster virginity. "Cheers."

We clink glasses and take a sip and I sigh in satisfaction when the crisp, refreshing taste touches against my mouth.

"That is good wine."

"It is. I don't really have wine very often, but this is pretty tasty."

My eyes go wide. Wait, he doesn't even really drink wine and he's expecting us to share a bottle? On his own dime? What is going on in that beautiful mind of his right now? Did he just decide that he was going to treat me with the bottle because I expressed I wanted a glass?

"You...you don't typically drink wine?"

He shakes his head. "Only socially. But I do prefer just a glass of whiskey or bourbon. Maybe a tiki drink. I really like mai tais."

"But why did you offer to get a bottle then? I would have been fine with just getting a glass."

"Because I wanted you to relax and indulge in more than just one glass of wine if you wanted," he explains. "You've been working really hard, so I wanted to do something that can make you feel appreciated. And to say thank you for trying to help me feel better about this whole thing. It's been a little chaotic in my mind, to say the least. Being back here."

"Yeah, I could tell when you came over to my parents that first time." I chuckle to myself. "You seemed...not as enthused to be back home than I thought."

Before Corey gets the chance to explain himself, we're greeted with a plate full of freshly shucked oysters and a cup of mignonette sauce in the middle.

"A dozen oysters," the waiter says. "Enjoy!"

"Thank you," we say in unison. Corey reaches over to grab his phone and holds it out to face me.

"What are you doing?" I asked, puzzled why he's suddenly facing a camera toward me.

"Cementing this as a memory," he answers. "Grab an oyster and smile!"

I shoot him a weird glance, but do what he asks and grab an oyster. I put it close to my mouth and flash a smile facing his camera.

"Thanks." He smiles. He turns to show me the photo he's captured. I think I look ridiculous, but Corey's ogling over it like I'm on the cover of Sports Illustrated. He does some quick taps on his phone and turns it back around again to show me that he's decided to make it his phone background.

"Whatcha think? I needed a new change anyway."

I start to blush. Is this real life? Because I feel like I'm in a dream that teenage me would conjure up. Corey Ramirez, certified grump, is making all these small gestures like he's trying to flirt with me. Did I just enter into an alternative dimension where I've been able to get Corey to turn a new leaf? Because now, I'm accustomed to him being super friendly to me, and I'm afraid that this behavior is going to have an expiration date.

"Looks good," I croak. Don't assume he's flirting with you. "Cheers to losing your oyster virginity!"

Chapter 9
Corey

Using the miniature fork they give us, I go through the motions Leanne has shown me to properly consume an oyster: twist the oyster from the muscle, pour some mignonette sauce into the oyster, and hold the oyster to my mouth and slurp.

Actually, once you stop thinking about how slimy the sucker is, this is actually pretty tasty. I don't hate the taste. It's not something I can consume everyday, but this is a nice treat. And this sauce, which is like a vinaigrette of some sort with tiny minced onion in there, compliments the taste of the oyster well.

"Well," Leanne chimes in, already finished her oyster and onto number two. "What do you think?"

I grin. "It's actually pretty good."

She huffs a sigh of relief. "Oh good. You know for a second, I was actually worried you may be repulsed by the taste."

"The texture definitely surprises you at first," I add, "but the taste is good. The sauce helps. I don't know how much I'd like it if it was just by itself."

I grab another oyster to experiment, only doing the act of removing the meat from the shell. I slurp it up and it glides down my throat.

"Still okay, but not preferable," I conclude once I swallow it.

"I can accept that thought," Leanne says. "I am satisfied with that outcome."

I chuckle. "Good. If I didn't like it, I wouldn't have tried to be sour about it anyway. I appreciate the sentiment of why you wanted to bring me here."

Leanne explained to me that she wanted to come here because the oyster symbolizes something important to us, but she was annoyed The Jolly Oyster doesn't necessarily live up to its namesake. This was her next best idea. I didn't know what to expect when I arrived at Leanne's house this morning. I only knew that she was going to try and take me on an adventure to help get me back into loving Neptune Beach again. And here we are, an hour away to indulge in some farm fresh oysters while we sit and watch the ripples of the water on the bay.

It's hard to take my eyes off of how stunning Leanne looks. She's wearing a white crochet-knit sweater and light denim shorts. She's perfectly dressed for the occasion of perusing around a fellow beach-like town, with more fog than what we're accustomed to in Neptune Beach.

Since we've gotten here, I've tried to do little things to cheer her up, because I know she's got a lot on her plate and in her mind. To show that even though I'm certifiably still going to try and seek out the opportunity to get out of Neptune Beach when I can, I can have a little fun while she tries to convince me that this place is cool too.

I might have went too far. The wine bottle? Could be thought of as a way to relax, take your mind off things. I wasn't lying when I told Leanne that she deserves a little treat. The phone screen change is something only couples and close friends do. I thought it was funny, but I can see why Leanne looked so surprised. It was a gesture reserved for "taking the next step" and I'm not trying to take it any farther than "two friends having fun." She's not looking to date really, anyway, after what she's been through.

"I'm glad you're a fan though. Does that mean that we can take another trip here, where next time, I call dibs on paying?"

I nod, so I can see her light up with glee. "Yes, we can come back and you can pay next time."

We wrap up our meal and Leanne allows me to pay. It's a little pricey, and I'm trying to be better about my spending, but I feel okay with it because I think Leanne deserves it. She's enjoying the last remnants of her wine and she's smiling while watching me sign and tip.

"Why are you looking at me like that?"

She raises a brow. "Like what?" She smirks into her wine glass. She knows exactly what she's doing, and even though I've had less wine than her, the little changes in her facial expression, the small grins she shoots at me, is making me wish we could stop time and live in this moment forever.

"Nothing." I shake my head. "You a little buzzed?"

"A little." She mimics the amount with a little space between her fingers. "But in a good way. I feel light. Free. But I'm in no shape to drive."

"I know. Which is why I'm driving us. I only had one glass."

I hold my hand out. "Keys please."

She fumbles around her bag and pulls out her keys, complete with a scrunchy-like handle and a glittery "L" keychain.

"Here you go."

"Thank you." I grab the keys from her. "Are you ready?"

"Yes. Actually, do you mind if we make a little pit stop before we go back to Neptune Beach? I have someplace on the itinerary I wanted to go to. It's on the way."

"Sure thing." I wonder where. We didn't really pass by too many notable places, except maybe San Quentin, but I don't know how close you can get to San Quentin before being asked about your intentions.

"Sure. Just let me know where."

We get back in the car and Leanne quickly puts her phone in the charger and secretly puts in an address to some road in Sausalito.

"What's here?" I ask.

"She smirks. "You'll see." She's purposefully trying to keep me in suspense. For something special, I suppose.

I start driving and occasionally, I'd peer over and see if I can figure out what Leanne's thinking about as she looks out the window. What questions I can ask to get to know her better as we're driving to our secret destination.

"So," I begin, "what were you doing before you started The Dragon's Belly?"

She starts chuckling before it evolves into a full-bodied laughter. It causes me to jolt, my insides tingle and some parts wanting to stiffen at how poetic it sounds to my ears.

"What's so funny?"

"Nothing. It isn't even that funny. I'm just laughing that at one point, I was working a job that made me so miserable, but I was just doing it to get by for the sake of everyone else but myself." She slightly turns her head and purses her lip at me. "I was a Client Services Associate for my parent's financial planner."

I make a sour face while my eyes focus on the road. That is a certified miserable job for Leanne. She likes moving around, being in different places than behind a desk. She's an adventurous girl.

"Okay yeah, that job doesn't sound like it's right for you," I note. "Why'd you start working there?"

"If I'm being honest, there might have been some nepotism from my parents. They are very convincing when it comes to telling other people how amazing of a person I am. And their financial planner, Jack, who is a very nice guy by the way. I didn't like the job because of him. He was just in desperate need of someone who could help him with the administrative work. Calling clients to remind them that their meeting was coming up. Filing portfolios. Shit that Jack was taking on on top of managing people's money and it was getting to be really overwhelming. I only had one in person interview and he hired me on the spot. I think before the interview, my dad had made a phone call saying that I was really organized and had some transferable skills through the experience I had in college. I feel like he was desperate just to get help."

"And that was the job that everyone wanted you to keep instead of being a chef?" As I fixate more on it, it grinds my gears. Imagining a life where you're stuck behind a desk everyday, funneling calls, maybe picking up a thing or two to someday get your license to help other people manage their money? For some people it feels like a dream, but if they really knew Leanne, that sounds like her worst nightmare.

"Yeah, it was. Greg, who also traded stocks in the morning, was really excited about it. Trying to tell me that if he wasn't an architect, he would have loved to be a financial planner. As if that made me feel any better. I wanted to scream at him, 'I'm not you! I don't find pleasure in buying low and selling high!' or whatever bullcrap. I liked cooking for friends and experimenting with different food. Interacting with people at different places, trying to sell my food. That's the entrepreneurship that I wanted to learn!"

"I get it. Well hey, you're closer to that dream now. And you're on your way to take The Dragon's Belly to new heights." I chuckle. "It's kind of like being in the outfield. You're waiting for that ball to come, knowing that you will leap at the chance when you get it. You don't know where it's going to land, so you're scrambling when you try and get under that ball the moment it flies into the air, but when you catch it, when you finally find what you were looking for, it's the best feeling ever."

Leanne purses her lips and smirks. "Wow, Corey. I never thought you had such an eloquent way with words."

When I talk to you, I feel like I can open up and write a whole damn novel on how you make me feel.

"Just a really big fan of the game, I guess."

The GPS tells us that we're inching closer and closer to our location, and I'm starting to wonder where exactly Leanne was planning to take me, because with all these winding roads to get where we need to be, it feels like I might get dumped on the side of a hill soon.

"Just find any parking spot you see on the road." There is a line of cars already parked, but when I see an opening to parallel, then I put on my blinker and try and grab the spot.

"There's a lot of cars here," I note.

"Yeah, it's kind of a tourist trap spot. But, hey, we're kind of playing tourist I guess, so this is what we have to do. Hit all the popular sight-seeing attractions."

We get out of the car and my eyes go wide when I see what's directly in front of us. I put two and two together to come to the conclusion that we're at Hawk Hill: a popular lookout point that has an amazing view of the Golden Gate Bridge, and when Karl the Fog has decided to leave for the day, you can see the bridge in its full glory. It's a spectacular sight.

We walk until we can get to an open patch of land where we can better see the bridge. The Golden Gate Bridge is an iconic landmark that people flock from around the world to see. It's easy to forget this iconic view can be captured with your eyes and camera with just a little under an hour drive from Neptune Beach. And with how high up we are, I can feel the gentle breeze from the Bay kiss my cheeks and a sense of tranquil overwhelms me. In a snap, my thoughts about resentment, about wishing I could be anywhere else, dissipate.

I close my eyes and take a breath of the sea. I hear Leanne shuffle closer to me and I open my eyes to peer down at her and her face-full grin.

"What's got you grinning like that?"

"Nothing," she says, still grinning.

"Your face is kind of saying otherwise. Nothing wouldn't make you grin like that would it?"

She rolls her eyes, but in a cute, non-menacing way. "Okay, fine. It's not just nothing. It's embarrassing though, I don't want to tell you."

"Come on, it can't be that embarrassing." I nudge her gently in her side. "You can trust me. I won't judge."

Her back arches and she shakes herself to regain poise. "Okay fine. You just...it makes me happy seeing you so...at peace. When is the last time you closed your eyes and became one with your surroundings?"

I shrug. I guess I don't take time to be at peace. I don't mediate, or do that "Speed, I am speed" thing before a game. There's always something on my mind.

"I don't know if I could tell you the last time I've felt this relaxed. When I was playing in the minors, all I thought about was pushing myself hard enough so I could be that much closer to my dream of being called up.

And then I got cut and it felt like I was spiraling for the first time in a while. I was stressing out that I might be moving backwards by being on an independent and new baseball team. But now...I don't know. I feel different for once. I see the bridge and it might be the first time where I feel okay if time stops."

I turn down to look at Leanne and she's speechless. She's blinking back at me, trying to open her mouth to figure out what to say in response, but coming up short. I watch as a hint of blush creeps up on her face. It does something to me. It ignites some spark inside of me. I already couldn't stop looking at Leanne when we were at lunch. How beautiful she is, how once upon a time, she'd linger around Lance and I when I'd be over at their house. I knew back then she liked me. But, when you're a teenage boy, you're not looking at your best friend's little sister and thinking she's beautiful. You're not looking at your best friend's little sister and thinking about what her lips taste like when you kiss her.

It's different now, and I'm starting to feel a magnetic pull towards Leanne Fairbanks.

I step closer to her, only leaving a few inches of space between our chests.

"Tell me what's on your mind, Leanne." My voice goes deeper and I've concentrated my gaze into her light brown eyes, traveling slowly down to her plump lips.

"I'm thinking...this might've been the best I've felt in a long time."

I grin. "Yeah? It's the best I've felt too."

We begin to lean in closer to one another, and I almost reach up to cup her cheek, when she clears her throat and turns away from me and the grasp I almost have on her.

"We should get going. We've been out for a while...I need to head home to prep dinner."

Suddenly, I'm out of the trance I'm in and nod. "Yeah...yeah, let's get back."

I feel disappointed Leanne is sending me mixed signals. But, I know her past. She's trying to open herself up, but doesn't want to rush into things too quickly. I can tell her all she wants to hear about how much I won't break her heart, but I don't know if that'll fully happen. My mind is still set on bigger things than Neptune Beach, but being here with Leanne is the first time where I've actually felt grounded and eager to stay.

Chapter 10
Leanne

For once, I wish I wasn't working at the Seals game right now.

By the sounds of the cheers from a typically full stand, the Seals are doing rather well. They win a majority of their games at home, and are currently second right now in the Pacific League. If they keep this up, or if they make it to first, then they'll be invited to playoffs, where they'll face the other divisions in the independent baseball league.

With the summer at its peak warmth right now though, it is unbearable to be standing in the heat. Add the fact that we're cooking with heat inside a truck that insulates all the warmth we're emitting, and I feel like I'm in the desert. The game has just started, which means we're going to be cooking for at least two more hours, and because I have to keep my apron on while I'm cooking, I'm layered with fabric that's sticking to my skin.

I just want to drop down and melt right now like a popsicle.

"Hey team, let's make sure we're staying hydrated, okay? It's ninety eight degrees outside and feels even hotter in here. If you feel like you need to take a break to find some shade, then please do so. You're more important than getting food out to the customer."

"Aye aye, captain," Emma says, giving me a salute. "And back at you. You're by the grill, Leanne." She steps closer to examine me and the drips of sweat that are coming down my forehead. "Your face is super red right now, girl. You should take a break. Need to take a break, it's not a recommendation."

"Not yet." I shake my head. "I have five orders to fill and we know that near the fourth inning people like to come back for a snack." We debuted these crunchy dried shrimp chips at a game a few weeks ago for a snack option and people loved them. I've had to keep the fryer going to meet demand.

I reach for a rag that I nestle inside my apron and wipe the sweat off my forehead. "I'll be fine. Make sure that people aren't waiting for their orders to be taken in line."

Emma rolls her eyes, but reluctantly goes back to tend to people waiting to have their orders taken. "Water. Lots of it. Please."

"Yes, yes." I reach over to grab my water bottle and take a sip. Still perfectly iced and refreshing.

We've hurdled over the mid-game rush and somehow the sun has perched itself so it's even more direct on our truck now.

"Shit. How much longer do we have?" I whisper, wiping whatever sweat is left off my forehead, but my throat is starting to feel dry. I don't know how much longer I can last. "I'm going to go see what inning it is and what the score's at." I don't want to do this but Emma and Vic are slumped in the driver and passenger seat, looking uncomfortable as all hell to be working. "Are you guys okay?"

They flash me a thumbs up slowly, but all that's telling me is they are just as miserable as I am.

"Fuck it. Executive decision, I'm going to close up near the seventh," I tell them. It's become unbearable with how hot it is. This is now out of concern for our safety. We don't get heat waves like this very often. And today, when we're about to see temperatures in the afternoon skyrocket up to at least ninety, I need to put our safety over people's needs for stir fry noodles and homemade shrimp chips.

"I'll text you if I think we can close up!" I shout. I'm not a huge fan of doing this. I know that we can make more money if we stay open through the entire game, even a little after, because sometimes guests will come up and ask for food to go for dinner. People will understand that our health and keeping cool is more important than boiling in the heat over a grill and possibly getting heat exhaustion.

I jog to the stands near behind home plate and lean in closer to the fence to eye what inning we're in. Damn, it's only bottom of the sixth? It's been two hours since the game started, what's with all the hold up?

Oh. I eye the score. It's sixteen to three, and the Seals are not the ones who have sixteen runs. I wondered why I didn't hear as many cheers from the truck as opposed to other games. It probably has to do with the fact that we're getting our asses kicked by the Tracy Turbines, which is the other team in Northern California.

The Seals are currently up to bat with one out and one player on base. To try and score eight runs in one inning is a very lofty goal, and frankly, I think the Seals should just ask if they can just give up now to avoid being humiliated more than they already are. I don't think there are such things as mercy rules in the professional leagues, though.

The announcer's voice blares over the stadium. "Now batting, number fifteen, Corey Ramirez!"

The crowd's hollers grow exponentially once Corey gets to bat. I love it, but I'm also wishing they could pick anyone else to be their favorite player on the Neptune Beach Seals.

It's been about two weeks since our trip to the North Bay and Marin County, aka the trip where we ate oysters, I got a little drunk off of some wine, and almost kissed Corey until I was taken out of my stupor and stopped myself from going off the deep end. I wanted to kiss Corey. So damn bad. He was standing close to me, so close that our chests were almost touching, and before, he'd almost Shakespeare'd me with beautiful words about his feelings playing outfielder and later how looking at the Golden Gate Bridge was the first time where he actually might have felt at peace. To think I made him feel like that makes me feel...something for him. He was feeling something too, because he was initiating by cupping my cheek and leaning into me until we were inches apart. And like a fool, I backed away from him.

I know that kissing Corey Ramirez will be bad news bears. One, he's my brother's long time best friend. Which means if anything were to happen between us, I could potentially cause a rift in something that was forged long before I even spoke more than a word to Corey. Breaking it off with Greg was different. Lance knew of him, but they weren't really friends like on the level Lance and Corey are. He only really considered him an acquaintance. A friend by proxy because they were both long standing Neptune Beach residents who love the city and decided to do a lot to give back to it. So when we separated it caused Lance to resent Greg as well, because he heard the anger and frustration straight from my mouth. The realization he became someone I wasn't ready to spend the rest of my life with.

Two, as much as I'm helping Corey in finding his love for Neptune Beach again, he's going to leave eventually. We have one major league team nearby, but the chance he's drafted to that one team out of thirty two is a slim percentage. And as much as he was enjoying the amazing view of the Golden Gate Bridge yesterday, he's mentioned all the cool places he got to visit from playing in the minors that he could see himself living in. Or to be given the chance to live somewhere new. He'll talk up dreams of being somewhere else but begrudgingly talk about how awesome the Bay Area is.

And three, I literally made a promise to myself, and out loud to Corey before I even considered that he could be attracted to me, that I'm not in a place to date. Which I stand by. If anything, I'm dating my job, and that's what I'm going to give my attention to. If I want to be successful, then I can't be giving my attention into multiple places, or I'm not going to be as focused on what I need to be.

So, if I kissed Corey, then I'd be in trouble. Because I'd been waiting over ten years to see what a kiss from Corey Ramirez felt like, and I don't think that he's going to be a bad kisser.

I decide I'll stay a little while to at least watch Corey's at bat.

"Let's go, Corey!" I shout, but suddenly start to feel a little lightheaded from raising my voice. My head starts feeling warm from the sun beating down on the stands. Once I cheer his name, I see him peer up at the stands from his practice swing and tilt his head up at me. I can see a slight smirk on his face and I realize it is going to be hard trying to resist feeling anything when he's making these little expressions at me.

Corey bats a strike at the first pitch, but he takes a beat to square up his shoulders and once the next pitch comes, it's out of here.

Holy shit, I mouth. Corey just hit a home run.

The crowd goes wild as Corey and his teammate run around the bases, bringing the Seals score up from three to five. They still have a long way if they want to come close to even tying, but the melancholy atmosphere that once existed minutes ago has left, and the fans are cheering wildly that their "hometown hero" has hit a home run.

I start clapping excitedly as Corey swings around third, making his way to home, when suddenly, fatigue rears its full head. I'm suddenly lightheaded. My eyelids get heavy and I blink once, twice, before I lose my balance and fall onto the pavement.

My vision goes black and I hear gasps and footsteps shuffle toward me.

"Hey!" Footsteps creep closer and a woman's voice calls to me. "Are you okay?"

She begins to shake me a little, but I'm unable to form any response or move any of my limbs to tell her I'm still alive. The last thing I remember hearing is Corey shouting my name over and over amidst the muffled whispers from other fans before all what's in front of me is darkness.

***

Corey

"Leanne!" I yell from home plate. She's not moving. Her limp body is being held up by another person in the stands, who is also trying to shake her to wake up. My heart thumps wildly. The rush of the home run, the worry about Leanne, is overwhelming me right now. She must've fainted from the heat. This weather, plus working in a stuffy food truck with a grill on is dangerous.

I forget a baseball game is happening right now. Thankfully, most of the fans have too. A few more people have rushed over to help Leanne out. I look over to the dugout and see if I can beckon our athletic trainer, Viviana, if she has anything in her kit to help her.

"Viv!" I yell.

"Yes?" she answers from the fence behind the dugout.

"Can you get your bag and go to the stands behind home plate? Leanne just fainted."

She nods and rushes to see if she can examine Leanne. I can't go back behind the dugout when I know Leanne's in trouble. I take off my batting helmet and plead with Coach to let me go in the stands.

"Coach, I need to be taken out of the lineup, it's an emergency."

His eyes go wide. "What? The game isn't over yet."

I start to act frantic, practically heaving at this point. "Leanne's in trouble. She fainted unexpectedly. I asked Viv to check on her, but...I want to be there when she's awake to make sure she's okay. I will try to get back as soon as I can, but...I can't focus on the game with this going on. I..."

I care about her. A lot.

"Yeah." Coach nods reluctantly. "Go. Be back as soon as you can, alright? We'll cover you though."

"Thank you," I rush. I sprint out of the dugout and as I make my way to the stands, I stop short when I see Viv cradling Leanne's head in her lap and putting a moist towel on her forehead. They've moved her so she's in shade now behind the bleachers.

"How is she?" I ask, kneeling beside them. My eyes flit down to Leanne's chest, to make sure she's still breathing.

"She's going to be okay," Viv reassures me. "She fainted from heat exhaustion, which doesn't surprise me with this weather. And with being in the food truck and cooking, it's definitely important to make sure she makes an effort to stay cool."

Leanne lets out a slow groan and I watch her squint her eyes sharply before reaching to grab the towel from her forehead.

I quickly reach to cover my hand over hers, splayed out over her stomach. Her hands are clammy and her skin's gone pale. She's wearing a black shirt that's almost sopping wet from all the sweat she's excreted.

"Hey," I whisper closer to her. "It's okay. You're going to be okay."

She slowly blinks her eyes open and tilts her head to look at me. "Corey?"

I give her hand a little squeeze. "I'm here. I'm staying here until you've cooled down."

Viv guides Leanne to help her sit up and tosses a water bottle to her. Leanne slowly reaches for it and squirts water over her head.

"Fuck," Leanne whispers. "I can't believe I fainted."

"The heat is no joke," Viv quips. "Were you feeling dizzy earlier today?"

"A little," she admits. "In the truck. And I started shouting when Corey got to bat and then my head started hurting. It was the sharpest pain I've ever experienced. I...I thought I could train myself not to over-heat, but...I'd never had the truck warm up like that before." She sits up straight and bends over again, grasping onto her head.

"Fuck," she groans.

"Woah, woah, woah." I grab a hold of her shoulder. "Take it easy. What's wrong?"

"Emma and Vic. I was going to text them to shut down. They're probably boiling in there."

"I'll go and let them know," Viv says, standing up from the concrete floor.

"They're at The Dragon Belly food truck," I tell them. "And can you let them know that I'm going to call Leanne's brother to take her home?"

"Yes, of course," Viv says. "I'll be right back."

I turn back and examine Leanne, who's sitting up so she's leaning against the fence. She closes her eyes again. I've never seen Leanne look so weak. Just two weeks ago, she was giddy and smiling and I was having the best time adventuring around the Bay Area with her. And even when she's working under pressure with multiple people demanding what feels like the world from her, she keeps composure.

Looking at her in this state, not moving or smiling, unable to do what she wants to, my heart plummets, and all I want to do is protect her and have a close eye on her until she's back to her normal self. I'll hold onto her for as long as I can to make sure she's okay.

I fix my position so she can lean her head to rest on my shoulder.

"How are you feeling?" I whisper, reaching over to wrap my arm around her back side. Right now, I'm putting aside the fact that we almost kissed with the Golden Gate behind us, and any feelings I may have to do anything else with her. I know the feelings are still there, but I'm just here to keep a close eye on her, friend to friend.

"Better," she whispers back. "Still feel like I'm drenched in sweat, but dry at the same time. The shade is really helpful, at least."

"I'm going to call Lance to take you home okay? But I'll stay here until he comes."

She pulls apart for a second. "Wait, but the game isn't over yet, Corey. You need to go back and help your team."

"I asked Coach to take me out. He understands."

"Understands what?"

"That I care about my friends," I tell her. There are more important things than baseball sometimes. The f-word I just uttered isn't really what I feel towards her, if I'm being honest with my feelings, but I'm going to respect the boundary that she sets for us. If that's what she wants us to be, I'm okay with it. I can't lose her as a friend, so I'm not going to argue against wanting to see if I can test my attraction for her.

"Thank you, Corey," she says, feigning a slight smile. It's the most I've seen in the last few hours, and it makes a huge impact. "I...I'm glad to have you as a friend then."

She goes back to rest her head on my shoulder. "I'm glad too," I tell her, telling myself that friends are the only thing we need to train ourselves to remain.

Chapter 11
Leanne

When Lance walks, nay storms, up to us, brow furrowed and a shade of red I'd never seen of him before, I worry his head might explode. He's that angry.

Lance doesn't really get angry at anyone easily; you would need to do something wild for Lance to unleash the devil he works really hard to suppress.

And right now, he's very annoyed Corey had to call him to come and get me. If my car broke down, then Lance would have come to get me, regardless of what he was currently working on. This time, he was in the middle of his latest obsession, pickleball, with the rest of the town since the local tennis courts were retrofitted to accommodate pickleball court lines, so when he walks up to Corey and I sitting on the concrete behind the bleachers, he is fully dressed in workout attire and his go-to headband that helps push the hair out of his face, while simultaneously making him look extremely goofy.

"What the hell happened?" he asks.

"Well, hello to you too," I murmur, but before I'm given the chance to tell Lance that he doesn't need to overreact, Corey stands up to meet him face-to-face.

"Everything's okay," Corey reassures him. "I've been sitting here keeping an eye on Leanne for almost the entire time."

"But the game!" Lance retorts. "You would still be out there trying to keep the team afloat. We're down by like fifteen, Core."

"We've been down by fifteen since the third inning, Lance. I'm surprised I was even able to score a homerun so we can be down by thirteen instead. I wasn't going to try and keep playing when Leanne fainted from heat exhaustion! She could've been in bigger trouble if no one knew what to do to help."

"Leanne should have been more careful, especially working in this heat. She pushes herself too hard when she works and forgets to take care of herself and take a break." Lance pinches the bridge of his nose. "And then stuff like this happens, and...shit." Lance's voice starts to crack a little. "What if she needed to be taken to the emergency room?"

I stay still, trying not to completely break down in front of my brother and his best friend, whom I have feelings for, while they fight over me. It's weird; Lance doesn't know about Corey and I and the fact that we've been one degree away from intimate since his return. Right now, I'm guessing Lance just sees Corey as someone who takes care of their friend's siblings, because he's a big baseball star who should be helping his team play a game instead of helping me.

Me: a not so young but always a child in the eyes of my older brother. And the moment I fuck up, I'm berated for needing help when I didn't even really do anything wrong. Sure, I may have over-exerted myself while working today and I can tell myself I should have taken better measures to stay cool, but it was busy and Lance knows that when there are people forming a crowd outside to eat my food, my body doesn't know when to take a break.

"I know, Lance." Corey steps calmly toward him and wraps an arm around Lance's shoulder. Corey and Lance weren't very affectionate throughout high school. They were teenage boys, obsessing over video games and the desire to be popular. Teenage boys didn't hug, then others thought they were soft. Now, there's like a weird aura in the air. My brother on the verge of tears imagining me in the hospital and my friend-crush comforting him. "I would make sure she's taken care of. She's like my family too."

God, now I can't be mad at Lance. He might annoy me to a new level by caring a little too much, but it's out of love. It's just...in a overprotective kind of way that also kind of scares me and everyone around who's involved.

They break apart and Lance wipes his eyes to look down at me, who continues to watch everything unfurl. There is a crowd of people who are starting to exit the stands, which probably means the game is almost over. I begin to stand up and move to somewhere more spacious so we're not caught in the stampede.

"Thank you." Lance nods to Corey. "I know you'd look out for my family like that. You're a good friend." He looks down at me and extends his hand so I can get up.

"Come on, we should get home before everyone starts getting up once the game ends. Seems like people are already kind of over it and leaving."

"Yeah." I nod. I pull myself up with Lance's help slowly, because I still feel a sharp pain in the front of my head. I squint just a bit when I'm stand straight up for the first time since I fainted, and Lance grabs a hold of my elbow to pull me closer to him.

"I got you," Lance says. "Take it slow, okay?"

I nod. When I get home, I'm going to shut all the curtains in my room and do nothing but sleep until the sun rises again.

"You good?" Corey asks, flanking my other side.

"Yeah," I tell him. "Just tired. I'll be okay. Thank you for staying with me, Corey. I really appreciate it."

He nods back. "I'll check in with you guys later." He gives us both a quick wave before he jogs back to the dugout to meet his team as they debrief the big loss they had today. As much as I'm ready to be home and in the comfort of my bed, I think I'm going to feel more comfortable if I stayed resting on Corey's shoulder instead.

We walk by the truck and Emma and Vic sprint from the side of it to meet Lance and I.

"Oh my god, Leanne!" Emma shrieks. "Are you okay? Viv told us that you fainted in the stands and we were so worried about you."

"Yeah, I'm okay. I'm just heading home to rest up. You guys got the truck?"

"Of course we got the truck," Vic responds. "Go get some rest. We cleaned up everything, just need to take it back."

I still feel absolutely awful that Emma and Vic had to endure this heat and work by themselves to clean up the truck and do all the closing work while I was trying to recover. I'd never forgive myself if what happened to me also happened to them because I made them work.

"Are you guys okay?" I ask. "You two were starting to heat up too. If you're starting to feel exhausted too, I can see if they'll let us take the truck tomorrow." I walk closer to see if I can examine any signs of pale and clammy skin.

"I don't want what happened to me happen to you two as well."

Emma holds out a hand. "We're okay, Leanne. I promise. We've been taking our time to make sure we're not working ourselves to the point of exhaustion. And we've been staying hydrated too."

I flit my eyes to the ground. "Maybe I should've listened to you guys when you were trying to tell me to take a break. Maybe I could have stopped this from happening."

"Hey," Vic reaches out to grab a hold of my shoulder, "shit happens and even if you weren't running around as much as you were, you might have still gotten heat exhaustion. All that matters is that you're okay."

"Go home and get some rest." Emma smiles. "We'll message you on what the game plan is tomorrow. If you don't feel like working either, I'm sure we can get a handle on things."

Wait, hold up. Being in a state so weak that I wouldn't work the truck? I don't know at what point that would happen. Once, I was just coming off an onset of food poisoning and had barely got any sleep the night before but powered through and still did a pop up. I couldn't imagine ever feeling like taking a break to let my staff members take over. Not that I think they couldn't. They're both trained and Emma knows all my recipes almost as well as I do.

"I... Don't worry. I just need to go home and rest. I'll let you all know what the game plan is. Thank you again, I don't know what I would do without y'all."

They wave to us before heading back into the truck and turn on the ignition to drive away once the security guards pull up the divider poles that lead into the park. I step into Lance's truck and rest my head on the window as he gets in and turns on the ignition. As the music of Lance's go to playlist: Guilty Pleasures, begins to play, he turns his head to take another look at me.

"How are you feeling?"

I shrug. "I'm okay. Just kind of ready to lie down."

Lance frowns. "Look, Lele. I'm sorry I got frustrated when I came to the park. When Corey texted me to come and get you because you fainted from heat exhaustion, I...I was really scared."

"I know," I whisper. "It ended up being okay. Someone came to help as soon as they saw something was wrong and then Corey asked the team's athletic trainer to get some cold compress on me while I was taken to somewhere shady. It's not like I was alone."

He sighs. In his mind, he knows I'm an adult, but he'll fixate on how I'm just his little sister. Emphasis on the little. "I know but, shit, Leanne. I was still worried. I raced here as fast as I could, in case things may have taken a a turn for the worst. What if you died, Leanne?"

"Okay, let's not talk death." I sit up straighter. "That is a little dramatic."

"It happens. More than you realize. The scary thing is that we don't live in an area where there's a lot of heat waves. It's not something that we can prepare for."

Ah, damn. My heart seizes a bit when I realize I might've fucked up, trying not to take this so seriously. As much as I don't want to be the person everyone worries about, I accept that it's my fate. Being the one girl in between two boys, my parents like to hoist me onto a pedestal because they automatically think I'm "fragile." And growing up, I was always an emotional kid, crying over every damn thing and getting too into my feelings, so as I grew up, it wasn't like I was bumped off anyway.

"I know. And I'm sorry. Emma and Vic tried to tell me to take breaks and drink water, but I didn't listen. I just wanted to make sure that we were helping our customers out as much as possible. Which didn't really go away as much as I thought even though it felt like a desert outside. So, maybe I could've prevented it if I had done more to cool myself down, but when it comes to my job, it takes precedent. Even over my health. But after that scare, I think it's shown me that I might need to reevaluate my priorities."

"Yes, please," Lance says. "I get it. You're a hardworking and passionate person. And I feel like I don't tell you enough, but I am really proud of you, Leanne. But, maybe you do need to take a step back. Go on a vacation."

"Psh, a vacation? With who?" I am single and have less friends than I do fingers, two of whom work with me.

"I don't know! Me? Leon? Wouldn't that be fun? We haven't had a vacation together since we went to Carmel for Mom and Dad's joint fiftieth birthday."

I pout. After this recent debacle, I might have to have Lance sign a binding agreement that if I were to go on vacation with my brothers, he would give me autonomy to do what I wanted, instead of trying to hover over me like a helicopter. But maybe it would be fun though. I did promise Corey I would think about taking a weekend trip somewhere during his away games to see more of California. I can't believe I might be bringing this up, but I think I know how to make Lance happy and help myself out in the process.

"I think that'd be fun. Actually, Neptune Beach plays Ventura for their next away series. We haven't really been to that part of SoCal before. We should ask Corey if we can tag along." And I'm going to try and be as secretive as possible with Corey while my brothers might be in the same vicinity.

Lance's face lights up like a firework. "Hell yeah! You're a genius Leanne! I heard Ventura's awesome. Great for surfing. Maybe I'll learn how to surf. Let's do it. I'll text Leon, I'm sure he'll be happy to join too."

He leans back in his chair as we begin cruising to the driveway leading to my parent's. "Fairbanks Family Road Trip, I can't wait!"

Neither can I, but I'm also going to have to learn how to hold my breath and my excitement about being in the same vicinity as Corey and not think about him in the same way I normally do, especially now that my brothers will be tagging along.

***

I slowly blink my eyes awake when I hear soft knocking at my bedroom door. When I peer over to look at the time on my nightstand and see it's a little past eight at night, I notice the sky has changed to an orange color. I've been sleeping for about three hours since I got home and I may or may not be able to go back to sleep later tonight. At least the game that's happening tomorrow is an evening one, so at that point, the weather should be a lot cooler instead of the afternoon game that took place today in the heat.

"Come in," I try shouting to the door. It's probably Lance letting me know that there's dinner if I'm hungry.

Slowly, the door opens and I sit up a little bit when it's not Lance who walks through the door.

"Hey," a soft voice peeps its way through, stepping into my room and shutting the door behind them.

"Corey?"

I want to scream. Corey is in my room. My childhood room, which has since been remodeled, but still has no shortage of pastels and framed posters of all my obsessions on the walls. Thank goodness I decided last year I didn't need a poster of the Jonas Brothers on my wall anymore, that would've been a tad embarrassing if I kept that up.

"Hi." He waves. He's holding a plastic bag full of something, and sets it down on my desk.

"What are you doing here?"

"I came to see how you were doing. I also brought some dinner for your brothers, because Lance didn't feel like cooking and your parents are out at a community event. Obviously, I brought some for you too."

I sit up straighter, eyeing the bag again that's on my desk. It's not branded, just one of those plastic bags that say, "Thank you!" and "I'm reusable!" on it. Those bags that people who come to California say are indestructible. I think I saw a video where someone could carry their dog in there and it didn't break.

"What'd you bring?"

He opens the bag and holds out a foiled cylinder-shaped thing, and I know exactly what he's brought me. My mouth opens in delight and I snatch the item from him.

"You brought me a burrito?"

He chuckles. "Yeah, I went to Taqueria La Playa. You can thank Lance for the suggestion. He was craving a carnitas burrito."

I realize I haven't really eaten since before we opened the food truck for the game, so this is going to do wonders for filling up my stomach. "How'd you know what to get me?"

"Lance," Corey quips. "Carne asada, rice, pinto beans, extra tomatoes, and..." he reaches back into the bag and shows off a small container of green salsa, "extra hot salsa verde. Had to hide this one from your brothers because you guys are animals for this stuff."

"We might be slightly addicted to their salsa," I note. "Maybe I should go get a plate to eat this on. Having a burrito in bed, while sounds like a dream, might bite me in the ass when I randomly find a pinto bean that's fallen into my sheets."

"Here, I can snag a plate for you. Or, we can go eat downstairs. Lance wanted to talk to me about something exciting that you two discussed on the way home?"

"Yeah." I stand up from my bed and set the burrito back into the bag. "Um, we were thinking that it might be fun, and to also get me to get out of the house, that we'd take a road trip down to Ventura to watch you play during your away series down there."

"Oh!" Corey says, lifting his brows. "Um, yeah. That'd be fun. So it'd be you, Lance, and would Leon be coming too?"

I nod. "Yeah, you get triple the dose of Fairbanks for a long weekend. You know, while also trying to win your games against the team you're playing." I eye Corey closely. I thought that he might be excited that we're "surprising" him by following him on his next series, but he seems really uneasy after I told him.

"Are you okay?" I ask. "You don't look really excited about this. I can tell Lance if you don't want us to go..."

"No!" He grabs a hold of my arm and steps closer to me. "It's not that. I'm actually really happy you guys are coming. I think this is going to be a really fun trip. Reminds me of when we'd used to stay somewhere overnight for travel baseball."

He leans over me a little more and bites his bottom lip.

"Some part of me kind of wishes it could be a little more intimate though. Like, how happy I would be if you were the only one coming. Promise me you'll make some time for just the two of us when we're down there okay?" He whispers closer to my ear. A silence looms between us again, and I'm teleported back to the moment when we're standing at Hawk Hill, when it felt like we were the only two people in the world. I just wish I didn't feel so conflicted about Corey's feelings for me. He's saying how happy it would make him if I was the only one coming to see him play in another city, but is he also going to keep thinking about how better it is because it's outside of Neptune Beach? I can't keep giving him promises of us and intimate time together when he might have an expiration date on us.

It's not fair to me nor my heart to be put through such conflict, and I want to tell Corey, but I don't want what we have right now to be ruined.

Chapter 12
Corey

I never thought I would see the day where I am sitting in a bar with my teammates, my childhood best friend, his brother, and the woman I'm kind of attracted to, which also happens to be their sister.

But here we are, and we're not even in Neptune Beach.

Lance and Leon get along really well with the other players. Lance, makes sense. He kind of acts like a fanboy with the rest of the players and mentioning how he used to play in college but had to quit because he went on co-op for his major. And to top it all off, he's involved with so many things in Neptune Beach, he's out here giving recommendations for the best places to eat and even started a running group for players who are trying to beef up their cardio regime. Leon's talking about his recent college experience with some of the young, also fresh out of college players, which is how I learned that despite his hard work ethic and doing well enough to get into one of the most prestigious law schools in the country, Leon also doubled as a frat boy, keg stands and all. Somehow he's the one who is on his third beer.

Leanne is the one I'm still trying to figure out, and the one my eyes remain glued to.

We're all seated on a few high long tables near the back of the bar. After our first game against the Ventura Spider Crabs, which ended with another loss, it seemed appropriate to enjoy a night on the town rather than wallowing in our hotel room. We're staying near the town's pier and downtown area, so it was an easy walk to grab dinner and now, a drink. Or multiples if you're a baseball team who enjoys indulging in five dollar well cocktails at a bar that has three different performance stages for dancing.

Lance grips onto me by the shoulders. "Hey man, we're taking a group shot."

I point to my chest. "We? Who decided that?"

"I did. And then I got like half the team to agree. You're away from home! Let loose a little."

Lance can say that because he's technically on vacation. I'm technically on business, and tomorrow I have to go back to "work" and try and win our second game against the Spider Crabs. I haven't been hungover since college and I don't think I want to experience it again at the age of thirty.

I flash him my cup of beer. "I think this is a good level of letting loose."

Lance rolls his eyes. "Yeah, but when's the last time that we've let loose together?"

College? One year, I drove from Los Gatos to San Luis Obispo to visit Lance at school. That weekend, the baseball team decided to throw a huge party at a house a few of the players shared. It was like the entire athlete student population was at this party. There were multiple water jugs full of jungle juice, beer kegs, and three areas that had a table to play drinking games. It was lit. And Lance and I got the most wasted we ever been. Going shot for shot, then trying to win at beer pong multiple times. As much as I was happy I drove down to see Lance for a weekend, the next day was spent completely hungover at his apartment, not even going out until the sun went back down to get something greasy to eat.

"Remember the baseball party junior year?" I remind him.

Lance nods his head slowly. "Hell yeah. Damn that party was lit. See, that's what I'm trying to relive!"

Yeah, definitely not. We are not twenty-one anymore, and with that, we can't drink like we did when we reached legal age. I don't want to even think about what potential hangover will come if I keep saying yes to Lance, who keeps saying we need to relive our youth a la shots and cheap beer. But, Lance gets more annoying when he can't force people to have fun, so I reluctantly tell him we can enjoy one shot together.

"But just one," I reiterate. "We have a game tomorrow."

He groans, but ultimately agrees to only pester me for one shot. "Okay, okay, fine. I'd rather see you try and win than be hungover, I'll admit that."

"Thank you." We get up and a trail of players follow us to a small opening at the bar. I turn around to check on what Leanne is up to. She's still chatting with Viv, I think because the rest of the team are all men, so Viv is someone Leanne can easily flock to. That, and Viv has taken care of Leanne when she had that heat exhaustion scare.

Lance wiggles his way to the bar counter and shouts over the groups of people mingling that he'd like ten shots. I don't know where he got that number, seeing as only seven of us are at the bar.

"Lance!" I yell. "Only five of us came up to take shots."

Lance rolls his eyes after giving the bartender his credit card. "It's fine. Some of us can take two." It's also worth noting Lance also had two beers before this. He beckons everyone to take a shot and then we crowd around one another and clink our glasses together.

We shout a resounding "Cheers!" and I gulp down the shot. Blech. Tequila isn't my bad, but it certainly doesn't sit well after I consume it.

"See, Corey!" Lance elbows me in the side. "That wasn't so bad, right?"

"No, it wasn't." It wasn't good by any means, either. "I'm going to go back and stick with my beer though."

"Lame," Leon juts in. "Come on! We're in another town and you get to spend it with your friends! I know you can let loose a little bit, Corey."

I gently pat the top of his head. Leon gets to try and egg me on because he's fresh out of college, but I don't budge. "I'm trying to know my limit. Which I think everyone should try and do the same."

Just as Leon tries to rebuttal, Leanne and Viv walk up behind us.

"Woooow, someone didn't want to invite us to take a shot with them!" Viv raises their hands up, like they'd just been betrayed. "Thanks a lot!"

Leanne starts to snicker beside them.

"Gotta pay attention when I'm talking about shots!" Lance replies. "Well, there are three left anyway that didn't get taken. You both can take one and I'll take the other one."

"Wow." I bend to nudge Leanne in the arm. "Didn't think you were so into shot taking."

She shrugs. "I'm on vacation. And Viv had fomo. I'm doing it more for them."

Leanne and Viv take a shot with Lance, and something tells me when Lance tries to put the empty shot glass back on the counter and nearly prevents it from falling on the floor and shattering, that this is going to be a long night.

***

I keep a close eye on everyone as they all dance around different areas of the bar. Some have ended up outside, others remain at the high table we originally congregated at, and a few have traversed to the back room that feels like a college party, playing all the music from our youth.

I decide to follow Lance and Leon, because they are the most drunk out of everyone and I want to make sure both of them don't puke their guts out on the floor. Which has led me to the outdoor patio area, where the music is a little more subdued. Some people are swaying, and some people are making out. Lance, by some stroke of luck, has budded up with a stranger and has reached the point where he looks like he's so hungry he'll almost eat her face off. I don't even know what Lance said to this person, maybe he just needed to compliment her on her shirt and she looks as if she's fully enamored by him. Leon is getting cozy with a few people on an outdoor couch, and honestly, I wouldn't be surprised if he started making out with these people too.

While I think I should be looking out for my friends, I tell myself that they're both adults and it shouldn't be the end of the world if I leave them alone for a few minutes. So I decide to get up and head back into the bar. As I head up to the bar to order a beer, I see Leanne and Viv, but they're not talking to one another. No, instead, their backs are turned to one another. Viv is talking to a woman and Leanne is talking, nay, laughing with a guy wearing a red flannel button down.

I narrow my eyes quickly in their direction. Why does Leanne suddenly look so happy to be talking to this person? I mean, she was happy talking to Viv, but I just assume that they enjoy talking to one another because they already know each other. Leanne has met this person maybe a few minutes ago and she looks enthralled with this conversation she's engaging in. There's a grin glued to her face as she listens to whatever the hell he could be blabbering on about. There are a lot of scenarios that can play out. Maybe I can assume that Leanne is only talking to this guy because she's trying to be nice. I'm bracing myself for what could be worst case scenario: she kisses the man after being so enamored by him, but I'm trying to think of a way to stop that from happening.

I take a gulp of my beer after I pay for it. I need to get out of this jealous funk that I'm in. I don't own Leanne or dictate how she should be living her life. She's her own person and she's an adult, too. She can make her own decisions, and she's deciding to talk to this guy. She may decide that she wants to kiss him or dance with him, and I need to tell myself that if she wants to do that, then fine. It's a temporary fling. I'm just going to be really bitter about it, because she's been friend zoning me this entire time we've hung out and to hook up with someone in the same room as me while I've respected her space and wishes kind of sucks.

It's at some point when my stomach begins to feel warm, I realize that I've drunk all the beer that I just ordered. Something ignites in me that makes me think I need to tell Leanne how I feel. What's the harm in saying it? Leanne and I are friends. I can tell her what's bothering me, even if she's the culprit. Best case scenario, she'll just decide she's not going to talk to anyone else tonight. That'll put me at some ease.

I slowly step closer toward her and pretend that I accidentally brush my elbow against her. She jumps, for a moment thinking I was a stranger who got too close in this crowded bar, but then softens when she notices it's me.

"Corey!" she squeals and leans into my arm. "What's up? Are you having fun?"

As fun as I can while making sure no one passes out. "Yeah, I'm having fun." I peer over to the guy that Leanne was previously speaking to. "What's up? I'm Corey."

"Um, Ray." He reaches out to shake my hand. "Good to meet you."

I menacingly step closer. "I need to talk to Leanne for a moment. Do you mind if I just pull her aside?"

"No, not at all." He turns to face Leanne. "Sorry, I didn't realize you had a boyfriend."

Leanne narrows her eyes at me. "I don't. He's not...Corey is just a friend!"

Ouch. Well, that stung to hear out loud, even if its true.

"Yeah," I butt in. "We're just talking like two good ol' chums." I lightly grab her by the arm. "Come on."

She acts like she's glued to the stool, because it takes more of an effort than it should to get her up and out of the seat. I pull her to a spot near the of the bar that seems like it's the quietest spot, but with all the music and speaking that's going on, I can still barely hear myself.

"What do you need that's so urgent, Corey? Ray and I were engaged in a good conversation."

"Was that all you were having? A good conversation?"

She rolls her eyes. "What are you talking about?"

I'm trying to tell her to stop flirting, but not come off abrasive. But, right now, as I'm staring at Leanne, dressed in a bandeau and high rise pleather pants, looking like she's freaking Sandy from Grease, I'm not sure what else to tell her other than, "You're the most beautiful woman in the room." Who am I kidding? She's the most beautiful woman in the world, and I don't need to travel to anywhere else to realize it.

You know what? Fuck it. I've had enough to drink to feel a little buzzed and the strongest pull to Leanne Fairbanks I've ever experienced, so I'm going to tell her exactly how I feel when I saw her engage in a good conversation with another man.

I lean in closer to her and brush a bit of hair that's fallen in front of her face. "Did you like it? When you were flirting with another man and I had to watch?"

She almost loses her footing and leans back against the brick wall behind her. "Flirting? I wasn't flirting! What's it to you anyway? We're not together."

I probably smell of alcohol when I breathe onto her face, but I don't care. "Together or not, I know you know how much I think about you, Leanne Fairbanks." I bite the bottom of my lip. "How much I fucking want you."

Her mouth forms an "O" and I want to kiss it shut. When she blinks back, unable to spill her thoughts out from inside her, I move one hand to cup her cheek and the other to splay right over her lower waist.

"I don't want to share you with anyone else. No, I refuse to let you give yourself to another man."

And then, I do something that I haven't done with anyone in a long time.

I lean in to take a whiff of her at the side of her neck and press my nose against it. She smells like citrus, with a nice floral undertone. It makes me go weak. I kiss a spot on her neck, to mark my claim, careful not to go too hard as to save her from getting any bruises.

"Corey," she moans and bucks her hips against me. I move my hand down to cup her ass cheek.

"You smell so sweet," I murmur into her skin. "I just needed to discover it myself. Taste what I've been salivating over for weeks now. My knees are starting to buckle because of how good you smell."

"Corey." She leans back and I watch her chest start to heave. "Let's take a step back. We should talk first."

"What exactly do we need to talk about?"

"I..." She tries to push back against my chest to separate herself. "I can't take this push and pull from you! You can't be telling me how you feel about me and complain that you're stuck in Neptune Beach and you're trying to find a way out! Do you know what's in Neptune Beach? Me! And I'm trying to do all these things to make you happy to be here but I know that all this still has an expiration date!"

I frown, sobering up once I see that Leanne's clearly upset. I shouldn't have done something to set her off when she might've not been comfortable yet. Especially when she's not lying about what this really is between us. It's a ticking time bomb which will explode the moment I get what I want: an offer.

"Leanne," I sober up, stepping back from her grasp. "I'm not trying to...I'm sorry, I..." This isn't about having fun anymore. Leanne has never been someone to just fool around.

She finagles her way out of my view and starts walking to the entrance of the bar. "I need to get some air."

"Wait!" I stride after her. "Can we talk about this?"

We reach outside, where even well after the sun is down, the weather still feels like we're baking in a sauna. "What is there to talk more about, Corey? You're clearly only in this for the short term."

"Well, I'm not the only one! You told me you weren't interested in dating after you broke up with Greg. I'm attracted to you, Leanne, and I know you feel a similar way."

I recoil. That was a cop out answer and I know it. I just wanted Leanne to understand deep down, I know she's attracted to me too. She wouldn't have leaned into my touch at the baseball game. She wouldn't have let me close the gap at the park. I know she didn't let me kiss her, but she thought "what if" for a moment, and all I want is for her and I to take a chance.

"You don't know me, Corey." She shakes her head. "You just want me to feel the same thing you are, but I don't have feelings for you like you're a fucking fling."

Tears start streaming down her face. "Once upon a time, I thought I was in love with you. It felt like fate, you and I. When I was younger, I dreamt of the day I could be with you. And ever since you waltzed back into my life, I can't stop thinking about the girl who had dreams of being with Corey Ramirez. How she'd be ecstatic they're finally coming true. But, for how long? What if you get called up tomorrow, Corey? I can't have my heart broken again."

She starts sobbing and it immediately sobers me up. I feel like a jerk. I said things that hurt her, and the last thing I want to do is make Leanne upset. We're both inebriated, and not thinking straight.

I pull her in softly to rest against my body. I feel her face connect to my chest and when she starts to cry more, I rub circles around her back and pull her in tighter against me.

"I'm so sorry, Leanne." I gently press my lips and give her a kiss on the top of her head. "I hate seeing you upset."

She pulls her head back and stares up at me. I slide one arm I had wrapped around her back and bring it to wipe her tear-stained cheek.

"I know I should give you space," I confess. "And I know I can tell you over and over again how much you mean to me, but my words may not carry the impact you're looking for. Just know, as long as I'm here, I want to be yours. And even if I left tomorrow, I would try to find some way to make it work. I...I've never felt this much about one person to try and fight for us, but you changed that for me, Leanne."

"Corey..." She whispers. "Do you mean that?"

I lean down to plant a kiss on her forehead. "A hundred percent. I mean every word."

Chapter 13
Leanne

Corey keeps his arms wrapped around me as we stand outside in the dark.

I do feel bad for making him feel like a jerk. I just don't want anything to feel temporary. As much as I want to touch and feel every part of Corey Ramirez, I don't know what it means to just be in a fling. Maybe I should try. I don't have much of a desire to get married again. The stress of the first time around was a lot, and I want to focus on my business.

Maybe I do need to just let myself loose, if Corey is feeling attracted to me, that's a dream coming true, right?

Man, I sure know how to pick the right men to fall in love with.

"What does this mean?" I ask him. "For us?"

"It means whatever you want. I would like to spend the night with you, but I'll give you your space."

I frown. I feel like I don't benefit one way or another. I either spend the night alone, wishing Corey was next to me, or I spend the night with him, wishing I could do it for more than just one night.

I purse my lips and give Corey a curt nod before breaking apart and giving myself space to move around again.

"Okay."

"Okay what?"

"I'd like to spend the night with you too. But, that doesn't mean I just want this to be a fling."

"It's not a fling, Leanne. It's..." He taps his finger against his chin. "I don't know. Friends with benefits, I guess."

"Isn't that the same thing?"

He shakes his head. "Whatever happens, I still want us to be friends. I know that's a lot to ask, but I do really like spending time with you and I hope you'll still be around for my journey, wherever that will take me."

"I do too, Corey." Since he's come back, I haven't felt this happy. I loved the date we had to Marin County, and I would keep hanging out with him. He's not completely disgusted by oysters too.

"Let's get back," he says. "It's getting late, and even though I don't have a game until later that night, I would like to try and not wake up with a hangover. But I think that may already happen."

"Yeah, I haven't drank this much in a long time."

"Are you feeling sick at all?"

I shake my head. "I'm okay. I have water back in my hotel room too."

"Good, you need to remember to stay hydrated." He starts chuckling. "I don't want you fainting in front of my eyes again."

"I won't. Promise." I can spare Corey from a health scare. But I did like the brief moment where our hands touched, and my body laid against his.

We quietly sneak away from the bar, Corey asking that a few of the players keep an eye out for Lance and Leon, who are nearing the point of gone with how intoxicated they are. I can tell by how Corey is asking his teammates, he's worried that Lance and Leon are going to somehow not make it back to the hotel, but everyone reassures him they'll keep an eye out for them.

I don't enjoy telling little white lies about my whereabouts, but I'm thankful Viv is understanding when I kindly tell her that the drinks I had are not sitting well, so I needed someone to escort me back to the hotel room. Once we exit out of the bar and begin walking, I link my arm around Corey's as we walk up the block to the end of the road where the hotel is located.

We head back to the hotel and decide we'll spend time hanging out in Corey's room, because when I booked the rooms for myself, Lance, and Leon, the hotel front desk asked if we wanted our rooms to be near each other, and I said that would be okay, but when they wake up to the sound of Corey and I talking, or possibly making other "noises," I don't want to have to explain myself, or plant a possible bomb from exploding.

Corey walks up to his hotel room, and presses the keycard against the door to unlock it. When I walk in, I expect his room to be similar to mine: suitcase sprawled out on the floor, clothes dilapidated around it. We don't even talk about the bathroom. I should not have makeup and toiletries laid out on a towel and covering every open space on the counter, but then I got in a mood to dress to impress, putting on winged eyeliner and a full beat of makeup. I guess it paid off.

But his room is quite the opposite. No makeup sprawled out on the bathroom counter. His suitcase still has clothes folded in it, and he neatly places his baseball duffel right next to it.

"Your room is so clean," I note.

"Oh. Yeah, I kind of like keeping things tidy. Saves having to rush to get where I need to go all the time."

"Wow," I say, walking to sit on the bed and wiggle off my sandals. "Are there any other secrets I should know about you? How you like your meat cooked? Favorite vegetable? What's your sleep style?"

He chuckles. "I don't think those need to be secrets anyway. Medium rare, bell peppers, and on my back, but that last one you were going to find out anyway."

"This is like, what teenage Leanne was writing about in her diary."

"What?" Corey joins to sit next to me. "Being in my hotel room?"

"Well, I guess not quite that. Being alone with you." I scoot closer to him. "Our legs touching one another. Back then, I did the most teenage shit to try and get you to notice me. I made you a goddamn sign for your senior night and bought you chicken nuggets."

He leans in and plants a kiss on my cheek. "Don't be embarrassed. Looking back on it now, it was kind of cute." Corey's grin doesn't leave his face, and his eyes go soft as he continues to take a look at me in my embarrassment. "And now, it's like I'm getting to know you all over again, and now I can see what I was missing when I was a teenager."

"Which is what?"

"How beautiful you really are."

My lips part. "Corey..."

"Leanne." He leans and touches his forehead to mine. "I can't keep looking at your lips and not know what it feels like to press mine against them. Please, let me taste you."

I gulp. This is it. This is what I've been waiting for. This is what almost happened when we were at Hawk Hill, but I was full of confused emotions and stopped it from happening. But now, even though I may decide that I never want to kiss Corey again for future me's piece of mind, I at least can get a taste of what I'd been yearning forever for.

"Yes, Corey. Kiss me," I plead.

He leans over on the bed and gently touches his lips onto mine. What begins as a light kiss intensifies in an instant. He leans into my body, holding me up by the weight of his arm wrapped around my waist. I wrap my arms around his neck and pull him closer to me. His lips are soft, the slight taste of bourbon lingering on them. I tilt my head to get a better angle, and Corey takes that as a signal to open his mouth up, guiding mine to follow suit. He plays with my tongue, and I grip at the back of his hair. He guides me to lean back on the bed and hovers his body over mine. When he leans down, I can feel the hardness peeking through his jeans pressing into my pussy.

There's no way we're just going to keep things at first base. I start grinning. How appropriate when I'm kissing a baseball player to mention bases.

I start to nip at his bottom lip, slightly sucking it between my teeth.

"Fuck," he says between kisses, "Leanne."

I break apart. Hopefully I didn't use too much teeth to make it hurt.

"Sorry! Did I bite down too hard?"

"No." He shakes his head and tries to calm himself down from how quickly he started breathing. "No, that was amazing. I didn't know what to think for our first kiss, but that blew my expectations out of the water."

I raise a brow. "Yeah? You think so? I might need to give up cooking and be a professional kisser then."

He shakes his head. "Yeah yeah. Only with me though, okay? And keep biting. I like a little necessary roughness."

With more force this time, he leans up to kisses me and it's like fireworks have gone off in my brain. Corey takes no time to explore every bit of skin that I have on my body. After he's working my mouth, he sends a trail of small kisses down my neck and to my collarbone, where he ends just above my breast.

"I'd be satisfied tasting you all day, Leanne," he says, breathlessly.

"So would I."

"I need to touch more of you," he pants. He hovers a hand over my chest and I flit my eyes down and back up at him.

"Can I?" he asks.

I take in a sharp inhale and exhale through my mouth. The bandeau that I was wearing did it's job of covering my breasts, but yet was somehow tight enough that I didn't have to worry about adjusting it every ten minutes to prevent it from falling. As I looked down at my chest though, it reminded me that it had been a long time that anyone has seen them.

"I think we should talk...before I let you explore places that may be more on the unchartered side. Run the bases, as baseball players would say."

"Okay." He nods. "But I'm not letting you leave me from this position, got it?"

I reach up to ruffle my hands through his hair. "Got it."

"Ugh." He closes his eyes and lets out a groan. "I want more of that later, okay?"

I smirk. It did feel nice that any little move I made had this monumental effect on Corey. Talk about feeling like you're queen of the world, making a man near helpless at every little move you make.

"Sure."

"Okay," he sighs. "Let's talk."

"Well, it's obvious that we shouldn't be entering into any kind of relationship. Not until you have a better timeline for how long you might be here."

He sighs. "Yeah. I wish I had that for you, truly. There's...a lot that I wish someone could give you, Leanne, because you deserve it. Especially because you need someone who is going to stay and build their life in Neptune Beach, and I...I still dream of spreading my wings."

"I know." It was a tough pill to swallow, but the soulmate I drummed up in my mind wasn't someone who was looking to flee Neptune Beach as soon as he'd been given the call. For someone that loved being at home so much, Corey was the opposite, and in this case, I don't think notion that opposites attract applied.

"And after being broken one time," I add, "I don't want to go through it again."

"I get that," he agrees.

"So," I begin. This is it. This is my proposition and even if it went against any kind of rule book that I drummed up in my mind for how I wanted to be with someone, I needed to do something that gave me release. That took the stress off. And that's what I was going to see this as.

"I think the friends with benefits can work. We'll agree that we're the only ones who we're being intimate with, but we're not going to label this as anything. No dating. No boyfriend-girlfriend-we're tying each other down with a label tacked on top of it. We're...just using each other for some fun time."

"And you're okay with that?" Corey asks.

I nod. "I will be. I can be thankful for the smallest bit of release even if I know it'll end at some point. I can't help how much I enjoyed what we were just doing. Call it a stress relief, I guess. I know I could use more of it."

"Okay." Corey smiles and reaches to give me a quick peck. "Friends with benefits. And we promise to keep it to ourselves?"

"Yes." I nod. I can't let anyone in my outer circle know I'm fucking my best friend's brother, especially the brother mentioned. "Lance will go ballistic if he found out. I don't want me to be the reason you two may never regain the friendship you once had."

"Yeah, I don't know if I want to see what that looks like."

I shake my head. "Trust me, after what happened with Greg, you do not want to see angry Lance."

"I've only seen him angry during a game, and...yeah. Those were some times where I didn't know if he'd ever come down from the rage high that he had and he wasn't even the one who messed up the play.

We look at each other again, and silently make our promise to ourselves to enter into this new phase of our lives, knowing that it'll come to an end, and I was going to be okay with that. I was going to let Corey be free, if that meant he was going to be happy.

"So..." He reaches up again, tilting my chin up with his fingers to look at him. "You mentioned something about running the bases?"

Chapter 14
Corey

These baseball jokes are really getting out of hand. Whoever decided the progression of kissing to having sex as a run around the bases...well I guess I can't help but laugh I'm getting to experience it all for myself again.

If it gets Leanne to bust up laughing like she is right now, I can't complain.

"What?" I laugh back. "Isn't it ironic a baseball player is getting to run the bases in bed with the most beautiful woman he's ever met?"

She arches a brow. "Do you say that to all the women you hook up with?"

I raise a brow back at her. Does she think I'm a person who does a lot of sleeping around?

"I mean, it's been a while. I haven't had sex in over a year."

"Wait." She leans back but still keeps her arms wrapped around my neck. "You haven't?"

"No! Do you think that I'm some kind of playboy?"

"I don't know! Maybe it's because I think that you're hot and I wouldn't be surprised if other women were clamoring to you trying to get in your pants!"

I laugh and pull her back into me so our bodies are flush against each other. "I'm not the kind of person to drop his pants for anyone. I'd only have sex with someone if I feel like I have a connection to them."

"Well, I guess that's a nice thing to hear out of a man's mouth," Leanne quips. "Just curious, when's the last time you've been in a relationship? After you graduated, I feel like there was a cord that just snapped. I stopped hearing about what you were up to, you moved around playing for different teams, and I feel like I'm back into learning who you are for the first time in...almost a decade."

I want to learn more about Leanne too, now that I feel like I'm mature enough to actually understand the inner workings in her brain and build myself to become someone she chooses to be close to her heart. I reach up to cup her cheek, and begin stroking it using my thumb. "Okay, first thing's first: I don't want you to think I'm still the guy I was back in high school. I know Lance and I said some pretty rude things behind your back about you, and I want you to know that I don't think you're the same annoying little sister that would bother us to play video games anymore. And I'm sorry if I ever said anything that upset you back then. I was...a dumb teenager who was obsessed with baseball and getting other people's attention."

She shrugs. "It's okay. I was kind of a dumb teenager too. Plotting my way to figure out how to break you and Giselle Hamm up when I found out you two were dating."

"Psh." I turn my head away. "That was just a lot of two people who just liked kissing a lot. The last time that I've been in a relationship was...almost two years ago? I was living in New Jersey and met someone who was a bartender at the town I lived in." Nessa, who I genuinely loved, but ultimately, we ended things because I got traded and she was not a fan of the potential of long distance. My attempt to resist Leanne for fear of the same thing happening is making my mind race.

"Ah." She nods. "Sorry I assumed you were such a playboy."

I pull her in closer to me. "It's okay. I just want you to know that I care about you, Leanne, and I'm going to give you what you want even if we can only do it for so long. We both deserve to have a little bit of fun, right?"

She grins. "Yeah, I think we do. And thanks, I care about you too."

"Let me take care of you then," I whisper, tugging on her top. "Can I take this off of you?"

She doesn't give me a verbal response but nods. She moves her hands from wrapped around my neck and sets them at her side. I grab her shirt by the hem and she raises both her arms up to take it off. Her breasts are covered with a strapless bra and I reach over to her backside to undo the clasps so it falls off her chest. My mouth can't help but water at how beautiful they are. Seeing them exposed for the first time like this makes my heart want to leap out of my chest.

I start to slide my hand up her stomach and palm one of her breasts. I splay my hand over it and start massaging it. I love how nicely it feels to hold it in my hand. Leanne lets out a breathy moan and that signals me to explore more. I use my fingers to pinch her nipple. She quickly bends forward and her moans are like music to my ears.

"Corey," she pants.

"Do you like this?" I ask, my voice on the verge of going hoarse. "Your breasts are so goddamn beautiful."

"Mhhhhm."

I shift myself on the bed so my mouth is closer to her chest. I lean in closer and press my lips against her nipple, then opening my mouth and biting on it.

"Ohhhh god, Corey. More," she demands. She shifts up and tugs a bit of my hair, causing me to let out a moan with her breast still filling my open mouth.

"Fuck." I look back up at her. With the way she groans into my head, I'm close to bursting. "I'm so into you, Leanne."

I reposition her so that she's leaning against my pillows and I unbuckle her shorts and slide them off her legs. I rub my fingers on her panties, right outside of her pussy.

"You're soaked," I note.

"Are you surprised?" She comments. "You make me feel so good. I need to come, Corey."

"Yes," I agree. I'm starting to reach a point where I'm going to come too, just from the sheer sounds Leanne makes when I'm pleasuring her. I tug on the elastic of her panties and pull them off so they're sitting on her thighs. I stick one finger in and after pushing my way inside, I make room for another. I rub them against her g-spot and give a few more pumps in and out.

"Corey." She says my name so breathlessly. I grin when I look up at her splayed out on the bed, hair spread out on the pillow.

"Hold on for a little longer for me baby." I can't take back the pet name, but I don't think I completely hated saying it.

I bring my mouth down to suck at her clit, and Leanne gasps. I guide her hips up, and hold her by the ass, going down on her again. This is only the start, but I'm already loving what I'm tasting.

"Corey," she pants my name again. "I'm going to come."

Leanne's head falls back into the pillow and she lets out a breathless "fuck!" when she comes.

"Damn," she says. "That was amazing."

I kiss her on the forehead. "Good."

"Wait." She sits up. "What about you?"

I raise a brow. "What about me?"

"You're just going to make me come and then leave you in the dust? Don't think I didn't feel how hard you were throughout that."

I playfully wrestle her back to laying on the bed and gently rest my body atop hers. "It's not about me," I say, giving her a kiss. I was so close though. Thinking about naked Leanne screaming my name will get me to come quickly. "I wanted to make sure you're satisfied."

She lightly pushes herself off me. "And I'm here to make sure you're satisfied too. Come on, take off your briefs."

I let Leanne take the reins and keep my eyes trained on her as she flits hers down to my hands as they work to take off my pants, and then my briefs. Her eyes widen when my dick pops out and sticks straight up. I toss my briefs aside and pull her in by her thighs to ride atop me.

"Like what you see?" I ask.

"Like doesn't begin to cover how I'm feeling," she says, shaking her head. "Is it wild to say I'm obsessed?"

"No," I grin, "because I want you to be obsessed with what's yours."

She laughs. "Sorry if this is gross, but I have to use what I got." She looks at her palm and spits into it get it wet and begins stroking. The rhythm is slow at first, but once Leanne picks up the cadence, I'm holding myself from finishing right this instant.

"God, Leanne, it's not going to take long to get me to come." I almost came in my pants from just watching Leanne, so now that she wants to take control, it's going to be a speed workout when she's got my dick in her hand.

As she begins stroking faster, I can't hold out much longer and I tell her I'm going to come. Leanne bends down and covers my dick with her mouth and sucks on it, which at that point, it's game over.

"Shit," I whisper, panting after I come in her mouth.

Leanne wipes her mouth after swallowing. "Good?"

"Yeah." Better than good. "Thanks."

We both clean up in the bathroom; I take a quick rinse in the shower and Leanne asks if she can use some of my travel mouthwash to rinse her mouth out. After, I turn the lights off and we hop into bed. I turn on the television to watch what I usually enjoy walking in hotel rooms on the road: the late night *South Park* marathons.

"Have you ever watched?" I ask, wrapping my arm around Leanne as we snuggle up under the covers and she goes to rest her head on my chest.

"No," she admits. "Looks familiar. What's it about?"

"A bunch of kids in Colorado who are rude as fuck. But in like, a funny way." What else could I say to describe it? Out of pocket comedy that is really offensive? I hope she's not judging me for my vacation channel choices.

The episode ends and the jingle starts playing while the credits roll and Leanne finally speaks her opinion after letting out a yawn. "That was alright," she notes.

"I'll take it." The next episode plays and after the first commercial, I turn my head and look down at a sleeping Leanne on my chest. I turn off the television and shift my body so that I can lie down on the bed as well, which is impossible to do without nudging Leanne off my chest. She stirs when I sharply turn my body on its side and nuzzles her face into her pillow. I reach over and wrap an arm around her stomach, and we fall asleep blissfully for the first time together.

***

We wake up the next morning after a long night's sleep. It takes me a lot of effort to fall asleep on a daily, but with my arm still hooked around Leanne, I feel the most well rested than I have in a long time.

Leanne turns her body around and faces me. She blinks a few times to reacquaint her eyes to the rays of sunlight that are making its way through the curtains.

"Good morning," I murmur, giving her a kiss on the forehead.

"Morning. How'd you sleep?"

"Honestly? I slept the whole night, which is actually something I don't do a lot."

"Really? Why not?"

I shrug. Maybe weird insomnia? I haven't received a formal diagnosis, but I think it's just spontaneous anxiety I get. Recently it has been about the upcoming games. Ventura is a tough team, and might be our biggest competition in securing a spot in playoffs, so I've been staying up late wondering if there's anything I can do to ensure I'm the best player I can be, and then playing through all these worst case scenarios in my head, like if I make an error or if they get too many runs past us.

And yet, even though we have a game today, I was actually able to sleep through the night. Leanne makes me feel relaxed, amongst other things I'm feeling about her.

"What's our plan this morning?" she asks. She sits up to peer over at what time it is. "It's about seven-thirty."

"Wow, that is a lot earlier than I was thinking, given how late we stayed up last night." You know, maybe I slept so soundly because I really only got five hours of sleep total. We have approximately six hours to ourselves to explore, including the time I will definitely be using to explore Leanne's body. "Did you have anything in mind?"

She sits up and scrolls through a page on her phone. "So I looked up 'Things to do in Ventura' and there's a lot of mentions about kayaking, but there's also some really cool landmarks that we can check out for free. There's the pier which is just right here, and there's also apparently a spot that's a cross that has a really great view of the city and the ocean. And then there's also that downtown area we were just at yesterday that also has a lot of shops and places to eat." She stops scrolling and gasps. "They have a romance bookstore. We have to go to that."

"Okay, okay." I pull her in so she can rest on my chest again. "We can go to the romance bookstore."

She relaxes her shoulders. "Well obviously whatever you want to also! I just want to spend time with you."

"Oh, I'm going to make sure we're doing nothing but that. Starting with some intimate time this morning."

I shift my body so that my body is atop hers. I press my morning wood into her pussy and she hitches a breath.

"Oh, so we're doing this?" She smirks.

I chuckle. "We can do whatever you want to."

"Well, since we're up..." She arches a brow toward me. "Why not?"

Oh, how I wish mornings were always going to be like this. Waking up next to Leanne is the best way I could start my day. Even better if I can make her come at the same time, which is exactly what I do.

Chapter 15
Leanne

It was hard to get out of bed after Corey completely wrecked me with the way his tongue danced around my clit. I don't know if I've ever felt so undone by someone before. I've had sex prior with Greg on multiple occasions, and enjoyed it, but Corey broke the meter. I didn't even know that could happen. But when Corey's being intimate with me, I feel like I'm living in a dream I never want to wake up from.

"We should probably start getting ready," Corey says, turning his body to look at me laying face up on the bed.

I groan. "But I'm so comfortable! This is your fault, you know that? Making me orgasm in the morning so that I don't want to do anything else."

"Sorry? But not really." He leans over to plant a quick, yet firm kiss on my lips. "I enjoyed it, and I know you did."

"Gee." I roll my eyes. "Was it that obvious?"

"It's okay," he whispers near my ear. "I like it when you make sounds for me."

"Okay." I start to push myself up and step off the bed. "Let's get a move on. There's lots to see and not a lot of time left."

I walk over to the bathroom and immediately stop before my feet hit the tiled floor. *Shit.* All my toiletries and clothes are in my room. Which means I need to go out of Corey's room, traverse the floor hallway, take the elevator up to my room, traverse another floor's hallway, and hope I don't get caught. That is the most important part. My room is next to Lance and Leon's, and the walls in these hotel rooms are not thin. They'll hear me enter into the room, and my only hope is they don't hear the door slam shut and cause a stir. It's before nine, so there's a high chance they're still knocked out cold in bed, but maybe the opposite might be true and they're wide awake and might be doing the same thing I am. Which then, I need to conjure up a lie and tell them why I'm rushing to not hang out with them until this afternoon.

I sigh and walk back over to Corey, who's sitting up at the edge of the bed. "I realized that all my stuff is still in my room."

"Shit. Do you think Lance and Leon are awake?"

I shrug. "I wish I knew. They might still be asleep because they got plastered last night, but they also may be wide awake. I just need to do it. And if they're wondering why I still have my clothes on from yesterday, then I'll just tell them that I...fell asleep in them because they're so comfortable."

"You're cute when you lie," Corey says, sauntering over to stand face to face to me. I look up at him and lightly shove him away from me when I put both my hands on his chest, but he doesn't budge. Corey's not extremely tall; he just sits at above five-foot-seven, but that's six inches taller than I am. So I can perfectly look up at him and not need to tip toe to try and give him a kiss.

He collects me in his arms and slams his lips onto mine. My body starts to go limp and I open my mouth for him. Even with the remnants of morning breath both in our mouths, he still tastes good. His kisses give an indication that he's ravenous for me. He knows what he wants, and he searches my mouth in such a rhythmic way, leaning to perfectly meld his lips to mine.

"Okay," I say, pushing back on him. "I need to go get ready. I'll text you to meet in the lobby?"

"Meet you there." He grins, quickly turning me toward him to give me another quick kiss. Boy, this man is going to ruin me.

***

I finish getting ready, and send Corey a quick text.

LEANNE

Heading down to lobby now!

COREY

See you soon :)

As I'm about to open my door, I jump when the door right next to me also opens, the door leading into Lance and Leon's room.

Leon steps out, looking very obviously hungover: his hair is a mess and spiked up in all different directions, and he's wearing no shirt and sweatpants with Stanford dawned across the leg.

"Leanne?" he murmurs. He takes a long yawn and blinks, making sure he's seeing things correctly. "Where are you going?"

"Um..." Think of a good lie. Leon's easy to convince, he's innocent and unassuming enough.

"I'm going to get some coffee."

"Oh." He perks up. "Can you get me something? You know what I like."

I slump my shoulders. Fuck, should've known if I bring up coffee that he was going to immediately ask that he'd have one too.

"Um...it's a little far of a walk. I was going to walk there and just relax for a little bit."

"Oh," he says. "Well, let me brush my teeth really quickly and I'll come join you."

"No no!" I rush out. "Actually, I will bring you back something. You should rest. You stayed up late last night."

"Yeah." He nods. "You could say that. And Lance was not doing good after we left the bar."

Oh fuck. "What do you mean, what happened?"

He swats his hand away. "Nothing to worry too much about. He drank a little too much and has kind of been glued to the toilet since last night. He's out cold now, but I had to take care of his drunk ass while also trying to stop myself from getting to that point too."

"Okay," I sigh. I hope Lance learned not to go down that road again. "Just give me a bit to go get the coffee and come back, alright? I'll try and be back in an hour."

He shrugs. "Sounds good. See ya."

He closes the door and disappears back into the room and I sigh, relieved that he didn't pry with any more questions. Now, I'm kind of annoyed my coffee trip has to kind of be cut short because I'm due back with a coffee for Leon, but I tell myself that it's okay because at least I'll get that time to spend hanging out with Corey.

I reach the lobby and walk over to Corey who is sitting on one of the armchairs in a nook near the entrance. He stands up and joins me at my side. Once we reach the outside of the hotel, he places a hand to the small of my back and leads me down to the sidewalk when we see another couple is walking in the other direction.

"So...bad news," I begin. "Well, it's not the worst thing that could've happened."

Corey reaches over and laces my hands with his as we cross the street. He really doesn't think that we're going to spot any teammates while we're walking downtown to grab coffee? He's feeling a lot more confident than I am about public displays of affection.

"What?"

"Leon caught me walking out of my room and asked where I was going."

"Oookay." Corey nods. "Not the worst thing. What did you tell him?"

"I told him I was getting coffee, which wasn't a lie. But then he perked up and asked me to get him something too. I didn't want to be a jerk and say that I didn't want to get my brother a coffee, what kind of person would I be? I'm just annoyed now that we might have to cut our time short by going there and then making it a point to come back."

"That's fine," Corey shrugs. "How long did you tell Leon we'd be?"

"About an hour."

He grips onto my hand a little more tightly this time. "Then we're going to make this the best out of this hour with one another."

We reach the coffee spot, which looks like a transformed shipping container in a dirt patio and order our drinks. I get an iced lavender latte and Corey opts for an iced mocha. I order Leon's go to: a caramel macchiato, and reach my phone out to pay once the barista tells us the grand total.

Corey extends his arm out to stop me. "Don't worry." He taps his card against the reader and the machine tells him they've accepted it. He looks down at me. "My treat."

"But I also had to order Leon's," I counter.

"So? I like your brother too. We don't have to tell him it's from me. He just gets to revel in free coffee. But I'm not going back until I finish my cup, and I'm planning on taking my sweet ass time consuming it."

Me too. I'm enjoying the scene around us. It's a tranquil courtyard set up in the middle of downtown. There's a group of cyclists enjoying their drinks out of wide rimmed coffee cups.

We sit down at a small table. Corey takes the seat to the left of me and smiles once I sit down and put my phone on the table.

"This is nice," he notes.

"Yeah." I nod. "I like the vibe here. It's quiet, peaceful."

Ventura, from what I've seen with my eyes, is a nice beach town. The beaches here look a lot better than back home. There's cleaner sand and waves that people can actually surf on. I feel like this place has a lot of what I could want in a town, and not too far away are larger cities like Santa Barbara and LA. That is, if I ever want to brave the LA traffic.

Corey turns to examine me and try to get a read on what I'm thinking. "Do you think you can envision yourself living here?"

I shrug. "I mean, no. Maybe? I don't know." I lean my face against my fist. "It's really nice. And I like that it's a weird mix of big and small. I could maybe get by with the food truck here, and I think there are a lot of venues around if I thought about building the catering business down here. It'd take some time to adjust to though. And I don't even know what it costs to live here."

That's another thing I don't want to think about. Moving means paying for rent. Something I don't do right now, and it actually pleases my parents that I still live at home. If I moved, I would have to find someone to live with, because trying to afford rent on my own as a small business owner starting anew sounds like a nightmare.

"Ah, yeah that's a thing, isn't it?"

"It's kind of a big thing," I confess. "I've never lived away from home before. Well, besides college." And even in college, I lived in a triple my freshman year and then moved into a sorority house for three years.

"You and Greg never lived together?"

I shake my head. Which, thinking back on it, was yet another giveaway that younger me was head over heels for him without realizing that maybe we weren't ready to delve into a marriage. Living together is an important step before making the big leap into being with one another and we bypassed that.

"No. Which I can see that being a big no no, especially before getting engaged. We did spend a lot of time with one another, but yeah. We were going to wait until we got married before looking at a place to live."

"Oh. Gotcha."

I take a sip of my coffee. Am I sheltering myself from exploring a world of feeling truly independent because I'm so used to what's comfortable? No one side eyes me when I tell them that I love my parents. In fact, it's become more universally accepted because everything is expensive and I'm happy to take the help when my parents offer it.

Corey still eyes me, eyebrow raised, like he's projecting his judgment into me with his shocked expression. Shouldn't he know this? He knows my parents and he should know from Lance how difficult it was for him to leave home for an apartment that my parents still side eye when he comes over weekly for dinner.

"Why are you looking at me like that?" I ask sharply when it bothers me that he's looking at me so judgy.

His face softens when he realizes he might have been shooting per-plexed glares in my direction. "I'm sorry, Leanne. I didn't mean to..."

"But you did!" I interrupt him. "Tell me what you're thinking."

He sighs. "I don't want to argue with you, please."

I shift my gaze away from him and try not to get so bothered by this, but I am.

"Hey." Corey reaches out to touch a hand on my arm. "I'm sorry if I came off judgmental. You need to do what you need to do, and moving out and living on your own is a big step."

"That's the problem!" Tears start streaming down my face as I begin to quietly cry. Fuck, the cyclists are going to start judging me too. "I know I might be behind on life because I've never lived on my own and this is all starting to feel like a wake up call that maybe being in one space has made me sheltered from seeing what's really out there."

"Leanne," Corey says, standing up from his chair and squatting down to wrap me in his arms, which makes me cry more into his chest. "It's okay to live with your parents. Hell, it's okay that you're living in the same town you were born in! Some people are jealous of that because maybe they want to go back home but they have bad memories tied to it. You've been able to take a bad moment in your life associated with your hometown and still find something that makes you happy about being there. Your family, your business, all that are totally acceptable reasons for not wanting to leave. And it's also nice that you have a good relationship with your parents where you can stay home and be happy with it."

I pull away and eye him. "Wait, are you and your parents..." Corey doesn't come from a broken home in any sense. His parents are happily married and still live in the home Corey and his brother grew up in. But when Corey would come over and hang out with Lance, he wouldn't mention things at home were rough. I remember that moment when he came to our house for the first time since moving back. Appreciating that he had a place to escape to.

"No, no. It's not like that. I love my parents. It's like, I have the opposite feeling you do, you know? How I'm excited to flee the coop? My parents...they want me to stay. They know that I love baseball, but they'd do anything to make me move back home. I think a part of them kind of wishes they had what your parents do. A family who's rooted in Neptune Beach as much as yours is. My brother moved to Hawaii, and my parents try to be involved with the community, but they barely had much money for my baseball equipment, they can't afford to donate to causes that may be important to them."

I nod. "That makes sense. Your parents are lonely, but you also want them to be happy with you living your dreams." Corey goes back to sit on his chair and I put my hand over his, which prompts him to lace his fingers with mine atop the table.

"Yeah," he says solemnly. "It didn't help that when I was younger that I felt lonely that they were just never home. I wanted so badly for my dad to coach when I played Little League, but he had to say no because of his work schedule. It broke me a little when he'd have to miss my games because he was busy making ends meet for our family, answering house calls when toilets were clogged and shit. Literal shit." He lets out a chuckle.

"That's why you were always over at our house," I figure.

He nods. "Y'all were like my second family. In a way, you kind of still are. I got through a lot of emotional baggage growing up because I was able to escape and hang out with Lance."

I smile. "I'm glad we were able to give you that."

He stands up and pulls me up with him and wraps his arms around me. "And now you're giving me another thing."

I peer up at him, resting my chin on his chest. "What's that?"

"You've got a grip on me so hard, Leanne, it's going to hurt so badly when I leave."

My heart sinks. I wonder if he knows his grip on me is so strong, it's going to hurt trying to find a reason for him to stay.

Chapter 16
Corey

I don't know how good I actually can do when I'm under this much pressure, because I don't think I've ever felt so nervous playing a baseball game in my life.

I've played in a good amount of playoff games, and even in high school, we made it so far as to win the conference championships one year.

But something about this game feels different. I'm trying to put my finger on why I can't stop my palms from sweating or my heart from beating so fast.

When I go up to bat for the second time in this game and look at Leanne, then everything: the fast heartbeat, the mind racing with thoughts, the nerves being sent all throughout my body in quick jolts, make sense. I'm nervous because I don't want to look like a fool when I'm playing in front of Leanne. She's seen me play before, that one time back in Neptune Beach that she snuck away to watch me bat then fainted from heat exhaustion slowly thereafter, and all the times back when we were teenagers and I didn't think much of her cheers. But, this time feels different because we're something different to one another.

I've seen her naked. I've tasted her. I've touched her breasts. And with all these things, I've absolutely loved every moment of it. I don't know what I think about Leanne yet, other than thinking that she's a goddess. I really like her, but I'm shying away from taking it beyond that, because we agreed we wouldn't make this anything beyond friends who mess around with one another. So, the L-word is something I'm working to actively block out of my mind at the moment. But I can't deny I like to look at her smiling face and after the game, when we're alone and it might be the one chance we get to sneak away before we return home to small town Neptune Beach where everyone knows our name and our whereabouts, I'm going to kiss that smile right off her lips.

We're down four to two against Ventura at the top of the fifth. Not a bad score, despite being down two runs. I'm happy that we're able to hold them off from scoring more, because they have a really strong batting lineup. If we can somehow beat them on their home turf, we'll only be two games behind them in the standings.

I walk up to the plate and fixate my eyes on the pitcher. I block out the thoughts of wanting to be next to Leanne and tell my brain to focus on what's in front of us, which is the ball. I need to make contact with the ball. My last at bat, with the same pitcher, was a single, which is fine because it meant that I got on base, but two outs later I was left at second and the inning was over. I need to cross home plate and this is my second chance at making that happen.

The first pitch is thrown and I don't take a swing at it. Too low. I'd be swinging a golf club with how low the pitcher threw the ball. Second pitch, the pitcher tries to surprise me with a curveball and I curse to myself when it lands squarely in the catcher's mitt and the umpire calls a strike.

I purse my lips. Okay, so this is how you're going to play, huh? Thinking I don't see right through your little plan. Tricking me that you're actually going to keep throwing in the same area but then surprise me with a curveball. Well, I can see through your little tricks, and if he does this again, I'm going to be ready for it.

When the pitcher throws the ball again, it's another curveball, but this time, I anticipate it. I swing my bat at the right time to make contact with the ball and it makes a clink against the bat and the ball is sent up in the air, so much until it lands over the fence in the outfield and bounces until it becomes invisible to the players and the fans.

Holy fuck. I did it. I hit the ball so far it hits the fence.

I run along the bases to the cheers of my teammates, banging their fists against the fence and the few people who are in the stands supporting us, aka the Fairbanks, cheering for me. Leanne's voice distinguishes itself amongst her brothers and as I cross second and stop as the ball makes its way to the pitcher.

And beat them, we do. After they try and make up for the run we were able to edge past them, we win against Ventura four to five. The team comes together on the field in a giant embrace and everyone gives me a pat on the back, telling me how I did such a good job getting a home run off of them today. That, plus being able to catch three flyballs that were coming in my direction while they were at bat, makes everyone agree I was the MVP of the game.

Coach gathers us for a huddle and tells us again how good of a job we did in winning this game. We're soon approaching the time where we'll be thinking a lot about our record and trying to get ahead of Ventura to clinch playoffs, because if we're able to get first in our league, we will play against the other independent leagues in the country for a shot at being the top team. Even though the Independent Baseball League could be argued as below the minors, even though we're all good baseball players, I'm starting to soon feel proud of how I'm doing. And I'm not feeling as shy anymore when I'm talking amongst my teammates; not feeling as resentful being where I am so I can actually enjoy relishing in our accomplishments as a team.

We're dismissed and everyone comes to consensus that we want to celebrate with dinner. There's a popular pizza chain down here that one of the players has been to before attached to a brewery that we agree is a good spot to go to. I gather my things and walk over to the Fairbanks siblings to tell them our plans so they can come along with us, when I'm suddenly asked to stop.

"Excuse me." A tall man wearing a San Diego branded hat and sweatshirt walks up to me. "Corey Ramirez?"

I turn to face him and awkwardly shrug my shoulder at him, keeping my hand around my duffel strap. "Hey, yes?"

"I wanted to congratulate you on a good game. You did really well out in the field and that home run, that was awesome, man."

I almost lose my footing for a moment. Wow, I don't think I've really been complimented on my performance on the road before. This is definitely making me feel good about what I just did out there, even if I feel weird hearing it from someone I've never even met.

"Hey, thanks, man. I appreciate it."

"I'm a scout for San Diego. I've been looking at you for some time now. Since you played in New Mexico. I gotta admit, you've got good hustle. You might be one of the best players in the Independent league."

My eyes go wide. He...hold on. I've been looked at? By a scout for an actual major league team? And I'm apparently one of the best players in the Independent league? I try not to look too close into rankings, even though the league website has a list of their top players after every week and I know I've been doing decently well to get on the list in some capacity, but I'm not number one, am I?

"Oh. Thank you, that's really nice of you to say."

"You've never been called up, have you?"

I shake my head. "No. I mean, I was drafted to Philly right after college, played in New Jersey for a little bit, and then got traded and played in New Mexico, until I was released. And now I'm playing for Neptune Beach."

He grins at me. "Kind of just been waiting for your number, have you?"

I shrug. This feels weird. I never thought I'd be talking to my journey to a scout. Or I have, but when it actually happens, it feels surreal.

"Yeah." I shrug. "That's a good way of putting it."

"Well, hey." He reaches into his pocket and takes out a business card. "Let's chat about seeing what we can do about that at the stadium and I'll give you a tour."

I grab the card from him and examine it. *Wesley Shipp*, the card reads, with all the important contact information. Okay, so looks like this isn't just some weird prank that someone would pull on me.

"Um, yeah." I nod. "I am supposed to leave for home tomorrow, but I can look into shifting some things around."

"We can help you coordinate that too, if you want," Wesley, but he could also go by Wes, says. "Book you a flight back home. You normally fly into Oakland to get to Neptune Beach?"

"Yeah, or San Francisco. I kind of like Oakland because it's less congested."

He chuckles. "Well now they're both kind of called San Francisco anyway, right?"

I wince. Yeah they did that weird airport name change thing didn't they? "Yeah, that's right."

"Well, yeah man. Let's get you to the stadium and give you a tour and talk about getting you on the team. We need some good outfielders and I think I'd be really pleased to see how you can contribute to the team."

"Sounds good." I nod. "I...I should call my agent about this right?" And probably not tell him that out loud.

"Yeah," Wesley says. "But that can be something we get on the phone with him together about. I'm not sugarcoating that we can see you on the team, Corey. Just come and check it out for yourself."

"Sure, will do." I flash the business card in front of him. "Thank you again."

"Thank you," he says back. "We're looking forward to meeting with you."

Wesley turns around and heads down the bleachers and disappears out of my sight. He didn't stop to talk to anyone else. He had his sights trained on me and then he basically just offered me a spot on a major league team. I know it's not that cookie cutter, and there will have to be things like contract negotiations that need to be discussed, but I'm holding the business card of a professional baseball scout, who had their eyes set on me of all people.

I can't even walk forward now to tell the Fairbanks that we're heading to go eat pizza. Shit, I don't even know if I'm hungry for pizza now. My stomach is in knots right now thinking about my future and how it potentially lies in this tiny business card with a major league team embossed on it.

"Hey, Core." Lance walks up with Leon and Leanne flanked at his side. "Who's that you were talking to?"

"Um..." Do I want to tell them who it really is? I don't feel like I'm ready to yet because a part of me isn't even sure how this is going to end up. What if I went to the stadium and they asked me to do hitting and fielding drills and I freeze up and do a poor performance? Maybe I should keep it to myself for now. I want to make sure if we're going to celebrate, it's going to be something that'll stay.

"Just someone I know from the minors. He works for San Diego now. Hence the outfit." That's not a complete lie.

"Ah, okay." Lance nods. "That's cool, he recognized you here. What does he do for them now?"

"Uh," I stammer. "He's an athletic trainer." I don't want to come out and say he's a scout, and get Lance overly excited when he can put two and two together. I'm just visiting the park and meeting with some of the staff. Nothing is confirmed until I sign a contract.

"Neat," Leon says. "Wouldn't it be cool if he was like some undercover scout or something and was ready to give you a spot on the team?

"Yeah." I chuckle. "Wouldn't have that been something?" Leon really is the smartest Fairbanks child and he doesn't even know why.

"Anywho," I continue. "We're going to a pizza-brewery conglomerate near the pier for dinner if you all want to join. You're practically part of the team anyway."

Lance and Leon light up. "We're down!"

"Cool. I need to go back to the hotel and shower anyway, but I'll text you when the team decides to start walking."

They excitedly nod and turn around to walk back to Lance's car. I reach out and pull Leanne closer to me for just a second, close enough where we're almost touching one another, but I keep my distance so others don't see what we're up to.

"Come to my room when we get back?" I ask into her ear.

"Y-yeah, sure," she breathes. "I'll see you there?"

I squeeze her arm a little and it makes Leanne's stance go a little limp. I love that she gets so weak in the knees for me. "See you there." I wink.

Chapter 17
Leanne

I make a few light taps to knock on Corey's hotel room door, careful that no one can hear.

This sneaking around is equal parts exhilarating yet terrifying. Do I think that I can successfully maneuver around all these people: my brothers, Corey's many teammates, without being noticed? Signs point to highly unlikely. I don't think it's as big of a deal if Corey's teammates happen to stumble upon us with one another, this has kind of been the first weekend where they've actually interacted with me in full conversation for the first time. And honestly, I don't know how Corey acts on the road, but this may also mark the first time where he's felt so comfortable carrying on long conversations with his teammates. He's laughing as him and Lance reminisce about their high school baseball days, when they'd get trouble for messing around during practice and had to run around the field multiple times. The amount of Big League Chew that was consumed on a given game day. The moments after a game where we'd go to Pearl's Ice Cream and stuff our faces with whatever flavored tickled our fancy that day.

He was actually enjoying talking about growing up in Neptune Beach, and reminiscing about his childhood and playing baseball at the Little League field. It almost got me hopeful he'll be happy to stay. If for whatever reason he'll stop playing baseball but still be happy about living in Neptune Beach. Then I don't have to worry about falling in love with him.

Why did I say yes to coming to his room when I know I'm getting to the point where I'm too deep in my feelings with him? Because I need a goddamn release and Corey can give it to me better than I can give myself.

Corey opens the door and smiles at me eagerly standing outside his room.

"Hi." He smirks.

"Hi." I sheepishly wave back.

He grabs a hold of my hand and pulls me sharply into the room as the door automatically shuts behind us. I'm careful not to yelp when Corey's strength can pull me almost off my feet and right into his arms.

"I missed you," he says, peppering kisses on my neck, moving up to behind my ear as I tilt my head back to welcome him.

"It's only been a few hours," I note. We finished up our little day trip around Ventura, where we walked around the downtown area and down to the pier and back, before heading back to Corey's room to take a little cat nap and have a little make out session, before getting up and heading to the park. I watched as Corey practiced, played the game, hitting a home run in fact, and now we're back here. I think that the time that he took to gear up for the game and actually play in it took less hours than an average work day.

"Mmm, too long," he notes. "I was thinking about this all throughout the game. Thinking about you."

"How are you able to do that while also keeping your head in the game?" I ask. There was literally a whole song about this. Troy didn't have his head in the game while he was playing basketball because he was thinking about how much he enjoyed singing with Gabriella. You can't keep your focus on both, or else they wouldn't have made a musical ballad about it.

"I don't know." He shrugs. "I just...when I go up to bat and see you cheering me on in the stands, something clicks for me. I think about impressing you or some shit and then it makes me do better."

I blush. "Wait, and you hit a home run today. Does that mean..."

He picks me up and twirls me off the ground before I can even finish my sentence. He gives me a smack on the lips while I keep my arms laced around his neck and I lean in to deepen the kiss, wrapping my legs around his waist. He holds me up to him and I flick my tongue against his, tugging the slight bit of his hair at the back. He utters a groan and holds me tightly against him, lacing his arms under my ass.

"Guess you're my good luck charm," he says. "You want to just make sure you're at all my games? We don't have too many left in the season before we know if we've made playoffs."

I scoff. "You know I'm at every Seals home game."

"Yeah, working the food truck. I need to see you with my own eyes. I need to hear you cheering for me from the stands. That's how I know you're watching me."

I chuckle. "Well, get someone to text me when you're at bat and I can try my best to catch you. But, with the rush of people who have been trying to make it to the games, we're only getting busier."

"I know." His eyes flit down to my lower region. "I'm kidding. I don't want you to leave work just to watch me play. But, thank you for coming to the game today. And yesterday. It's been really great to spend some time with you, just the two of us. In a different city where we can play sightseer too."

"You're welcome." I give him a quick kiss. "I've had a lot of fun. I'd never been here before and I kind of like it. It's a cute town that feels small, yet big. Maybe next time we can think about renting a kayak and taking it out on the ocean."

"You know we can do that back home too?" he notes.

"Yeah, but..." I don't think about it when I'm home. I guarantee, once we're back home in Neptune Beach, all we're going to be thinking about is work and my life is going to feel occupied trying to get the business going, maybe figuring out what things I can do to promote the catering side. And Corey's going to keep playing baseball and take other trips up and down the West Coast without me. Because as much as I want to accompany him on all the road games he takes, its going to start to make my family wonder why I'd rather spend my time away from home than being in it.

"I'm just thinking about how busy we'll get once we get home. We're not going to really have much time to kayak with your baseball schedule and my work."

"You're right," he says. "Hey, um, speaking of once we get home. I'm not actually traveling back home tomorrow with the team."

I lean back from him. "Wait, why?"

He purses his lips. "Promise you won't tell anyone about this? No one will know about it except you."

"Yeah, sure. I promise."

"It's not anything bad," he tells me. "It's...good. For me. So you know that guy I was talking to? The one who was wearing the San Diego gear?"

"Yeah, your friend right? He's an athletic trainer?"

"Yeah...about that." Corey sets me down and sits on the bed. I join and sit to his right. "He's actually not an athletic trainer. And I only met him today, so I also lied about how long I've known him. He's actually a scout."

I blink back at him. Wait, scouts. Those are those people who are trying to recruit baseball players.

"Wait, a scout?" I shift closer. "So that means..."

"I'm going to San Diego tomorrow to meet with him and tour the place. Nothing is set in stone until a contract is signed, but he poached me, which I still think is wild."

"Corey," I begin. A grin spreads across my face and I beam at him while also trying to calm myself down inside. Corey might actually be called up to play in a major league team. A good one, even if that statement puts a sour taste in my throat. I guess he'd be the exception as to why I'd ever wear a Padres jersey.

"I'm really excited for you. This is such an amazing opportunity!"

"Thank you," he says. He envelopes his hand over mine and traces over my knuckles. "I actually wanted to ask if you'd like to come with me."

"Me?" I point at my chest. Duh, of course you Leanne. There's no one else in this room. "Why?"

"I don't want this weekend to end. When we get back to Neptune Beach, we're going to have to sneak around even more if we want to be with one another. I don't even know how I'm going to be able to get you in my bed without my mom asking a million questions."

Dammit. Yeah, now this is why I kind of wish I didn't live under the same roof as my parents. No matter what age I was, they'd still pry with questions, especially when it was someone who would come over to my house and hideaway in Lance's room playing shooter games until one in the morning against my parent's rules and we'd all wake up and eat breakfast together and I'd try and not stare too hard at Corey across the table from me dousing his eggs in Cholula.

"Yeah, mine either."

"I think it could be fun trying it in your car," Corey chirps up.

I roll my eyes. "Oh yeah, it's so hot having sex in my parent's old Benz." I wouldn't know, because I don't think about sex in my car that smells like lo mein almost every day.

Corey leans over and pushes me onto the bed lightly and shifts his leg over my body to straddle himself atop me. "It's so hot having sex with you anywhere. If I didn't worry so much about getting sand up your ass, I would've fucked you on the beach."

My body starts to heat and when Corey slams his lips on mine, I arch up closer to touch my body against his jersey. He searches for the waist of my pants and finds the button. He undoes it and pulls the zipper down, reaching his hand into my underwear and sticking a finger into my wet pussy, pumping in and out, my clit rubbing against his thick knuckle.

I sigh into his mouth and my eyes flutter back into my head. He kisses my neck and tugs at my shirt to signal me to take it off. I grab it by the hem and remove it, so that the only thing I'm wearing is my nude colored push up bra. Note to self: shop for potentially more sexy looking bras.

He pulls the bra down and begins to kiss my nipple. He takes a small bite at it and I let out a low moan, but before he's going in for another, he pulls back and keeps a distance from his mouth and my breasts.

"Everything okay?"

He tugs on his jersey that's been undone from being tucked into his pants during the game. "I just realized I'm still in my uniform. And I'm stinky. I should take a shower so you don't have to touch my sweaty skin."

A lightbulb flashes in my head, ignited from the desire for nothing more than touching every part of Corey's body from his head to his feet.

I blink at him, smirking as I throw the idea into existence. "Do you want to shower together?"

His eyes darken and he works to carry me off the bed. "Um, abso-fuck-ing-lutely I do. You're so adventurous."

He walks over to the bathroom to turn the shower on, and I get up from the bed and begin to unclasp my bra and wiggle off any of the clothes still stuck to my body. I take a deep breath in while Corey still has his back to me. Showering together, what am I thinking? This is not a typical Leanne suggestion. This is unhinged Leanne behavior. Leanne's never had sex in the shower. Leanne has only explored, like two sex positions in her life.

But Corey Ramirez makes Leanne Fairbanks do things she's never dared to explore before. To experience the thrill, and the subsequent orgasms Corey Ramirez is sure to provide for her.

I step over to the bathroom and watch as Corey begins to undress from his uniform. Each item of clothing on his body hits the floor. His jersey, the undershirt he wears beneath it that hugs at his abs so form-fittingly, his pants, and the compression briefs he wears under them.

He reaches a hand out to see if the heat level is to his satisfaction. "Do you like your showers hot?" he asks.

My throat goes dry. I mean, temperate is a good way to describe it right? Hot but not too hot? I don't want my skin to be scalding.

"Yeah, but not too hot."

He steps closer to me. "Do you want to step in and see if you like the temperature?"

I swallow. "Y-yeah. Sure thing."

I take a step into the shower and instinctively, start to lean back so the water from the shower head's beginning to douse my hair. It's the perfect level of warmth, and after a hot day where I've been sweating just by sitting in the sun, it's nice to rinse off.

Corey chuckles and steps into the shower as I'm starting to get into it with me and the water.

"Hey," he says, cupping my breast. "You asked if I wanted to shower together."

"Sorry," I tell him. "The temperature feels great."

"Good." He steps closer and cups the back of my wet hair and tilts my head up to him. He leans down and our lips touch while my hair continues to dampen from the stream of water coming out from the shower head. It's like we're kissing in the rain, with a few droplets hitting my face and the mist coating our skin.

Corey reaches over to the drilled in shampoo dispenser and pumps some into his hands. "Can I wash your hair?"

I blush. I feel like a princess. Corey asking me if he can massage my hair? I take short showers so I don't even pamper myself that much when I'm in the shower. All I'm worried about is washing myself efficiently so I can get going out the door.

"Of course you can," I reply.

Corey threads his hands through my hair, beginning at my scalp. He starts massaging the shampoo into it, taking his time lathering it so that it's covering almost every spot. This is so much more work than what I do.

I sigh in satisfaction as his fingers massage my head.

"You like that?" he murmurs near my head.

"Mhhhm." I melt into his soaked chest when my back touches it.

He trails his fingers down to get the ends of my hair and moves me to turn around when he's all done so that I can rinse it out.

"Thank you," I tell him as I work my fingers in my own scalp to make sure the shampoo's been completely washed out of my hair. "I am spoiled now by someone washing my hair. I never want to go back to washing my own hair again."

"Well, I don't know how I can sneak up into your bathroom to give you scalp massages every time you shower. Can you somehow prop a ladder against your house so I can sneak into your window?"

"Maybe, but my room is also on the second floor and there isn't really much to brace your fall if something were to happen. I'll just remember this moment and you every time that I'm taking a shower."

"That works for me."

We finish each of our hair washing routine, Corey getting excited that he gets to thread his fingers through my hair again when I tell him I still need to add conditioner. As he takes the last moment to rinse the soap off of him, I decide I'm not done soaping up his body just yet.

"I think you missed a spot," I tell him, biting my lip. I reach past him and squirt some of the body wash into my palm. I press my palms together to get the soap a little more sudsy and wrap my hand around his dick.

He hitches a breath but looks at me sinisterly as I start pumping my fist, picking up speed thanks to how slick his dick is under the water.

"Leanne." He gently pulls me closer so I don't let go of him. He starts breathing harder on my forehead. "That feels so good."

"Yeah?" I blink back at him.

"Yeah, I...I'm trying not to come but...you're making it hard." He clenches his teeth.

"I'm on birth control," I tell him. "I had a physical and was negative, and I haven't had sex in years..."

"Me neither. My results came back negative too." Corey pants, beads of water drip down from his damp hair. He leans down to hover closer to my face. "Will you let me in Leanne?"

I haven't crossed "sex in the shower" off my list yet. Me from the past would've never tried. I wanted to explore my kinks, if I had any. My previous sex life was so...vanilla. We took turns on who would be on top, and that was the extent of our sex. It was nice, but boring. Corey sucking on my clit made me feel so good. It made me realize I wanted more than missionary.

"Yes." I nod. "I want to feel you bare."

A hotel shower is definitely a cramped space for two people, but Corey's on a mission now. He guides me to face the wall opposite the shower head.

"Bend down for me," he orders. "Hands on the wall and let me see that ass."

I slowly make my way down with the weight of my hair dripping down in front of my face. Corey reaches out and grabs either side of my ass and guides me to where he needs me.

"I don't know what I love more..." Corey says. He slaps my ass and I yelp. "Your ass or your breasts."

"I know I like the way your ass looks in those baseball pants," I counter.

"Oh yeah?" He snickers. "I see what you're really staring at when I'm at bat."

He spreads his hand over my back and guides me down until I'm nearly touching my toes. Gymnastics as a kid is paying off because I am nearly touching my toes.

"Come here," he whispers. He slowly inserts himself into me and I hear him shudder against the pitter patter of the water dropping from the shower head.

"Oh god, Leanne. You feel so good. We fit so good together."

He thrusts himself in and out of me, while I'm bent over, trying to hold my hands against the slippery wall.

"Fuck, Corey!" I yell. Apparently this position unlocks a whole new level of orgasmic. Please, let me explore more of what it means to be taken from behind and please let Corey be the one railing himself into me.

"Leanne, oh my god." Corey grunts and gently slips himself out from me. I stand back up, soaked in all places, and face Corey who's trying to catch his breath.

"I'm spent," he says and lets out a breathless laugh. "Thank god I'm done playing baseball for the day, that was a workout."

"Let's do it again?" I propose. I don't know when we'd ever find a moment to do it quite like this, but I'm craving for Corey now.

"Yeah?" He gives me a quick kiss. "How should we do it next time?"

"Doesn't matter," I smile. "I trust you'll know to give me a good time." And I want to savor every moment I get before it might be gone.

Chapter 18
Leanne

Post shower, Corey and I fall into bed, cuddling one another naked, and I almost forgot that we needed to meet up with people for dinner soon.

Actually, I wouldn't have remembered if it wasn't for Lance texting Corey that he was waiting for him to come down so they could all walk together.

"Did he text you?" Corey asks me.

I peer at my phone. "No, I haven't received anything from him." When Lance is around a bunch of other guys, he kind of gets in a mood where he's in his feels. He's reminiscing about baseball and feeling clingy to the other guys he's with. Corey, in particular. I'm kind of a minority here, and honestly, if I said I wasn't feeling well enough to go to Lance, he would wish me better and move on. If Corey did the same thing, Lance would throw a fit and ask why.

"I wish I could say that I'm not feeling well and he'd leave me alone," Corey sighs.

"He's just making up for lost time," I reassure him. "He may not say it out loud, but he really misses you."

Corey frowns. "Yeah, I know. I don't mean to sound like a jerk. I'm happy that Lance and I are hanging out with each other again. When I left, not knowing yet if I would ever come back to Neptune Beach, a part of me was sad to leave Lance and probably talk to him less. Distance and all that. So, now I'm kind of thinking that I owe him this lost time, especially if I'm potentially going to be leaving again. I just didn't think I'd be attracted to his sister." He winks at me.

"Yeah, yeah." I roll my eyes. "It was only a matter of time that you fell for your best friend's sister."

Corey blinks back at me, a pause looming over us. Shit. I shouldn't have used "fell" if he's just enjoying the sex. Falling implies that he's in love. We're not in love. We're infatuated.

"Sorry. I shouldn't have used fell. This is just for fun, right?"

"Yeah." He nods. "Don't worry about it. I got what you mean."

"Good," I reply.

"Um," Corey clears his throat, "so tomorrow. Would you like to come to San Diego with me?"

"Oh." I blink. The stadium visit. I haven't drummed up a reason why I've decided to stay in SoCal a little while longer. Lance and Leon need to go back home tomorrow. Lance has work. I should go back and prep for the game that the Seals have the following day. Food is being delivered. Emma can probably handle this on her own, but I still need to conjure up a convincing enough lie for my family.

"You don't have to say yes." Corey sits up and puts his hand on my bare thigh. "I just thought it would be nice that we'd stay a little while longer together before we may not be able to get much time to ourselves."

"I know." A part of me is jumping out of my seat from excitement. I've never stepped foot in a stadium before when there isn't a game going on. Will I get to see where the player's locker rooms are? Plus I'll have the chance to stand on the field, which I don't think I'd ever be able to do because my singing can be equated to a screaming goat and I'd never be invited to sing the national anthem at a major league baseball game. But most of all, Corey and I can be actually out in the world somewhere and hold each other's hands. We can engage in a small level of PDA, as long as whoever's around us doesn't mind, and we'll have time to spend with each other as we're making our way back home to Neptune Beach. Maybe even stay the night somewhere to make the drive less mundane.

"I want to." I nod. "Yes. I don't know what I'm going to tell my family yet as to why I'm staying a little longer, but I'll figure it out."

Corey grins and wraps me in a tight hug. "Great! I'll rent a car then and we can take our time heading back to Neptune Beach. I don't have a game until Tuesday anyway."

"But don't you have practice tomorrow?"

"I do, but I can tell Coach that I need to stay in the area for a little longer. I think if this were to all go well, then he's going to hear from my agent about my move anyway."

I get up and rummage through my suitcase to pull out a tank top and a pair of shorts to wear to dinner tonight.

"The team is going to have a hard time once you're gone," I note.

Corey shoots up an eyebrow. "What do you mean?"

"You're a really good player, Corey," I explain. I've only seen him play in full twice, and a few at bats here and there, but he's arguably one of the best players on the team. He consistently gets on base and is a strong outfielder. There are other really good players on the team; baseball teams aren't the best because of one person. They may just be helpful in getting a team closer to being a winning team.

"You're in the top players for batting average in the entire independent baseball league. You work hard, and even though there are days where you don't get any hits, you're still putting in the hard work and trying to be a good example. And I think that you're starting to really love this team, and you're going to miss them when you leave."

Corey doesn't meet me in the eyes as he's changing. He's quietly putting on each article of clothing bit by bit, and when he's all done, he grabs his wallet and phone that he's placed on the desk in the hotel, asking me if I'm ready to go.

"Um." I swallow. "Yeah, I'm ready."

He gives me a pained smile, and I'm too busy to rack my brain around what I said that could have made Corey shut down.

"Hey," I grab onto his arm and pull him back before he could step out of the hotel room, "did I say something to upset you?"

"No," he says. He smiles down at me, but it's so soft that I can tell something is bothering him. "It's all good. Don't worry about it."

Why is it that when people say "don't worry about it," it only makes me want to be more concerned? Especially if they don't want me to worry, but then they'll be closed off and on the outside, it visibly looks like something's bothering them.

"Corey." I peer into his eyes. "I can tell that something's on your mind."

He sighs and lets the door of the hotel room close so we don't see out into the hallway.

"I've moved around a lot since graduating college. When you're a player in the minor league, you can get called up, traded, it always happens so quickly. I thought back then, If that's what I have to do to further myself to where I want to be, then I will."

He starts to frown. "The downside to that is I don't get to call people my teammates for very long. The longest I've been on a team is two seasons, and I really felt like I built a family with who I was playing with. It was the first time since college I felt like I had that connection. So when you said that I might be starting to love this team, I didn't want to admit that you were right. Because yeah, it's going to be really hard to say goodbye."

I blink back tears but my face is soiled. Corey silently wraps his arms around me and pulls me in tightly against him. While I was talking about his team, I also was thinking about Lance and me. And as much as I was putting everyone else first, I selfishly wanted to do whatever I could to make him stay, because I don't want this to mean I'm letting go from us.

"It's okay." Corey starts to draw circles around my back. I breathe a ragged breath into his shirt, where I can already feel patches of wet drops from my tears start to pool into the fabric.

"I haven't received an offer yet," he continues. "Nothing is final until I sign a contract. You're got me for a little while longer."

"I wish I could have you forever," I murmur into his shirt. My words sound garbled because I whisper them into the fabric of his shirt, but I needed to give some sort of release to subdue the bubbled-up feelings built inside me.

"What'd you say?" Corey asks.

I don't tell him what I actually said, because that's for me and the shirt only. "I'll take what I can get," I tell him. "Are you planning on telling the team? Do you think they'll figure it out when you can't be at practice tomorrow?"

He shrugs. "Maybe I will. So I'm honest about it. I'm not great at hiding secrets. And maybe to get a feel for how everyone else feels if the possibility of me leaving will be. So it doesn't feel like a surprise."

"Yeah. Wouldn't want anyone to be disappointed one day because you've suddenly stopped coming to practice."

"Yeah." Corey gives me a sad smile. "I don't want that either."

We quietly make our way to dinner, walking hand in hand until we get to the block where the restaurant is. It's the smallest bit of PDA we've done thus far and I blush as we're walking alongside the waves of the ocean next to us. It's a short moment and we're doing nothing more than touching hands with one another, but it's the small moments I'm holding onto when I know that they're going to end soon. Especially since Corey may be leaving Neptune Beach as early as next week if he gets an offer from the Padres.

We send a silent signal to each other when we look at one another as we're approaching our destination to let our hands go and walk into the restaurant. I walk a little to the left to keep my distance from Corey as he heads toward the back, where he already knew everyone was going to be from Lance's text.

"Hey!" Lance sits straight up on the bench he's sharing with Leon and a few other players. "Look who finally decided to show up!" He jumps a little when he sees who's shown up alongside Corey. "Oh, hey, Leanne. I didn't know you were going to come."

I narrow my eyes. "Why wouldn't I?"

"Well, I knocked on your room when Leon and I were about to leave and you didn't answer. Thought you took a nap or something and weren't going to come."

"Oh." I'd rather go on with his assumption than tell the truth. "Yeah, I decided to take a little cat nap, but then I got hungry."

"Ah." Lance nods. "Well, come on, sit!" He pats the seat next to him. "Corey, I got a pitcher of beer, do you want some?"

"Yeah, man, that'd be great. Thanks."

Corey shoots me a quick apologetic glance before taking the seat next to Lance. There doesn't look to be much room on the bench they're all sitting at, so I decide I can either dine alone or with Corey's teammates who are sitting on the next bench over. At least if I sit with Corey's teammates, I can try and get to know them. Corey likes them, so I think they're probably nice guys.

I sit down and a younger player who wears glasses, Kyle I believe, smiles at me.

"Hey." I wave. "Anyone sitting here?"

"Nope," he says. "All yours."

I sit down and peer at the table, smiling at the players who are making conversation with one another, not trying to insert myself randomly into anyone's conversations. Especially if they're talking about baseball strategy.

Kyle turns to me after I've situated myself. "Leanne, right? You're Lance's sister who has the food truck during games, right?"

"Yeah, that's me. You're Kyle, aren't you?"

He nods. Phew. I try and remember names but there's a lot of players to keep up with. I only know his name because he's the only player who wears glasses on the team during games. "Yeah. I usually play third base."

"Oh cool. What were you doing before you started playing for the Seals?"

"I, uh, played baseball at Fullerton. I graduated last year."

"Nice!" He's like a majority of the players on the Seals, college graduates who are still trying to play in hopes they'll have a chance to be called up. Corey is actually on the older side, at twenty-eight. It's wild that by thirty, you're on the tail end for average ages of baseball players. I'm twenty-six and I still feel like I have so much of my life ahead of me and yet, I'm behind at the same time. I know there is no specific timeline for growing up, but I get a little wistful when I see former friends from high school meeting up, married, babies in tow. That was something I wanted before, and now, I don't even know if I'd ever be ready to be a mother.

"How are you enjoying the Seals?" I ask.

"It's pretty fun," he notes, after taking a sip from his beer. "I'd never been to Neptune Beach before being signed by the Seals. I actually grew up not too far from here in Camarillo, so as a kid I spent a lot of time at the beaches here."

"That's cool," I tell him. "When you were thinking about playing baseball after college, did you think about wanting to play for Ventura?" You don't get to choose what teams you play for, but I'm trying to see if I can prove the theory that you'd always prefer to play for your home team over a team you'd have to move for. For no particular reason, of course.

"Yeah." He nods. "In high school, I'd take trips to see the Snow Crabs play with my baseball team. It was a fun time, and at that age, we all had those aspirations to play for them. Because I didn't want to shoot for the stars and tell myself I was good enough to play for the Dodgers."

My heart breaks a little. I hate that people have this little voice in their head that told them some dreams are too high to shoot for. And I hate I had felt that way too before I realized that no one was going to stop me from doing something that scared me.

"Hey." I lightly put my hand on his arm. It doesn't mean anything beyond a friendly gesture. Really, talking to him kind of like he's like just another one of my younger brothers. Although, I feel like I have a weirder, stronger connection to Kyle in this moment than I do Leon. I love Leon, but he's the smartest member of our family. He knew he was going to be in law since he was ten and would carry our dad's briefcase around the house like he was ready to defend a case. He didn't need someone to tell him that he should be questioning his career choices.

He's happy to be learning law and he's going to kill it once he passes the bar after law school.

"There is nothing wrong with shooting for the stars even if it feels statistically impossible," I tell him. "I mean, Corey's been playing baseball out of college for six years now and he's still holding out hope he's going to be in the pros one day."

He dramatically rolls his eyes and takes another sip. "It's a crime that man isn't in the major leagues honestly."

"Oh, yeah?" I smirk. "Why's that?"

"He's a beast on the field," he begins. His face starts to light up, his expressions animated as he talks about Corey. He really looks up to him from what I can gather. "We're not close to one another on the field, distance-wise, but when he needs to get a guy out from the outfield, dude can throw. And then the power that guy has with a bat? He sent that ball into space during today's game."

"What are you going to do if Corey's called up to play in the majors?" I ask. "You know, if he ends up getting the call. Because that's what he's said he wants." That's no secret, and I don't think it is for the team either.

"I mean, I'll be happy for the guy. He deserves it. But it'll also make me sad, because I really like the guy. He was kind of closed off at the start of the season, but he's slowly starting to warm up to the team. He's been really supportive of me trying to grow as a baseball player and even gave me a few places to explore around the Bay Area. I'll be happy for him, but I'll miss him too."

"Yeah," I say into the table. "I feel that." A little too hard, I wanted to add.

"You and Corey are close?" he asks.

I raise a brow at him. "Are you asking if we are?" I wasn't trying to be snarky, I'm curious. Are we exhibiting behavior that makes it seem like we are?

"Yeah, well, a little bit of question and a little bit of observation. You two seem close."

Oh shit. Are we exhibiting flirty behavior? I try to deter him from thinking so, if he is. "I mean, he and my brother have been best friends since they were kids. I've kind of just been close to him by proxy."

"Hmm, yeah, I guess." He taps his finger to his chin. "But I also have noticed that Corey changes...I guess when he thinks about you. Like he cares a lot about you. I remember that time you fainted because it was so hot and Corey just freaked out. He was so worried about you."

"Yeah, but he would've done that to anyone," I note. Would he?

Kyle starts chuckling low to himself. "I don't think he would've been that worried over anyone. It's okay, Leanne." He reaches over to touch my arm. "I'm glad Corey's got friends that have made his move back home a lot easier. We'll lean on each other when he leaves too, right?"

I purse my lips and eventually nod at him. "Yeah. We will." I make a note to myself that he'll be the one ready to console me when I'm a mess after Corey leaves.

Chapter 19
Corey

One thing I don't know how long it'll take me to jive with if I move here is LA traffic.

Leanne and I checked out of the hotel room early to allocate at least three hours to get from Ventura to San Diego for my meeting with Wesley at eleven. Prior to that, I had to pick up the rental car I ordered so I can drive there and then Leanne and I can drive back to Neptune Beach. If it was only me, I would have opted to fly but then I wanted Leanne to come and she was able to, so I didn't know what the best way to explain to Wesley that he didn't need to worry about getting me a flight back anymore, I'm enjoying a road trip with my friend with some added benefits.

Leanne has successfully been able to fib out of driving back home with Lance and Leon, saying that she connected with a friend from college who now lives in the area. They didn't question it, just wished her a good time. Lance even added, "Good for you. You should take more time to relax and visit new places."

I could tell Leanne was a little miffed by him brushing her off when moments earlier he was asking why I wouldn't be back until Tuesday afternoon, going so much as to fake crying that I'll be gone during the biweekly pool tournament at the Jolly Oyster he's invited me to.

Sometimes, I wonder if I'm more of a sibling to Lance than Leanne is, and what that would mean when I inevitably tell him that I'm attracted to her.

We've now successfully reached San Diego, and the GPS says we should arrive at the park in a little under half an hour.

"How are you feeling?" Leanne asks.

"Excited, I think..." I don't know how I'm feeling. A mix of emotions: excited, nervous, a little miffed that I've been sitting in traffic, but happy I've been spending time with Leanne.

"I know this isn't like a formal interview, but it kind of feels like one." I haven't interviewed for a job since I worked at Pearl's over summers in high school, and I think they were going to give me a job anyway because my mom and Pearl, the owner, took barre classes together at the fitness center.

"Just think of it as meeting someone new for the first time," she reassures me. She grabs a hold of my hand resting on the center console and interlaces my fingers with hers. "You're going to do amazing. You already have, or else you wouldn't be on your way to freaking San Diego to talk to a scout."

God, this woman. My own certified hype woman.

"Thanks." I squeeze her hand. "I'm glad I get to share this moment with you."

"I am too." She grins. "I've never been on a stadium tour."

"I have, but only in the Bay." With the team that's leaving and San Francisco. SF will forever be my home team. It would be cool to play for a team like that, but at least San Diego is a division rival.

"Did you get to stand on the field?"

"Yeah," I say, at both fields. I was young, elementary school age when I did, but I ran as fast as my little legs could on the dirt, my cleats gripping against the sand. I still remember the moment that I crossed home plate both times. My hands raised up high as I rounded third, running into my dad's arms once I crossed home plate. Then, I didn't know what I was going to do when I grew up. I just knew that I loved baseball. And to younger me's delight, I still do.

"It was really cool. I mean, I was a kid at the time, so I was just amazed that I was standing on the field."

"You weren't thinking about hitting home runs when you were standing on it, were you?"

"No." I laugh. "Especially considering at the time, I don't think I could even hit the ball past the pitcher's mound."

We approach the stadium and meet Wesley near the entrance.

"Hey, Corey," Wesley excitedly shakes my hand. "Welcome! Glad you were able to make it."

"Thanks." I nod. "I am too." I look over to Leanne who's holding her hands out in front of her, smiling awkwardly unsure of what to do. "This is Leanne. I hope it's okay she's joining us. We're heading back up to Neptune Beach together so she's kind of like my travel buddy."

I want to cringe. Travel buddy. Part of me wants to just call her my girlfriend at this point. Sounds better out loud to a stranger than a travel buddy.

"Hi." She shakes Wesley's hand. "Nice to meet you."

"Good to meet you as well, Leanne. Have you been to the park before?"

We both shake our heads. "No, it's our first times."

"I don't mean to sound like a prick," Leanne begins, "but I've never really had a desire to come here. Sorry, Giants fan."

Wesley lets out a hearty laugh. "Yeah, yeah, I get it. I grew up in Boston, believe it or not. I may have a San Diego email address, but my heart belongs to the Red Sox. It always will. You can find it in you to root for both teams if Corey starts playing for this team, right?"

She grins. "Of course."

"Because you'll be wearing my name on your back, right?" I nudge her in the side. She looks up at me, trying to find a word to respond back with. I smirk. Got her with that one. And anyone would be a fool to think I wouldn't buy Leanne a jersey that spelled my name and number on the back of it so everyone can know exactly who she should always be rooting for on the field.

"Um." She swallows thickly. "Yeah, of course. You'd buy me a jersey with your name on it, right?"

"In every fucking style I can," I tell her. A home jersey, a city connect one, those special heritage jerseys they do. Getting her a Mexican heritage jersey she can proudly wear to cheer me on as I take the field to celebrate a night that celebrates my culture.

Wesley takes us into the stadium on the ground level, where we're shown the team's locker room. Wesley opens the doors for us to step into, and I peer around at the room, where name plates of current players hang over their lockers and their jerseys are hung from rods.

"Wow," I whisper.

"Pretty cool, huh?"

"It's definitely not like any of the lockers I've had before." We don't even really have a locker at the Seals stadium. We have to bring all our equipment to the dugout every single game and pack it back home with us.

"There's also the fitness room and the batting cages which are near the dugout." Wesley lets us do a loop around the locker room and moves on to show us the rest of the facilities. What's wild is how available this all is for players. They come to practice and they can use this whenever they want.

"And finally," Wesley steps up into a bright light and we follow him into the dugout, "here's the dugout and the field."

"Damn," Leanne says. "It really just jumps right out at you."

"What does?" Wesley asks.

"Just...you know, the fact that we're looking out at a stadium that can hold what...fifty thousand people?"

"Yeah," he agrees. "Close. Just under forty thousand. Three million fans in a season."

"That is surreal," I quip. That's three million bodies, almost six million pairs of eyes and ears that see my name and watch me play. At least a million of those bodies might see me fuck up. I'm bound to strike out at least once a game, drop the ball every other one. There are over a hundred games in a season, there's no such thing as having perfect records or even an average that's more than point five.

"It's pretty awesome," Wesley says. "I'll sometimes watch from the press box. Everyone looks so small, but they're all there to watch baseball and have a good time."

"And you think I can do this?" My voice cracks, sounding like I'm going through puberty all over again except I'm thirty. I'm so weirdly overcome with emotion, at how someone may think that this is my future. I'm good enough to play baseball to an audience of almost fifty thousand when I was just happy to be playing for a fraction of that amount around the country.

Without being told or asked, Leanne grabs a hold of my hand. It jolts me briefly; I didn't have any bat signal to call out for help that I am completely and utterly freaking out right now, but I lace my fingers silently with Leanne's and Wesley gives us a warm smile.

"I do," he answers. "I think you'd be a good addition to the team. And I don't know, something just feels right, when I see you standing on the field."

"But I'm not even wearing a uniform," I tell him.

He shrugs. "Doesn't matter. You've still got a sparkle in your eye to you. Feel free to walk around the field for a little bit, I'll be hanging out here until you're ready to go."

Wesley disappears behind the dugout and Leanne and I are left standing at home plate, hands still intertwined with one another.

"Tell me what's on your mind," Leanne says as she glances up to meet my gaze.

"This might be happening. This...shit. I'm going to be playing in the MLB." My feet make an indent on the dirt from shifting it back and forth. "I just...all of my emotions feel like mush because I'm so overwhelmed." I look down at her. "What if I get here and take the field and I'm not what everyone expects? What if everything I've worked so hard for crumbles and I'm sent back down again?" I feel a tear streak down my face. "I don't want to disappoint everyone that's been a part of my journey that's led me here."

I would feel like everything I've worked for would just be wasted if I just never had a hit, never scored a run. I'd be taking up space on the bench while everyone is celebrating their achievements.

"Everyone is going to be so proud of you when they get to find out. And you're not a disappointment. You're not going to be a disappointment. Not every game is going to be perfect, but every hit, every catch you make is going to get people off their seat cheering for you." She turns and faces me, stepping closer so that we're centimeters apart. She grabs me by the arms and stares straight into my eyes. "I am proud of you. So fucking proud of how hard you've worked and the fact that you're standing on this field right now." Her eyes start to water. "And that I get to share this moment with you."

"Leanne," I say with a thickness lacing my throat. "I–"

What was I feeling? I loved her? I was enamored by her and her kindness. I wanted to confess how special she makes me feel, how in this moment, she's like a star, twinkling in my eye. She's the most beautiful person I know, inside and out, and I...I want to tell her that I'm starting to feel a deep connection to her and say I don't want to be with anyone else ever in my life, but I don't know how we'd be able to make this, us, work, especially now that talks of me moving eight hours away from her are becoming more and more serious.

I settle on, "I'm thankful that I get to share this moment with you too," and brush my lips against hers. The kiss this time is not rushed, we're not frantically trying to kiss our lips off and stick our tongues down each other's throats. This is a sweet one, where we're slowly pressing our lips to each other, parting and then coming back again. I'm taking my time savoring this moment, not rushing to feel something, because I want to hold onto Leanne as long as I can, and right now, all that's consuming my mind is showering her with soft kisses that cause her to melt in my arms.

She wraps her arms tighter around my waist and I clutch onto her back as we part and touch our foreheads against each other.

"Kissing on a baseball field is something I've never done before," I note.

Leanne raises a brow. "Really?"

"Why do you sound so surprised?"

"I don't know! I didn't know if you if you've ever won like a championship game and shared a kiss with someone afterward to celebrate!"

She laughs as she's trying to make her point. I think she's obsessing too much over a certain athlete/musician power couple that just shared a lot of kisses on the field during football season.

"No." I shake my head. "I have not. Sorry to disappoint."

"Well." She flutters her lashes. "I'm honored to be the first then."

I grab a hold of her hand before I get too lost in her eyes and kiss her senselessly again, and we walk back to the dugout and take the final tour of the stadium before we make our way back to Neptune Beach.

Chapter 20
Leanne

Before we head on the road back to Neptune Beach, I decide it would be best to get a bite to eat while we're here and the food options are almost endless.

Corey and I find a chic Japanese spot in the Gaslamp that is full of hanging plants and a colorful wall mural that makes the vibe fun.

After we each order: an udon bowl for me and a sashimi salad for Corey, Corey's gaze fixates on the elaborate flora decor that surrounds us. He lets out a "hmm," while still looking up at the ceiling.

"What's up?" I ask.

"Have you thought about opening up your own restaurant?"

I straighten in my seat. That's a loaded question.

"No." I shake my head. "Do you know how hard that would be?" I'm already starting to feel the onset of a headache thinking about logistics and space. I mean, the food truck is easy. We go where we're told to and we have to stick to the confines of the truck. Even with a catering business, we go where we're told and we work with the venue and the client to bring them food and service. A restaurant is your space, your responsibility. If something in the kitchen breaks, it's your responsibility to fix it. You buy your own furnishings and make it look aesthetically pleasing to attract people and then hope your food tastes good as well. It's stressful already thinking about it.

"Yeah, I mean it'll be hard of course. But, imagine how amazing it would be if you'd get to take a space, however big or small, and make it come alive. You can paint the walls red, have a dragon drawn on the walls, make a fake-looking pagoda in the corner..."

"Woah." My eyes widen. "How much money do you think I'll have for this?"

"Well," Corey says, twirling his straw between his fingers, "I think that maybe if everything falls into place then I'd be able to help start one. Somewhere around here, maybe closer to where we'd live if you don't want to live in the city...La Jolla is a nice place to start a restaurant..."

"Woah, woah, woah." I scoot back in my chair and it creaks so loud I have to mouth a "sorry" to everyone who's forced to listen to the abhorrent sound of a chair scraping against a concrete floor. "Where is all this coming from?"

"I just want to propose the idea of us moving together."

Propose. My mind fixates on that word and I can't process anything else beyond that damn word. I've heard it before and I've been broken by it. And now, Corey wants to "propose" the idea of us moving in together if and when he moves to San Diego?

"Corey," I groan. "We can't move in together."

"Why not?"

"Because we're not even dating!" I raise my voice at him. "You can't just spring up these wild ideas when all we're doing is fucking."

I recoil when I realize there are not really a whole lot of people sitting down in this restaurant because a number of heads just turned toward the table Corey and I are sitting at and shooting us "you're really doing that here?" looks.

"Leanne," Corey says in a calm tone. "It's just an idea..."

"It's a stupid one," I bite back. I immediately felt bad being so rude. It's not stupid. It's a dream. I'd love to wake up to Corey every morning, kiss him before I leave for work. And I can't believe I get this time to be with Corey and hold his hand and show him affection without having to worry if anyone can see us. But I'm not ready to leave home yet. I'm scared to move away from my family and everything I've created, and why do I need to change my life? Just because Corey will have a job that will pay the bills and take care of us way more than I possibly could?

"Okay." His brow furrows. "I'm sorry I brought it up. You're right, I don't know why I bothered asking."

I pout. I feel bad now that I've made Corey feel like a fool.

The server brings us our food and we barely talk. I don't even really have much of an appetite anymore because I'm so worked up about the move-in topic and now, we're wasting precious time alone together by being upset with one another.

Corey asks if I've finished and after still having too much broth and noodles in my bowl I can't take with me because we're immediately heading on the road, I respond with a nod. He solemnly leads us to the car and we make the quiet, tension-filled trip to our next destination.

After driving up Highway 101, passing through Ventura and Santa Barbara, eyeing the calm water to our left that is the Pacific Ocean, we make it to our destination for the evening. Corey and I were so excited to both be pitching in to share a room together at the Madonna Inn in San Luis Obispo. I have seen this hotel on travel sites for each of its rooms having a unique theme, and the urinal that's just a waterfall. But now that we've successfully been able to go radio silent on the three-hour car ride here, I don't know if I can even have fun because Corey is mad at me and I'm...not mad at him, really. More confused than anything. Was he thinking a lot about this? After we explicitly stated to one another that we'd keep this strictly platonic with some fucking on the side?

He parks and I get out of the car to try and grab my suitcase from the trunk. I forgot I packed a lot of clothes for this trip that made the suitcase feel so heavy. That, or I've tried to hold in all these tears for the past three hours and I feel every other part of my body fails to do some kind of movement.

"Here." Corey reaches his arm over mine to grab the luggage handle.

"I got it," I say between clenched teeth.

"Just let me help, Leanne," Corey says, defeated.

"I'm fine," I tell him, but when I collapse against my suitcase and start sobbing, I am indeed, not fine.

Corey silently covers his body with mine and wraps his arm around my neck.

"Leanne," he says in my hair. "Let me help you. Please."

"Fine," I say into my suitcase. I stand up from keeling over on my suitcase and wipe the snot that's dripped down my nose. A really attractive look.

"But before I do," Corey begins, "come here."

He bends down and wraps his arms around my waist and pulls me into him. He plants a kiss on the top of my head and I slowly wrap my arms back around him.

"I'm sorry," he says, pulling me in tighter. "I didn't mean to make you upset."

"No," I say into his chest. "You were just making a suggestion. I just...I was just surprised and I reacted poorly. I'm sorry."

"It was kind of a big ask. You're right, we're not official. And I don't want to take you away from Neptune Beach and everything you'd be leaving behind. I just..." He pulls apart and looks down at me. "I love spending time with you. And when I was standing on that field, kissing you, something set off in my brain telling me that I wanted this every goddamn day. It's becoming more and more difficult to just be friends with you, Leanne. Well, friends who fool around."

I sigh. I can agree with him on that.

"Yeah, I know. I'm trying to tell myself that we can't take it anything past friends who fuck but it's really hard. You're all I want, Corey."

And I think I'm starting to fall in love with you. Or I already have, whether I want to admit it or not.

"You're all I want too, Leanne. I don't even want to think about trying to date someone else. You've ruined dating for me."

I grasp his hand. "Oh, come on! There are so many women out there, you're going to find someone perfect for you. I mean, you'll be in San Diego! There's plenty of people to find...there's that new women's soccer team..."

"Okay, woman." He rolls his eyes and puts a hand to my mouth to shut me up. "You can stop it with that nonsense."

"What?" I counter. "I'm just trying to hype you up!"

"Do you know what would hype me up?" Suddenly, he hoists me up from the ground and I squeal. "If we check in and I get into that plush hotel bed with you."

"Okay! Well, you need to set me down, my name is on the reservation."

We check in and I beg Corey if we can take a look at the urinal before we head up to our room.

"Is that...allowed?" he asks. "What if other people are...pissing?"

"Well, go in and tell me if anyone is and I'll wait until they're done. People do this all the time. This urinal is special. It was mentioned on 'Extreme Bathrooms'!"

He shoots a brow up. "Extreme bathrooms? What does that even mean?"

I roll my eyes. "Think about it. It's not that deep."

He purses his lips and his brows come together to form a V. He fixates a spot on the floor and looks like he's about to shit his pants.

"It's all about cool bathrooms, Corey. Like a urinal that doubles as a waterfall. And those self-cleaning bathrooms in San Francisco that are open to the public."

"Ah." He nods slowly. "That does make sense. Okay, I'm going to use this special waterfall urinal then and report back. And then let you take a look at it, because you are so excited to see this...urinal."

"It's special!" My yell is comparable to a screeching child with a pet rock they randomly found.

He pats the top of my head softly. "So are you," he notes.

I pucker my lips and blow him a kiss and watch him disappear into the restroom.

I wait for him to come back out, and realize that he had been in the restroom for a long time. He could have been taking a number two, but five minutes pass by and I still hadn't seen him come out.

When he finally steps out, he gives me a thumbs up and tells me that the coast is clear and I can step into the bathroom.

"You hyped up the urinal too much," he tells me as he stands between the doorframe leading in. "I mean it's cool, but it's just all rocks."

"Yeah," I give him a deadpanned look. "How many urinals do you know have that?"

He pauses because I know the answer to that is absolutely none. "Zero," he mutters.

"Exactly. Now, lemme see." I maneuver my way past him and step inside the urinal. I listen as the water runs down into the drain and quickly snap a video of it before making my way out so someone who's able to use it can head in.

Corey pushes himself off the wall. "So, was it everything you dreamt of and more?"

"It was...pretty awesome." At the end of the day, it's just a manmade waterfall that also serves as a place for people to do their business. I'm satisfied after seeing it, but it's not the most beautiful thing I've ever seen in the world. It's not "eighth wonder of the world" status.

"You sound disappointed," he notes after we've begun walking to find our room.

"I'm not," I reassure him. "I'm just...content." It's that middle ground, where you've not reached the point where you're bouncing off the wall with excitement, but you're not mopey and sad. I'm just feeling good about my life and now that we're at a point where we're back being happy with one another.

Corey grabs onto my hand. "I am too."

We head inside our room, ironically called the "Romance Suite," which is a junior suite that has a bed and separate living room area that looks straight out of a regency-set story. The walls are painted a Tiffany blue color and there's a small chandelier hanging from the ceiling.

"This is amazing," I say once I've set my bags down in the general living room area. "I've never stayed in a room that's so decorated like this."

"It's something unique," Corey adds. There were lots of types of rooms that we could have chosen from, and thankfully, it was a weekday so it was easy for us to find a room type. This was on the pricier side as compared to a standard king room that doesn't have a separate living area, but Corey and I agreed that we can both pitch in a little more money to enjoy a room that is more spacious because we may never get another chance to share something intimate like this with one another.

"Do you like it?"

He looks down at me. I can't read what he's thinking about from his facial expressions, but once he meets my eyes, he grins down at me.

"I do. But I'm just happy that I get to spend time somewhere with you. And sharing a bed with you. Speaking of," he begins, and grabs a hold of my hand and starts leading me closer to the bed.

"I need to do something to make me forget about that fight we had, if you know what I mean."

"Yes." I nod. "I fully agree."

Chapter 21
Leanne

Corey pulls me into him and greedily slams his mouth onto mine. I snake his arms around his neck and he uses the strength in his arms to hoist me up and scoop his joined arms under my ass.

"I hope I can do enough for you to forgive me for how I acted earlier," he says.

From what sexual acts we've already done so far with one another, I don't think that Corey needs to do much to make me forget that we even fought in the first place.

Corey gently drops me on the bed and hovers his body over mine.

"You're wearing too many clothes," he observes.

I look back into his eyes, his stare fiery as it trails down to my sweater and smirk.

"Then do something about it," I command.

He reaches down to the hem of my sweater and pulls it up. I give him some assistance by raising my hands above my head and he's able to smoothly take the sweater off of me. When I'm only wearing a bra, I sit up and reach behind to unclasp it to help Corey get a head start with the rest of the garments, but he stops me by splaying his hand onto the padding over my bra.

"No," he rasps. "Let me try and take it off."

I part my lips. "Okay," I whisper back.

He pulls me up and wraps his hands around me, and while keeping his eyes trained on my face. With one push to unhook the clasps of my bra, it comes loose and the straps begin to fall off my shoulders. He quickly goes to play with my nipples, rubbing them gently between his fingers before he brings his lips to them and gently bites down.

"Corey," I yelp. I bite my lip and arch my back toward his mouth as he sucks on me.

"Mmm," I grunt. "God." I don't know any other words to describe how amazing I feel from this.

"Let it out Leanne," he grins up at me. "Let me hear you, my good girl."

I don't hold back. I let out a scream that rocks my insides. He hasn't even done much else yet but I feel amazing. I feel wanted. Somehow Corey knows what my pleasure spots are, and he's taking care of me. We're exploring different positions and places. I've never had sex as good as I do with Corey, and it terrifies me. We just came back from San Diego where Corey had a really good meeting with a professional baseball team and I think he might be living out his dreams and leaving Neptune Beach soon.

"God, Leanne," Corey tilts my chin up to give me a kiss. "I love the way you scream for me. Is there a way I can just make time stop so I can savor this moment with you?"

"I don't know if you can make time stop," I tell him. "You're not that cool."

He playfully rolls his eyes. "I wish I could." He grabs a hold of my cheek. "You make me so happy. This weekend has been a lot of fun. Not just because I get to play baseball. I forgot how much I do miss California. The ocean views, the beachy vibes. You."

"But not all those things can stay with you when you move to San Diego."

He frowns. "No. And that's why I wish I could stop time, because you're the most special part of this weekend."

"Well, we should just try and have as much fun as we can tonight then." Knowing this might be our last night we'll spend together like this.

"Would you visit me?" He asks. "In San Diego? You'll always have a place to stay. We can eat tacos, go to the beach. Maybe there will be some cool cooking convention you can go to at the convention center..."

"Maybe you should make one," I laugh. "So I can come down."

"I'd do whatever it takes," he says in a more serious tone. "I don't want anyone else, Leanne. And, if I have to wait months, years, I'll wait however long it takes for us."

"Corey..." I don't want to rehash this again.

"I'm not asking you to move in. Yet. I just want you to know I don't want to go to San Diego and put myself on a dating app. I don't even want to go to any event where I have to take someone as a date if I can't take you first."

"What are you trying to say?"

"I'm trying to say...take your time. I'm not going anywhere. Yes, long distance sucks. But we can call each other every night. We can try and make a schedule. You set your own schedule, so when you don't have a Seals game or an event, we can try and make that our weekend. We'll take turns, if you want to come down and then the next time I'll come up. I don't know where I'll stay... I mean I'd stay with my parents. They should be fine with you staying over."

He takes a deep breath. "Sorry, I'm trying to speak all the shit that's been occupying my mind. What I'm trying to say is, I want us, but I want us when you're ready. And I'll be here waiting. I'll learn to be patient. That's all."

I don't know what to say in response. I don't think there is anyone else I want more than Corey, and this arrangement might be more than just good sex. I don't think it was ever just about the sex. But, if Corey is telling me he will wait for when I'm ready, I can't help but fall deeper for him. My ex-fiance just tried to change my agenda. Corey is letting me make my own path. To me, that's already a step in the direction I want from a soulmate.

"Okay," I nod. "I might need a bit to think about everything, is that okay?"

He bends down and kisses me again. "It's more than okay. I'm just happy you're considering it."

He turns the television on and we watch a few shows before I find myself falling deeper into sleep with my head resting against Corey's chest.

***

My heartrate quickens when I see the trunk full of suitcases filled up and Corey's dad still carrying more boxes to the car.

This is it. This is the last chance I have to tell Corey how I feel before he gets in that car for LA and leaves for good.

I try to run but my feet feel like they're glued to the ground.

No. They are.

My soles are like gum sticking to the pavement and when I try to move, their rubbery material stretches and I try and step to get off the ground, but I can't.

I fall flat on the sidewalk and watch in agony as Corey packs up the last box and opens the passenger side door, stepping into the car.

"Corey, no!" I yell, but he can't hear me.

"Corey!" I try again, and I get the sound of the engine starting instead.

"Please," I sob, still glued to the pavement. "Don't leave. I love you." I never got the chance to tell him and now it's too late.

Why can't he hear me?

Why is he driving away...

"No!" I yell, sitting straight up in my bed and shooting my eyes open. I notice that light is shining into the room again. What time is it?

"Leanne?" Corey groggily sits up and puts a protective hand on my back. "Are you okay? What happened?"

I'm still breathing heavily after that strange dream I had where it felt like I was screaming at the top of my lungs and Corey couldn't hear me. That he couldn't even see that I was there, and then it was too late and Corey disappeared forever before I could tell him that I loved him.

"Just...had a bad dream. I'm fine."

"What was your dream about?"

You. Leaving. Me. Upset.

"I don't even really remember all of it," I lie. "I just remember not being able to move, like my feet were glued to the ground and I woke up."

"Well, you're safe with me," Corey reassures me by pulling me into his chest again and letting me hear his rapid heartbeat. Shit, I must have scared him with my scream.

"Thank you. Sorry I yelled. I...didn't even realize I'd said something out loud until it caused me to wake up."

"It's okay. We all have those scary dreams sometimes."

The scariest part was it felt like it alluded to something so real. Maybe not the soles turning into gum part, but the idea I might be stuck in a town I've known all my life and when the chance to move is presented to me and follow someone who I want to be with, I'm stuck.

"Corey," I begin. "Did you mean it?"

"Mean what?"

"That you'd want me to move in with you. That your end goal is for us to be together." That if I dropped everything to start anew, he'd support me. That if we left Neptune Beach, we could build a life with one another. A future.

"That if I were to join you...if, when, that you would help me build my life back up? Rebuild my dreams in a new place?" Love me when I might be scared that I'm jumping into something unknown for the first time.

"Yes," he breathed. "Of course I would, Leanne. I...I'd do anything to try and keep you close to me."

I twiddle my thumbs in front of me, laying my hands still on the blanket covering us. It had barely crossed seven in the morning and I felt like I couldn't wait to bring something like this up. I mean, what if it would come back to haunt my dreams tomorrow? Or next week? Forever until I died? I can't be essentially haunted by the thought of what if forever.

"Okay." I nod.

He narrows his eyes at me. "Okay?"

"Y-yeah," I croak. "I'm sorry. It's a lot for me to process." I take a deep breath to calm myself down from the still pounding heart rate I have after waking up so suddenly.

"Last night, I dreamt that you were packing the car to leave Neptune Beach and I tried to run as fast as I could to try and tell you that I...was falling in love with you and I thought that you needed to know that before you left because I didn't know if I was going to be able to tell you that again and try and make you stay."

Corey's mouth drops and he blinks as I've tried to tell him in the most nonchalant way that I'm falling in love with him. I mean, if my dreams are any indication, then this is something I think that I need to chase after.

Corey's still silent and I lean in closer to try and nudge him to respond.

"Corey?" I ask anxiously. "What are you thinking?"

"Do you love me, Leanne Fairbanks?" he rasps.

I start breathing heavily. I have been in love before, so I know what it was like to be in love with someone, but somehow this feeling was not like the feelings I had before. I did love Greg, and I was ecstatic at the time to marry him. I thought he would give me everything, and looking back on it now, maybe I was too young and was just in love with the idea of being in love. I rushed into things a little too much, and after the pressure of planning a wedding and realizing I was stuck in a job that I didn't love and wanted to jump into a career that might not have been immediately profitable.

But when I look back at Corey and as I look back on the past few months that we've spent with one another, something dawns on me that this is a different feeling than I've felt before. I'm coming to the realization that I don't want to wake up one day and let Corey disappear. I've never thought so much about how much I'd miss someone if they'd left me as much as I do with Corey, because I love being with him and I love the way that he treats me like I'm precious cargo.

I'm completely obsessed with him. I love him.

"Yes. I do." I nod. "I'm falling in love with you, Corey. I think I have been for a long time."

Chapter 22
Corey

The moment Leanne finishes uttering my name, my lips are on hers.

Our still-naked bodies melt against one another, and my fingers thread through the strands of her still-wavy brown hair.

I break apart from the kiss for a moment to take a breath, and to tell her that her feelings are reciprocated.

"I love you, Leanne," I breathe into her mouth. "I want to be with you. We'll figure this out, okay?"

"I'm scared, Corey," she confesses. "What will happen is that either I'll go down with you to a new city and try and figure out how to start my life up again, or we'll be trying to do long distance until we can figure out a plan later to be together, which might mean years."

"I know, but we'll make it work. I'll make sure we do."

Do I have a plan concocted yet to make this work? No. Technically, I can continue telling myself nothing is official until I've signed a contract. I can keep my prospects out for another team to show interest. Problem is: if I want to stay near home, then that leaves one team I can try and shoot my shot for. But, I don't want to be waiting for a call, especially because I'd only be called in if there was room for them to take me. As

I've always told myself, I have to bear down and take what I can get, even if that means I'd be away from the woman I love for a long time until we tried to drum up a plan.

"In the meantime," I tell her. "I'm still in Neptune Beach. I'm still playing for the Seals, and I'm not going anywhere until I sign. And until then, when we can talk about what we're going to do, I want to be yours, Leanne. Not in just the friends who fuck kind of way. I want you and I want you to want me back."

"I do," Leanne begs. "I want you. I love you, Corey."

"I love you too, Leanne." I bring my arms around her waist and slightly lift her so I can cradle her in my lap. She hitches a breath when she realizes that she's sitting on my erection.

I look up at her. "Is that enough for you to realize?"

"It's a good start," she says sheepishly. "You're almost there. But I think you should do a little more to show me how much you want me."

A rumble hums low in my chest and I thrust myself up into her on my lap so she can feel me between the fabrics of our underwear. She gasps once she feels my hardness rub against her.

"How's this?" I begin.

I can see she's trying to resist me so much but her quicken breathing tells me she's almost to a breaking point. "Almost there," she grits. "You're getting warmer."

With my hand, I shift the fabric covering her aside and stick a finger and then one more and twirl around inside her.

"Yeah?" I whisper. "What about now?"

"Corey," she pants. "You know what I want."

I smirk. Of course I do. It's what I've been wanting us to do for so long. I know it's a big step for us to take, but maybe the universe or whatever being that exists beyond our realm that's put the thought of losing me into Leanne's mind, is a sign that we should go for it.

"You're sure?"

She nods. "Please," she begs. "Come inside me."

"Let me grab a condom," I tell her. It was a good thing I bought some before the trip in anticipation that something like this would happen.

I remove her underwear and strip mine off soon after. I press my dick into her navel and Leanne responds by biting her bottom lip.

"This is for you," I tell her. "For as long as you'll want me."

"I'll always want you," she breathes. "If you'll have me, Corey."

"I will."

I slowly insert myself into her and begin thrusting. I sigh. It feels so good. It's taking so much in me to savor how good our skin feels pressed against each other.

"You're so wet for me, Leanne."

I pump a few more times into her at a steady rhythm. Leanne moans into my ear, a moan that partly sounds like a squeal with how high her tone changes. It's the sounds. The damn sounds that Leanne Fairbanks makes for me that make me so damn giddy. Because she's making those sounds because of me.

"Corey," she whispers.

"Look at me," I tell her, because she's keeping her eyes closed. "I want you to look at me as I fuck you. So I know who you belong to."

She blinks her eyes open and we stare unblinking at one another, as I keep pumping in and out of her. Leanne's lips stay open in an "O" and I watch her bare chest rise and fall as my cadence rises.

"Good girl," I whisper. "You're doing great, babe."

It doesn't even register immediately that I just called her babe. It's another thing that's adding on to this scene straight out of a movie.

Leanne and I, tangled up in one another on a bed, exploring each other, whispering words of affirmation. Coming from the pleasure we're giving one another.

"I'm going to come, Corey."

"Good." So will I. As much as I want to hold onto this moment forever, it feels to good to let this feeling stay inside me.

Leanne arches up into my chest and I lean down and take a bite of her nipple. She lets out a delighted scream and as she grips onto me, I come off her for a moment and grunt. I pant as I spill into her and we hold each other for a few moments as we calm ourselves down from two earth-shattering orgasms.

I give her another kiss on the forehead. "You did amazing, babe."

"Thanks." She chuckles. "You weren't so bad yourself."

"Yeah? You think so?"

She gives me a quick kiss. "Yeah. In fact, I think that I'd like to do it again sometime."

"Good, me too. We'll just have to figure out where."

"Oh yeah." Her smile falls and she nudges me to get up so we can both rinse off. "I forgot about that. Well, I guess forgot isn't the right word. I didn't want to think about it in hopes that it would make this situation better."

"We'll figure it out," I tell her as I turn the shower on. "I mean, there's that small inn off the coast of the beach that all the tourists need to stay at when they come to visit."

"How could I explain that to my parents?" The toilet flushes. "That I need to get away for a night or five?"

"Or, I don't know," I start before stepping in and rinsing off, "we tell everyone we're dating?"

Leanne purses her lips. The silence coming from her standing inches from me hits me, blinking and crossing her arms, makes me more frustrated the more I fixate on it.

"Leanne," I start. We just had out of this world sex and now I feel like we're taking a step backward in our progress again.

"I'm thinking!" She blows away the hair that's collected over her face. "I want to tell everyone, you know."

"But..."

"But everyone's going to be so critical about it. My parents will be happy but they also will either question how I'm going to make long distance work or how I'm going to strap on my boots and revamp my career after I move. And then what's Lance going to think about his best friend dating his only sister?"

"I would like to think that he would be happy if he'd care about both of our happiness..." I speak it into existence but that puts Lance in a tough position if this somehow didn't work out. If we were to break up after all this, and Lance would of course take Leanne's side. I might lose him and I was just getting happy again that we're talking again. I'm proud of myself for making an effort to be more present with him after he's tried so hard to make me happy to be back home. Shit, I forgot I haven't even really told him about the visit, or the real reason why I'm here.

"But you know he's also going to think that I'm going to steal you away from him."

I roll my eyes. "You both give me different things. He's someone that I'm gonna talk about baseball with and occasionally go to the bar and play pool with. He's my friend, and we give each other friendship. You...you give me a lot more than that Leanne. You give me someone who I want to love and care for. To treat like the queen you are, in my bed and out of it. I don't think I'd want that as much from Lance."

She laughs back. "Fair. Lance wouldn't make you come in bed like I can."

"Exactly." I press a soft kiss on her nose. "I don't want to force you into anything, but I want this. I want to proclaim to everyone that you're mine and wear you like you're a heart on my sleeve. I want everyone to know how much I love you, Leanne."

She tries to hide her grin and ultimately nods. "Okay," she agrees. "Let's try this thing out. I don't want to just say we're fooling around anymore. Everything we do is because we're in love and we deserve to be out loud about it."

"That's my girl." I kiss her again. "Okay let me shower before I get too carried away kissing you and want to go for round two."

"I wouldn't say no if you'd like." She winks.

"Gimme a little bit to cool down." I laugh. I may have endurance to play through nine innings of a baseball game all the way through, but I need a little break before I can orgasm again in Leanne. But I would do it again, every day, if we could.

I rinse myself off in the shower and return back to Leanne, who is sitting on the living room couch, watching kid's cartoons because nothing else was on this early in the morning.

"What's the plan today?" I ask Leanne. "Besides making sure I get you home in one piece."

"I don't know." Leanne shrugs. "I just don't want to go because that means that we'll have to resume life back in Neptune Beach. Do you think we can hang out a little while longer on our trip home to make some more memories before we need to resume life as we know it?"

"We can take our time heading back to Neptune Beach," I tell her. "The beaches around here are beautiful. And we're not far from Hearst Castle."

Leanne beams. "Wait, that's not a bad idea! I've always wanted to see it. How far is it from here?"

I plug in the name into my phone's Maps app. "Only forty five minutes away," I quip. "We can even take a scenic route if you'd like."

"I'd like that. Take a little pit stop on the beach..."

I take her in my arms. "Partake in some activities that sound like a very fruity cocktail..."

"Ew," Leanne recoils. "I am not going to get sand in my lady parts."

"Yeah, that doesn't sound so comfy." We pack up our things and loaded the car's trunk with our suitcases and equipment. I wished we could have enjoyed the room and the amenities of the hotel for a little longer. Apparently they had a really well known cake that's very delicious and very pink. But there's always a next time, and I am going to make sure that Leanne and I are going to have another time where we can enjoy a vacation with the company of one another.

We take our pit stop in Morro Bay, grabbing some burgers from a well-known joint not too far away. We don't have any blankets to sit down on, so we're resorting to sitting on the smooth, fine sand on the beach, with a light tide that barely washes up on the surface.

I look at Leanne, the side of her face illuminated by the sun peeking out behind her, and think to myself: Leanne's making a big sacrifice by wanting to be with me. I just hope I'm worthy enough for her to stay.

Chapter 23
Leanne

We return back to Neptune Beach, and when Corey drives up to my parent's house, the whirlwind of wondering how the fuck we're going to navigate this hits me like a ton of bricks.

Corey drops me off at my house late that night, and I sneak up to my room as to not disturb my parents, who are sleeping. I had told them already I was going to be arriving home late due to my desire to rent a car and drive up the coast, I just omitted some crucial information on who accompanied me for that trip.

I punch in the code to get into the garage and use the spare house key that my parents keep under our doormat my dad bought because it says, "Welcome to the Dark Side."

The house is dark and I tip toe up the stairs with my weekender duffel bag and plop it into my room before I even turn the lights on. I shut the door behind me and turn on the lights. I think I can spend the time to unpack tomorrow, as I don't need to be at the ballpark until four in the afternoon to prepare for the Seals' six thirty game start time. But I would much rather be spending that time with Corey if he doesn't need to be at the ballpark by a certain time as well. I think there's a place that we can go where we don't need to worry about someone bumping into us. We can take the ferry into San Francisco, play tourist.

He should be home by now, so I pull out my phone to text him.

LEANNE

Doing anything tomorrow before practice?

COREY

no, well maybe going to gym. Why?

LEANNE

because…wanted to know if you wanna go out with me

;)

COREY

that does sound a lot better than going to the gym

Thinking anywhere specific? Not Neptune Beach I assume

LEANNE

no not here…and not anywhere i'd think of anyway. I was thinking we can go to SF?

Instead of responding via text, Corey decides to call me instead.

"Hey," I answer almost immediately. "What's up?"

"I just decided I'd rather hear your voice than watch text bubbles pop up on my screen."

I smile. "Miss me already, don't you?"

"Shhh," he says in a low whisper. "Don't tell anyone."

"Okay, I won't."

"I'm just kidding, babe. You can tell whoever you want."

I blush into my pillow. We haven't been together a full twenty-four hours and Corey's already got his nickname picked out for me. Albeit, the nickname is a fairly genetic one, but it still brings music to my ears more than if he were to just call me Leanne. Although, when it was Corey saying my name, it instantly made me want to melt.

"Did your parents ask why you were home so late?" I ask, curious.

"No, they're asleep. The house was dark when I got inside."

"Same here. I'm surprised that my parents haven't made an effort to get up and walk over to my room to question my late arrival." My dad is a deep sleeper, like can sleep through earthquakes, leaf blowers, sirens galore. My mom on the other hand, takes a little while to fall asleep. Probably because she's had to stay up to watch three children struggle to go to sleep when they were babies.

"So I can assume they're not going to get up and talk to you before you go to bed?"

"No..." I say cautiously. I knock on the wood of my bed's headboard very gently. The last thing I want is for my parents to walk in, without even knocking because they'll say it's their house and they have access to come in and talk whenever they want. Now that Corey and I are together, I'm going to have to be really careful that they don't barge in when I'm on the phone with Corey telling him how much I loved him or worse, if he tells me to do things that will definitely break the heat scale.

"Okay, good."

"Why?" I ask innocently.

"You'll see," Corey warns.

"Okay..." I roll my eyes, but grin that we don't need to hide any emotions we feel toward one another, engaging in a push and pull if one or the other really has feelings for the others. It's in the open now, and we're kind of just seeing where the journey takes us.

"Anyway," I start. "How do you feel about taking a trip to the city tomorrow?"

"I'd love that," Corey responds. "And you're okay with being out somewhere where we may potentially run into someone?"

"Yeah." I nod. "I think it'll be okay." If we run into someone we know, then we can conjure up something on the spot, and just admit we're dating even with a lot of what-ifs. I guess no one knows about Corey's trip so we don't need to explain we're on what feels like a ticking time bomb to enjoy dating before we're separated.

"What did you have planned?"

"I didn't think too much about it." I have been to San Francisco many times, but all the places that scream tourist, like Fisherman's Wharf, Lombard Street, Union Square in its prime, I've tried to avoid. But, there are places I love to go to. I have the few good eateries I've tried and liked, and places where it feels like we can relax: like in Golden Gate Park. It should be fairly quiet on a weekday with people heading to work.

"Do you want to play tourist or try and go to somewhere you're comfortable with?"

"I mean, funny enough, I don't really go to some of those hot tourist places because I know that there will be a lot of people there. Like, I've never thought to visit Alcatraz."

"You know what?" Corey begins. "Me neither. I have always wanted to go, but I just kind of forgot about it. Then I grew up and lost some of that desire. But, I think it's a place you should visit if you're ever in San Francisco. It has a rich history behind it."

"Yeah." I laugh. "And a race inspired by the people who tried to escape. Although, I'm more interested in watching the *Mythbusters* episode on whether or not they could have successfully escaped and made it out alive."

"That was a good one," Corey says. "Didn't peg you to know what *Mythbusters* was."

"I had an older brother who was a big science nerd. He made us put it on just as much as he made you watch it when you'd come over."

Corey lets out a light chuckle. "Yeah, that tracks. So, what do you think? Should we go and see for ourselves?"

"Sure." I nod. "That sounds great."

"Our first date," he quips. "I like the sound of that."

"Me too." It's after the fact and I could argue we had date-like outings prior. I mean, we took a road trip up the California coast together and slept in the same bed. But maybe Corey has something fun up his sleeve to commemorate the occasion. And I get to see what he has in store.

"How long has it been since I dropped you off?" Corey asks.

"Hmm." I tilt my head and look at the digital clock on my nightstand. Currently, it's just after midnight, and Corey dropped me off maybe an hour and some change ago. "Maybe a little over an hour. Why?"

"Because I miss you already," Corey says. "I know it's only been an hour, but I've been spoiled with being in the same bed with you. Now I want that all the time."

Maybe one day, I think. I'm still unsure of going in headfirst to move in with Corey. But now that we're official, that we're calling each other "babe" and saying "I miss you" and the L-word, I can't go back to what was before. The forbidden romance, hiding our feelings, and letting the thought of "what-ifs" tear us apart.

"I know," I tell him. "I do too."

"You're certain your parents are fast asleep, right?"

"Uh, they should be." I don't want them to randomly wake up at any given time to ask what I'm up to, but in case they do, I'm going to turn off the lights just in case, so they can just assume I'm sleeping.

"Okay," I say, returning to my bed. I open the covers up and slide inside. "I turned my light off so they can assume I'm sleeping." I even take the extra measure of turning on my nightstand fan, which I keep on to help me fall asleep to white noise.

"Good girl," Corey whispers into my headphones. I feel a jolt run through my nerves and down there starts to pulse when he tells me who I am.

"Corey," I begin.

"Take off your underwear."

I let out a gasp.

"What?" he says with a deep chuckle trailing after. "Are you nervous?"

"No," I retort. I've just never participated in over the phone sexual activities before. This was a turn I can say I didn't see coming.

"I've...never done this over the phone before."

"That's okay. That's why I'm going to walk through it with you."

I swallow, and grab onto the hem of my underwear and slide it down my legs. I toss it on the floor of my bed next to me.

"Okay," I whisper. "What's the next step?" I know what it is, but I need the satisfaction of Corey telling me explicitly so I can feel the euphoria from someone telling me that I need to touch myself, so they can hear me get off.

"Start with one finger," he rasps. "Rub your clit. Feel inside you. Make a swirling pattern. Make me hear how you feel when you touch yourself."

I take a deep breath. I slide my hand down, brush it over my pussy and start rubbing my clit. I let out an "oh," that I've apparently kept deep in the pit of my throat, and start rubbing a little faster, my heartrate picking up.

"Are you thinking of me as you're touching yourself?" Corey asks.

"Yes," I moan. I'm thinking about Corey's body over mine. His fingers rubbing me instead of mine. I stick my finger inside and thrust it in and out. My fingers are soaked, but I love it. I stick another finger inside me and breathe out through my mouth.

"Yes, Corey," I whisper. My speed quickens and I tilt my head back on my pillow. "I'm going to come."

"Do it, baby," he commands. "Come for me, my good girl."

I pull up my blanket over my mouth and scream as I come over my fingers.

"You did so good, babe," he tells me. "You sounded amazing."

"Thanks." I smile. "That was...almost as good as if you were here."

It's odd thinking about how I'd wish Corey was here, while I'm in the bedroom I used to hang posters I'd get out of teen magazines of boy bands popular at the time. Imagine if I hadn't remodeled my room to "adultify" it and Corey was making love to me with the JoBros on my wall.

"Well, we'll figure things out," Corey reassures me. "You have a car right?"

I laugh. "Yes, I do. Are you implying..."

"I'm telling you that we should have sex in your car, Leanne," he says. "We can go out to the far end of the beach late at night, maybe we'll pitch a tent or something on the sand, and make love to each other under the stars."

"We'll figure it out," I tell him. I'm not bringing back up the idea of sand in our cracks. "I should probably go to sleep. We've been driving a lot today."

"I loved it," Corey says.

I smile into my pillow. "Me too. Goodnight, Corey."

"Goodnight, Leanne. I love you."

"I love you too."

I press the end call button and set my phone on the nightstand. We're going to figure this out, and then we don't have to be so sneaky about everything. But for now, at least I can be happy that we're open about our feelings to each other. That makes me sleep more soundly than I have in a long time.

Chapter 24
Leanne

The next morning, Corey and I plan our trip out to San Francisco. It'd be more of a hassle to drive into the city, when we can take the ferry across the bay instead. I send Corey a quick good morning text, letting him know I'll be at his house in a few minutes to take us to the ferry terminal.

I drive down the street to his house and text him that I've arrived.

COREY

Gimme a few, sorry. Woke up late and just got out of the shower. I should be ready in five?

LEANNE

That's fine, take your time!!

COREY

Trust me, I'm trying to go fast so I can kiss those lips of yours.

LEANNE

Hah, well that works too.

The next morning, Corey and I plan our trip out to San Francisco. It'd be more of a hassle to drive into the city, when we can take the ferry across the bay instead. I send Corey a quick good morning text, letting him know I'll be at his house in a few minutes to take us to the ferry terminal.

I drive down the street to his house and text him that I've arrived.

Corey: Gimme a few, sorry. Woke up late and just got out of the shower. I should be ready in five?

Leanne: That's fine, take your time!!

Corey: Trust me, I'm trying to go fast so I can kiss those lips of yours.

Leanne: Hah, well that works too.

I'm smiling into my phone after our text exchange when I jolt from the sound of knocking at my window. *Who the fuck...*

"Ah!" I gasp when I lock eyes with Corey's mom, who is waving from the other side of the car window. Her car is parked right behind me in front of the Ramirez's mailbox. I didn't think anyone was going to come home in the few short minutes I needed to block Corey's driveway, but karma is my boyfriend. Well, actually, it's my boyfriend's mom coming home.

I roll down the window and sheepishly smile at her eyeing me suspiciously.

"Hiiii, Mrs. Ramirez," I greet her.

"Leanne Fairbanks." She grins, lifting a brow after. "What are you doing here?"

"Um..." There is no use in lying. What would I even say anyway? I'm visiting another person that lives around here and just so happened to block the Ramirez's driveway?

Before I try and explain myself, Corey walks out the door but stops short at the walkway leading up to the house.

"Mom!" he yells. "You're home? I thought you had work..."

"I finished my meeting, so I'm working from home for the rest of the day. Where are you going?"

"Um...we were going to go take the ferry into SF," Corey says. He still hasn't moved from where he stood, frozen and surprised.

"You and Leanne?" his mom asks.

After a beat, Corey nods.

"Yeah. Leanne and I are dating."

I sharply turn to look at him. I guess there was no other way to say it. Friends can go into the city with one another, but I imagine Corey's mom would poke with questions when Corey gets home later after the game.

"Oh!" She immediately lights up. She's beaming at me with pearly white teeth and turns to look back at Corey, who's now walking to the passenger side of the car. "I didn't know. How exciting! Why didn't you tell us you were dating Leanne, Corey? We love the Fairbanks family."

"It's all still a little new," Corey explains. "We've only been together for...well I guess this is the second day. Two days."

"Wow! Well, I'm very happy for you two. I will ask more questions when you're not trying to get somewhere. Leanne, you're more than welcome to come over whenever you want for dinner. You're family now too. I mean, you two have kind of been close for a long time."

"Yeah, yeah, I know." Corey dramatically rolls his eyes. "We gotta go now, or else we're going to miss the ferry."

"Okay!" Corey's mom walks back over to her car. "Have fun. We'll see you at the game tonight! Both of you, I guess."

"See you later." Corey waves and gets into my car. "Sorry about that."

"It's okay." I start the ignition and make a three point turn out of Corey's parent's house. They're his parents, of course they should know.

I wouldn't want to keep something like that from someone so important, but I don't know how I'm going to tell my parents yet.

A "ding" sound comes from Corey's phone and he reaches up to read what text message he's received. He scans through it before laughing and setting his phone down.

"My mom's already texted me to remind me again that she's very happy that I'm dating someone that she's so supportive of. She added after that she would be happy as long as I'm happy, but you're like, the perfect person I could've chosen."

I smile down at my steering wheel. I mean, I have to agree. There's something so perfect about two people who have known each other for more than half their lives, coming back to one another and discovering they're attracted to one another, and later falling in love. Some people might find their brother's best friend repulsive, but I didn't.

"Funny how some things just work out like that," I say. I set my elbow onto the car's center console and he reaches over with his hand to wiggle his fingers with mine and we interlace our fingers with one another.

"Yeah," he agrees. "Fate works in mysterious ways, doesn't it?"

"Yep." I think back at this morning, and how I couldn't believe that we got found out. By Corey's mom of all people. I'm still trying to organize a plan to tell my family. It's not my parents I'm worried about; they will likely react the same way as Corey's mom would. All jovial and happy that if I could be with anyone, it'd be the equivalent of their fourth child. Lance is a plan in it of itself. I still don't know what his reaction will be. Will he think that this is a match made in heaven? Or will he just think it's easier to project his jealousy for another important person in Corey's life because he'll be doing it to his own sibling?

"Are you okay that you had to tell your mom about us?"

Corey turns to me. "I mean, it's okay. I would rather have it be brought up naturally, but I don't think they were ever against me dating you, if they've thought about it."

"Ah okay," I reply. "You don't really talk about them that much. Do you guys have a good relationship?"

Corey sighs and keeps his eyes looking straight forward on the road ahead of us.

"My relationship with my parents is fine. But that's kind of all it is. I love my parents, and I recognize they do a lot for me. My dad didn't go to college; he immigrated here from Mexico days before he needed to start high school. When I was a kid, I wished my parents could be more involved with baseball. I was jealous of the dynamic Lance and your dad had, and I looked up to your dad. He was a really good coach growing up.

"I know that I shouldn't be complaining that my parents weren't really involved because my dad had to work his butt off to get both of us through school, but it was tough when I had to find a way to get myself home after practice because of their busy schedules. And even then, we weren't loaded. Not to take a jab at your family by any means, but my family couldn't afford to just drop thousands of dollars to buy new equipment or funnel any hobbies or go on road trips across the country."

I swallow. My upbringing is a topic that I keep to the back of my head. It's a "I know that I grew up not needing to worry about financial stability," but I also never want to come off as arrogant about where I came from and who got me where I needed to be.

"I'm sorry," I say, my voice small. "I know that our upbringings were very different. I don't want you to think I'm some spoiled kid ever. I appreciate everything that my parents have provided for me, but besides not having to pay for rent, I'm fairly independent. I'm going to try and not talk about my wealth like it makes me a better person or that I've had a better life."

"Leanne," he says, tracing the outline over my knuckles with his thumb. "I don't think you're spoiled. Not at all, baby. You're one of the hardest working people I've met, and I love that about you. To put it truthfully, we were just raised in different income brackets. That doesn't make me think badly about you."

"Okay," I sigh, leaning my face against the window. "If you say so."

We reach the ferry terminal with approximately two minutes to speed walk to get on the boat that will take us to San Francisco.

"Shit," I pant once I take my seat near the window. "We barely made it."

"Yeah, I wasn't thinking we were going to run into my mom in our process of leaving."

The ferry takes off and we're gliding atop the calm water in the bay. In short time, we peer up and can see that we're just about to cruise right below the Bay Bridge.

"Come on." Corey stands up and extends his hand. "Let's go outside so we can watch the boat cruise under the bridge."

I stand up and follow him. When we step outside, there's a slight breeze from how fast the boat is going that my hair is flying in different directions around my face.

I laugh. "I didn't think I was going to be outside so I didn't bring a hair tie."

Corey turns to face me and he takes both of his hands and tucks the small wisps of hair that were covering my face and tucks them behind my hair. He grips onto the ends of my hair right below my ears and steps closer to me.

"Just call me the hair tucker," he smiles.

I laugh. "I'm glad that you're good for something."

He parts his lips and his eyes flit down to my lips. I curiously look back at them, even though I know what they taste like. I know what he wants and it's the same thing that I do. So I tip my toes slightly to plant my lips on his. Corey lets go of my hair and moves his hands to set them on each of my cheeks. He strokes the apples slightly with his thumb and I splay my hands across his broad back. The wind sends my hair flying in all different directions again, but I don't pay the loose strands any mind. I lean into Corey and he envelopes me in a strong hold.

I smile as Corey keeps peppering light kisses on the corners of my lips, thinking how much I love this. Us, on the water. Together. So in love. Living in the moment.

"What's got you all smiley?" he teases.

"You." I wink.

"I am pretty amazing, huh?"

I slap my hand against his chest. "Yes. You don't need to get a big head about it though."

"No." He touches his nose against mine. "Your compliments are the only thing that's keeping me alive. I need them like I need oxygen."

I playfully roll my eyes. "Well then. I love you, Corey Ramirez. You're the most amazing person to grace this planet and the best thing that's ever happened to me."

"Now that's going to last me for years." He grins, kissing me again. "I love you too, Leanne Fairbanks. I think that is enough to keep me standing."

"Good." I rest my head against his chest as the boat slows down and we're pulling into our dock. I can't think about what a life would be like if I wasn't loving Corey. It'd be a life I'd rather push to the bottom of my head so I didn't have to think about it.

We hitch a ride on MUNI to the dock housing the boat that will take us to Alcatraz Island. There's a good amount of people who've also decided to tour the iconic prison site. Some people who very much give the vibe that they are a tourist. They're wearing cameras around their necks, complete with comfortable walking shoes and bucket hats with the Golden Gate embroidered on it. Even though Karl is in full force right now.

Corey and I take a sit down on one of the benches on the boat and I rest my head against his shoulder.

He kisses the top of my head. "Tired?"

"Maybe a little bit. I couldn't get much sleep last night."

"Gee." He chuckles. "Why not? Someone keeping you awake?" He turns and touches his lips against my ear. "I have no problem doing it again, just so you know. Next time, I'm going to make sure that I'm there to make you come."

"Corey!" I whisper-yell. But I'll be honest, I really enjoyed touching myself and making sure he heard it.

"Just saying," he replies. "I'll listen to you come any time of the day."

We sit watching the waves hit against the boat until everyone has embarked on the boat. Two more people board and they walk right past us. I hear a familiar voice shout, "Oh hey, Corey!" before he sits down with a person I don't recognize in front of us.

When I lock eyes with the mystery man, I immediately sit up straight and scoot away from Corey to put some distance between us.

"Leon?"

Chapter 25
Corey

"Leanne?"

Leon's still staring straight right at Leanne and me while the man that's accompanying Leon looks confusingly at the two Fairbanks siblings whose faces are stuck in awe.

"What are you doing here?" Leanne asks.

"I'm going to tour Alcatraz," Leon says, dumbstruck.

"Okay, duh. But...why? And who's this with you?"

Leon rolls his eyes. "I had a free day and Nico hasn't been here before."

"Uh huh." She nods. "And who's Nico?"

Leon tilts his head back in exasperation. "Nico is a friend from Stanford. He's from New Jersey. He wanted to check out Alcatraz before he moves back to the East Coast next week."

"So you two aren't dating?" Leanne gets right to the point. I didn't even know Leon was queer. He's pretty private about any sort of dating life. He's very much the kind of person who if you could be married to your career or schooling, he would. I mean, he's going to be taking over the family business. I don't want to know the hell it took for him to do well enough in school and his testing to get into somewhere prestigious like Berkeley Law. He's on a track that dating would put him in a place that could be very distracting and potentially deter him from doing as well as he has.

"Psh, no." Leon rolls his eyes. That makes something in Nico frown slightly with the way Leon's reacted like that. He flits his eyes between the two of us. "What about you two? Don't think I didn't walk on this boat and saw you two resting your heads on each other."

Leanne sighs. "Is this just the universe's way of telling us that we can't keep this a secret anymore?"

Leon raises a brow at us.

"Um...I think you two should talk to each other," I butt in. "Here, Nico." I beckon him to take a seat next to me and have the Fairbanks have a good talking about their love lives, because it seems like they both have something to say. "Switch seats with Leanne."

"Babe," Leanne begins. "I can talk about this with Leon later. This is our date, even though we've run into people we know." She narrows her eyes at Leon.

"No." I put my hand over hers. "You should talk about this with Leon now."

Leanne groans. "Fine." She grips onto the bench Leon and Nico were sitting on and walks over me to sit next to Leon. Nico lets her pass and he takes the seat next to me.

"Here." I stand up, guiding him to the aisle. "I think they might need some privacy. We can have our own good chat. What did you study at Stanford?"

"Drama," he says.

"Oh." I take a seat on a bench that's a few rows up from where we were originally sitting. That was...not what I was expecting. "That's cool. What are you hoping to do with that after graduating?"

"Actually, I'm going to NYU for law school. I'm hoping to go into entertainment law."

"Nice." I nod. "So still trying to keep the love of drama but also learn the law."

"Yeah," he says. "I love drama and performing and I think my dreams of being on Broadway aren't going to leave me any time soon, but it's a tough industry. I'm competing with the best from around the world. I'm going to be in an entry level job hoping one day I'll get the call."

"Yeah, man, I feel you. I'm a baseball player who's spent four years waiting to be called up to play for the major leagues. It's only now that I've been seriously considered."

"Oh, you're Lance's friend that's the baseball player. Yeah, Leon mentioned you just moved back to Neptune Beach to play for the new minor league team. So you got called up?"

"Not yet," I whisper to keep our voices down so Leon doesn't pick up what we're talking about. I take a quick peek behind me. Leanne and Leon are engaged in seemingly serious conversation, their expressions not lightening up much.

"I had a visit to San Diego this past week and they liked me. A lot. But I'm waiting to see if they'll reach out to my agent and make a move. I don't want to tell my friends and family until it's been made official. But Leanne knows, she came with me."

"Gotcha. And if they do, you'll move down to San Diego?"

"That's the plan."

Nico narrows his eyes at me and slowly nods like he just solved a calculus level problem. Long distance or uprooting our lives all over again doesn't seem complicated to explain, but I guess there are a lot of plans that need to be made.

"I see," he says wearily.

"Why do you sound so suspicious?"

He sighs and takes a quick look out onto the open water as we quickly approach the island. "Moving away from someone you care about makes trying to keep up communication with them so much harder."

I give him a sympathetic look. Ah, so this is the actual way that Nico feels about Leon. Something is telling me that this is not just a friendship between these two.

"Yeah, I'm aware." I'm still concocting some grand plan to convince Leanne to move to San Diego with me and we'll find a way to keep *The Dragon's Belly* in business in another location. It might have to involve getting another food truck and registering it to operate in San Diego, or convert a restaurant, but we discussed it when we were down there: trying to start and operate your own restaurant is very hard. Finding people to work, people to eat your food, hype it up, talk about it. I didn't even realize how many steps it's going to take to get Leanne's life back up to where it's at now.

"And you're hoping you'll make it work?"

"I will make it work," I say curtly.

"Hey," his face softens, "I'm sorry. I don't mean to sound like such a skeptic. It's just...promise me you won't tell anyone this? I don't want Leon finding out."

"Yeah, don't worry, your secret is safe with me. Keep mine and I'll keep yours."

He takes a deep breath. "Leon and I...we've been friends for the past two years. We met through the pre-law society and he's one of my favorite people to hang out with. When I found out I got accepted to NYU, I was ecstatic. It was my first choice, and it worked out perfectly because I'm already from the East Coast. I grew up going to shows in the city. I got accepted to Stanford and decided to do undergrad out here just because...it's Stanford. It's the best school in the country, and I could explore California. That and also, all the arts programs in New York rejected me. In a perfect world, Leon would attend a school on the East Coast too. But, he loves his family too much to leave California. Hell, leave the Bay Area to add.

"I didn't think leaving someone I care about would be so hard. And I didn't think I'd be falling for my best friend, but here we are."

I gently pat my hand atop Nico's thigh. I feel for him. Hell, I honestly wish I never had to feel what he's going through. Realizing you're falling for your best friend of two years in the midst of also moving? And it's not as bad as Leanne and I. We might be moving to be at least eight hours apart, tops. We can drive to see one another. Nico's moving to New York City, which is in another time zone. That's hard to try and align schedules to talk to one another.

"Damn, man. I'm sorry. Have you told Leon this?"

He shakes his head. "I mean, I don't want to ruin our friendship. If I confess how I really feel to him, my biggest fear isn't that he doesn't feel the same way back. It's that he does, and our time would be up."

"Yeah, that'd be hard." That's why I just needed to tell Leanne how I really felt, even though I'm still worried about what's to come too.

"Mhhm. So that's why I'm a little cynical. It's not because I don't believe you can do it. I want it to work for you two. I'm just sad I'm not able to figure it out for myself."

I frown. I want to be reassuring and tell Nico that I myself don't have it all figured out either, but maybe that will make him more distressed. Thinking to himself he's a failure for not being able to figure it out too. I don't know how to combat that other than saying, "You're still young, you still have a lot to look forward to!" But, I'm only six years older and people like to tell me that I still have a lot of future to look forward to, even if I'm getting one year older from being a prime baseball player.

"I don't want to tell you that if you were going to figure out a way to make things work, then you would, because this whole long distance, trying to find a way to make both parties happy is actually really stressful, and I don't have all the answers, but I hope that no matter what happens, things will be okay between you two." I want to believe that things will work out between them, and in a perfect scenario, Leon and Nico will realize each other's feelings and maybe something will bloom from it, but it might be a little bit of time until those feelings will fester.

"Thanks." Nico gives me a soft smile. "It will be. We only have to be in law school for three years. Maybe our paths will cross after that. And we'll get our own love story. I hope things work out with you and Leanne. You two look cute together."

"Thanks. We are pretty adorable, aren't we?"

The tour guide announces that we are approaching the dock and will embark on the tour of the island. I look back to see Leon and Leanne, both still engaged in a deep conversation. Leon's eyes are a little red, and Leanne's face mimics the shade of a beet. Man, these two are so emotional. I shoot a text over to Leanne.

The three ellipses pop up and I turn my head again to see Leanne meet my eyes for a moment, mouth a "sorry" my way and go back to stare down at her phone.

LEANNE

Sorryyyy Leon and I are…we need to talk through a few things. I'm gonna stick with him for a bit of the tour. Can I text you when we can meet up after?

COREY

Yes, of course. Lemme guess…he's got some feelings?

Nico shared some secrets with me.

LEANNE

Some is an understatement.

Thanks, love you. I'll make sure to get some time to look at old jail cells with you, promise.

COREY

Take your time. Happy that you're having some bonding time with your brother. Love you too.

Chapter 26
Leanne

There's that special feeling when you think you know a person: what they like, what ticks them off, who's on their mind. You can read them like you can read billboard sign. And when you can sense something's bothering them, you know what you're looking for and you're there to help at the drop of a hat.

I thought I knew a lot about my brother. Both of them, but Leon was the one I grew up tending after more than I did Lance. Lance had to take care of both of us, but I always made sure Leon got extra attention. He is the baby, after all.

When Leon left to go to college, I was sad, but he went to Stanford, which is only a forty-five-minute to an hour drive on a day without traffic. But I felt like we lost a little bit of a connection. We'd laugh that we went to rival colleges and when The Big Game rolled around, we each got to brag when our teams brought home the axe. I got to brag more than he did, but he didn't care all that much. The kid knows little about sports, but a lot about fantasy books and music.

Leon came out to me when he was nineteen. He told me first out of our family, then my parents and then Lance. No one was going to be unsupportive of it; we all wanted each other to be happy whoever we wanted to date. Leon coming out as pansexual was just something we learned that we were going to support. He only told us that he was a little worried with confessing about his sexuality because none of our family are queer. We're blessed that we are in a place where being queer is accepted openly, but it did take a little explaining when we eventually told my grandparents, who were accepting of the loving part, but did ask a few clarifying questions with regards to the pan part in pansexual. Namely, why Leon was attracted to someone who wasn't tied to a specific gender and what being nonbinary meant.

Other than his sexual orientation, I didn't know a lot about Leon's love life. While he came home almost every weekend because he missed my mom's cooking and had to shy away from ordering ramen everyday because it wasn't good for anyone's wallet, he was quiet about anything that related to dating and relationships. It was always, "I don't really have time to be in a relationship" and not "there's this one person."

So, I guess I didn't really know all that much about my brother, because he came on a walking tour of Alcatraz with someone that he claims is his friend, but is being really defensive about my requests to elaborate further.

"What's with you and Corey?" Leon asks immediately as we sit next to one another. Corey and Leon's "friend" Nico grabbed a seat a few rows up to give us space. Leon is not happy to see me, and even more upset that he had to catch me with Corey's arm around me and my head resting on his shoulder.

"What's up with you and Nico?" I retort.

"We're. Just. Friends," Leon repeats. "What makes that so hard for you to understand?"

"You two are awfully close for just friends," I say. If I can say that I know one thing, it's that Leon looks at someone a certain way when he's interested in them. He'll step a little closer, brush his arm against the other's, laugh at every word they say.

"I can be friendly with friends. Isn't that the point?"

"Don't spin this in a way where it sounds like I don't know what you're like when you're around someone you like. I'm your sister, Leon. I want to believe that you can tell me everything. I really wish we can be at a point where we can, and it's really heartbreaking that it feels like we aren't."

He scoffs. "Do you know how much you're gaslighting me right now?" He starts laughing to himself. "You were full on body against Corey Ramirez! Our brother's childhood best friend? Someone that slept over at our house every month? I know you had a little crush on him in high school, Leanne, but I didn't think you were going to wait around for him to come back for you to make your move."

I sigh. "It's not like that."

"Really?" He raises a brow. "Because you told me that you weren't going to date again after your broke up with Greg."

"Well, I'm not going to be celibate," I say. "I just said that when we broke up because I already had my heart broken, and I didn't want to subject myself to something where it could happen again."

"So you just think Corey is going to not break your heart, Leanne?"

No. Actually, I think my heart might break even more when he has to leave for San Diego. That, or it's going to break when I decide to move hundreds of miles away from my family and my business and have to start all over. Both ways will probably wreck me to pieces.

"No." I blow out air trapped in my lungs. "I don't know."

I start quivering. I can't confess what Corey and I are going through. It's not my place or secret to tell.

"Leanne," Leon begins. He reaches his arm around my shoulder and pulls me into him. "What's wrong?"

I wipe the tears dripping from my eyes. "There's a lot...but I can't tell anyone. Corey and I are fine, but we just have a lot of decisions that we'll have to make really soon, and I don't know what I am going to do."

I start crying into Leon's chest and he rubs the top of my arm slowly up and down.

"It's okay Lele. You're strong, you're going to get through whatever you're going through, I know you will."

"Thanks," I sniff. "I didn't think I'd fall in love again, and I'm really scared that I'm going to fuck this up."

"Yeah," Leon says absent-mindedly. He cranes his neck over to where Leon and Nico are engaged in their own conversation. I'm surprised, these guys have only known each other for minutes and they're talking like they're best friends.

"Okay, I confessed my secret, now you have to tell me what's on your mind."

He slumps. "Do I have to?"

"Yes! I poured something really important to me to you, you need to return the favor."

"Fine." He takes a deep breath. "I think I'm in love with Nico."

I wait for him to drop a more surprising bombshell.

"Uh huh." I nod. "And...?"

"That's all."

I blink at him. "Okay. Tell me something I don't know."

"You didn't know that until I told you just now!"

"Yeah." I roll my eyes. "But I told you it was obvious from the way you were looking at him before you noticed that I was looking at you."

"And now your suspicions are confirmed."

"Follow up question then." Because this is what I know is really bothering Leon. "Why aren't you dating him then if you're in love with him?"

"Because," he sighs, "he's moving across the country in a week and I'm not following him."

"So you're just going to let the love of your life leave without telling him how you really feel? Take it from me, Leon, you're going to regret not telling him."

His brows furrow and his whispers almost turn into shouts. "What am I supposed to do, Leanne? I can't convince him to stay. He got into NYU Law and I'm going to Berkeley. We've both got our dreams and where we want to be to make them happen. If they're not going to be on the same coast, then so be it. I'm not going to force anyone to drop everything just because our hearts are pulling us another direction."

"Okay." I nod. More than anything else, I want Leon to be happy, and as someone who has found love again after not believing that she would, I want him to take that chance to confess that too. But I also respect his decision to hold back, especially because with Nico moving across the country, who knows how often they can keep a conversation up. Time zones can really mess up making time to communicate with one another.

"I'm not going to pry," I tell him. "I just want you to be happy. I trust you'll figure out a way to get there."

"Thanks." He tilts his head to rest it on my shoulder. "I'm just going to try and be a good friend to him and then see where things go. If he wants to be as much of a friend to me as I to him, then we'll keep in touch even if we're far away from each other. And then, in three years from now, when we're done with law school, then maybe we'll find a way back to one another again."

The boat pulls in the dock and the captain tells us to get ready to disembark: gather our belongings, be careful getting off, the tour on the island will begin momentarily.

"Leanne?" Leon begins.

"Yeah?"

"So you and Corey..."

I scoff. "What about me and Corey?"

"How'd that happen? Also, when were you going to plan on telling me? Do Mom and Dad know? Does Lance know?"

"God, enough with the interrogations!" I chuckle. "Let's continue talking on the tour. I have a lot to update you with."

I shoot Corey a quick apology text. A part of me is upset I'm not spending time with him on a date we planned knowing fully that our time is ticking like a bomb. But, even though my brother isn't moving out of the house, we're not going to be seeing a lot of each other once he starts law school. He's the only one of us to be entering into a form of higher education and a rigorous program to add. He's going to be spending a lot of time reading and studying, and it's not going to be any reading material he's going to be excited over, so I'm not going to spend time with him having these intimate conversations.

I don't even put at the forefront of my mind that it might be that I might be moving away and visits will soon only be during major holidays and possibly during offseason.

There's a lot that I need to think about, and time is running out.

Chapter 27
Corey

On the same day as our date to Alcatraz, which later turned into a friend-date with Nico while Leon and Leanne spent the entire tour talking amongst themselves about life and the future, I got the call from my agent that San Diego would like to call me up to play with them.

We were at a restaurant in Chinatown, slurping on noodles while Leanne apologized after almost every bite because she thinks that our date is ruined because she spent more time confessing to Leon about her feelings for me and the future for us. And then when I got the call, it really brought the mood down.

I try to console a sad Leanne by holding up a noodle toward her and asking if we can Lady and the Tramp it but she only smiled tight-lipped and went back to staring bleakly at her plate.

"Hey." I reach across to grab onto her hand. "It's going to be okay. We'll figure this out."

"I know." She tries to grin through the visible heartbreak I can see through her droopy eyelids, like she was suddenly hit by an exhaustion spell.

"I'm just upset that we didn't get more time to ourselves at Alcatraz. Which is partially my fault, I did tell Leon that we could talk about you and I and how this all came to be." She covers her head with her hands.

"But I did it because I was thinking that we were going to have more time. Like, they would take a week to negotiate a contract instead of less than twenty four hours."

"Baseball teams will work quick when it comes to what they want," I tell her. Secretly, I wished they took their time too. We're wrapping up the season this week and we've clinched playoffs. I'm really proud of the team for achieving such a huge feat in our inception season, and I want to keep playing so I can lead my teammates to a victory. Hopefully.

"So, what happens now?" Leanne asks.

"I have to go down to San Diego to sign, and they will probably announce my acquisition on social media. Do some press things, and then I'll likely have to move fairly quickly."

"What's fairly quickly look like?"

I shrug. "Likely they want me to start attending practices as soon as possible. I could be playing in a game as early as the following week."

"Shit," Leanne whispers. "That's not really a lot of time at all."

It isn't. I want to dive into everything headfirst, because once I stepped foot on the field in San Diego, I felt that tingling feeling like I belonged on that field. I'm ready to start practicing, because I want to get acclimated with the team. I'm the new kid again, and I'm the new kid playing on a major league baseball team for the first time. While these players have all been in my shoes before, they've also ascended to a position where some may consider themselves amongst the greats. Three-time All Stars, homerun fiends, athletes I looked up to when I was in high school.

"No, it's not."

I'm not going to rush Leanne into making any decisions yet. It's not a lot of time. And when I go down, I'm going to see what I can do to not delay the process per se, but to see what can be done so I can have one last hurrah in Neptune Beach. Play my last game, celebrate with my family and friends, confess to the rest of our close circle that Leanne and I are together.

"I'm really excited for you, Corey." She gives a sad smile. "You've finally got what you wanted after waiting for so long."

"Thank you, babe." I smile back before taking another spoonful of sizzling rice soup into my mouth.

We finish our food so we can get back to Neptune Beach in preparation for our game. Leanne has to go back and prepare the food truck for the game, and I still need to show up for our last week of regular season games, and tell Coach I'm on my way out.

Leanne drops me off at home so I can gather my equipment. When I see my mom's car parked in the driveway, its a reminder we had bumped into my mom after she came home earlier this morning before we left for San Francisco. And, because she rarely leaves the house, I'm going to have to explain the confession I told her this morning, and break the news about the offer.

I open the door and yell to my mom that I'm home.

"In the kitchen, Corey!"

I walk over and take out my phone and wallet, setting it on the kitchen island. My mom is preparing tea and on the television behind us is some variety show with a host I don't recognize. Although, I'm not keeping up with who's been given a show at this point. It feels like they just give it to anyone. Hopefully this one she's watching isn't about finding out who the father is...or isn't.

"Hi," I greet her.

"Hi?" She holds her hands on either side of her hips. "That is all you have to say to me?"

I blow out a breath. I'm tempted to retaliate and tell her that I don't have a lot of time to talk, which is also true: I need to be at the park within the hour. Maybe going a little earlier to make sure that I can get some quality coach time, because I'm about to drop a bomb shell.

"I mean, it was part of it."

She sighs and pinches the bridge of his nose. "Oh, mijo…" My mom isn't Mexican, but with being with my dad for so long, and having the absolute pleasure of being forced to spend holidays with my dad's side of the family that live in Oakland, she's picked up on random Spanish phrases here and there. The way she says "mijo" in that disappointing, yet sympathetic tone, it almost makes you think she's been speaking Spanish her entire life.

"Yes, yes I know. I have a lot to tell you."

"Yes you do, sir. When were you going to tell me you were seeing Leanne Fairbanks?"

The sad reality is…I don't know. Maybe after a month, when I know we've had some time on us to get all of our families excited about our newfound union? But what would my parents say when I'd tell them I might have to reconsider because I was also thinking about the move? Would they be disappointed in me that I wouldn't want to try and make it work? Would they be so sad that I'm moving away mere months after I moved here to not even notice?

I guess now I get to find out.

"I don't know." I shrug. "It's all so new. Like less than a week new. I wanted to make sure we were in a rhythm before telling our family and friends."

"What do you mean?" she asks. "Are you having doubts about dating her?"

"No, no!" I shake my hands back and forth in front of me. "It's not that. It's…"

I take a deep breath. I know I'm going to rock my parent's world with this news. They may be excited that I'm finally getting to live out something I've dreamt of as a child, but they'll be sad. When I moved back to Neptune Beach, my parents were the most ecstatic about the news. They hinted that this meant finally, I'm going to be home and we can have this time to spend catching up. That, and I think they're not adapting really well to being empty nesters and even though they don't have to worry about expenses with us anymore, it is stressful to have to travel to places outside of Neptune Beach. I mean, my brother lives on a freaking island. At least it's a direct flight there, but those flights aren't cheap with all the tourists that travel there year round.

"Last week, someone came up to me while I was playing in Ventura. A baseball scout for San Diego. He asked me to come down and visit the park and told me he had been watching my plays throughout the season. Today, I got the call."

I watch my mom blink back at me, silent. Blinking. Blinking some more. Tears streaking down her face. A deep breath. A ragged exhale. Sobbing. Hands up to cover her face.

"Mom." I rush over and wrap my arms around her. I didn't think this might have evoked such a large reaction. "What's wrong?"

"Sorry." She takes a deep breath. "These are happy tears. I promise."

"Really?" I murmur. "I can't tell."

"Menopause, Corey. You should be happy you don't have it."

Ah, of course. Good ol' menopause. Like she said, I wouldn't know how that feels.

"Sorry," I say. Does that mean that any news I spill to her is going to end up with her sobbing uncontrollably?

"It's okay. That's amazing. So, when do you start playing? Your dad and I haven't been to San Diego in so long. Do you remember? We took you two to Legoland and the zoo and your dad wanted to take an extended trip to Tijuana because it was so close by but I was very nervous to say yes. Kids in Tijuana?"

"I think we would have been okay. Dad speaks Spanish."

"Well, maybe now since you'll be heading back down there."

"We'll see." I chuckle. "I don't know exactly when I start yet. They sound like they want me to start as quickly as possible, but I have to finish up my game here, figure out moving logistics, and...yeah. I'm excited to start, but I'm sad that I have to leave. I'm trying to figure out how I'm going to tell the team."

"They'll miss you." My mom nods solemnly. "You've brought that team a lot of success since you started playing."

"It's a team effort," I counter. But in my humble opinion, yeah. I did.

"Don't downplay your successes, Corey," she scolds. "Sure, you can't win a baseball game by yourself, and we're not biased...that much, but you're good. We're always so proud watching you at the games. We wanted to watch you more once you graduated college, but you were always so far away. I'm sad that we won't be able to drive down the street to watch you at Neptune Beach anymore."

"I know. As much as I didn't want to move back here to play in Neptune Beach...I'm kind of sad I won't be playing here anymore either."

She raises an eyebrow. "Was it that bad? When you were forced to play here? I know you wanted to work your way back to being on an MLB team, but I didn't think you hated it that much."

"It was just hard at first because I felt like I wasn't moving forward. I was back home for a team that was brand new. What if we weren't all a good fit? And then I wondered if anyone would notice me because I wasn't playing in one of the big minor league teams anymore. And being back home..." I held my tongue. I didn't want to confess what feelings I had against my parents growing up.

"Being back home what?" my mom pries.

"It kind of brought back some not so fun memories from when I grew up. When I thought that I was alone, or I'd be sad when you or dad couldn't come to my games. I know now it was because dad had to work a lot to ensure I could even play baseball, but I was so young to understand then, and I didn't want to tell you guys because I didn't know how to bring it up."

"Corey." My mom closes her hand over mine. "I'm sorry. I know we were busy at work, but you should have told us that it bothered you. Maybe we could've made some arrangements to come to a few games. We were worried you two wouldn't have as good of a childhood if we didn't give you the best things and enrolled you in camps and sports."

I see the sadness come over my mom, with the way she frowns, looking away and at the floor. She's getting lost in thought, and I wish that my departure wasn't the reason we're talking about something that's affected me for most of my life.

"You gave me a good childhood," I reassure her. "You and Dad loved us. That's all I could want."

"We still love you, Corey." Her eyes are wet. "We always will."

I wrap my arms around her and pull her tightly into me. "I love you too." I try and hold in the emotions I'm feeling too, but let go when I realize, they're not all bad. I'm sad that it doesn't feel like I got enough time to spend closely with my parents, but happy I got to start.

As we're holding onto one another, I hear the sound of the garage door closing and the door leading into the garage shutting.

My dad walks in and sets his backpack down onto the armchair in the living room area. "Woah," he chimes in. "What did I miss?"

We're both startled and pull apart and my mom wipes her face. My dad steps closer, and stands next to us.

"Why are you two crying?"

Before I can answer him, my mom speaks up. "We'll tell you on the way to the game." She laughs. "We need to get Corey to the field."

Chapter 28
Corey

I sprint to the field that's already full of players who are busy warming up with throws. I know I'm late; I should have showed up at our scheduled time to practice before our game begins to stretch and run drills, but with the bombshell news that's been dropped into my lap via a phone call from my agent, Coach can give me a pass. I mean, he might have to if he wants me to round out my premature departure.

Coach eyes me hastily drop my bag in the dugout and rip the zipper open and pull out my glove.

"You're late," is all he tells me once I inch closer to him.

"I know," I say once I catch my breath. "I'm sorry."

He blinks rapidly. "Is that all you have to tell me?"

"No, actually." I take a deep breath. "Do you have a second?"

He gestures back to the dugout and leans up against the fence. He still looks annoyed that I showed up an hour before the game begins.

"Um..." I swallow. I make circles with my cleats on the dirt to distract me from stumbling on my words. "I got called up."

His eyebrows raise. "You did?"

"Yeah." I nod.

"Good for you, Ramirez." He shoots me a sad smile. "Where to?"

"San Diego."

"Nice." Coach nods. He's smiling, but I can see bits of sadness come through from his tired eyes. "We'll miss you here at Neptune Beach."

"Well, it is my hometown after all. I can't say goodbye forever. My parents will still be here and I'm still going to be visiting them whenever I can."

"Parents, and someone else special..." he begins. He shoots me a wink and I don't know if I should be stammering to deny it or tell him he's spot on.

"How'd...you know?"

He starts to laugh to himself. "I like to think I'm a good observer. And the way you jumped to help Leanne out when she had that heat exhaustion scare."

"Oh yeah." No one's going to forget that, will they?

"For good reason. You gotta do what you need to with the people you care about."

If that were the case, maybe I wouldn't be moving to San Diego after all. If I care about Leanne, and maybe even to an extent, my parents, I would stay here and make an effort to make this my home as much as they wished I did.

"Yeah." I nod, continuing drawing circles on the dirt.

"You good, Ramirez?"

"Yeah." I aimlessly nod again. As good as I can be with everything on my mind, which is full of a lot of emotions right now. None of which I can pinpoint as "good."

"You seem like your head's in the clouds." He chuckles.

I shake my head out of the funk. "I... Yeah, you could say that."

"What's bothering you? Having second thoughts?"

"No, I don't think so." I want to go to San Diego. It's been my dream to play for the Majors. And yet, do dreams change? Can I want more than one thing?

"I just want things to work out all around. I would hate to disappoint people, and I feel like I am in some way."

Coach looks back at me, like the dumbest thing just came out of my mouth.

"Kid," he tells me. "That's a weird thing to call you. You're kind of old to be my kid."

I roll my eyes. "I'm past thirty, I'm not that old."

"To be my kid," he clarifies. "My kids just learned about addition and subtraction. You... I'm not looking forward to when my kids get to deal with what you're going through. Relationship issues, and all that."

"What was the point you were trying to make?"

"Oh yes. I can guarantee you, you are not disappointing anyone. Your parents, Leanne, your friends. I can guarantee they are all proud of you. You're chasing after your dreams. And if they don't want you to do that, maybe that's them being a little selfish."

I sigh. "I just want to be able to make everything work somehow." Maybe I can also see if my parents would want to move down to San Diego? I mean, sure, they also love Neptune Beach and I wouldn't go so far as to sell the house, but maybe they can split their time between here and down there.

"You will," Coach reassures me. "I have a good feeling. So, how long do we have you until?"

I shrug. "Likely only today. I have to fly down to San Diego tomorrow to sign the contract. And then I'll jump right into practicing with the team. They needed to call up an outfielder, so I might be playing as early as next week."

He pouts, but slowly nods when he connects everything together. That this is it. This is my last game. That I'm not going to be here when playoffs roll around. I'm not going to be the player helping bring my team their first ever victory, as much as I want to be.

"Damn. Well, guess we should make it the best damn last game you'll play in Neptune Beach." He grabs ahold of my shoulder and smiles back at me. "Let's get you warmed up."

Coach tells me I need to wait until the end of the game to let the team know of my departure. It's better that way, so we don't throw off the mojo of anyone playing. I didn't think that my leaving would throw anyone off their game, but when I announce my departure, I'm proven wrong.

We win, to everyone's delight, and Coach gathers everyone up to huddle in the outfield so I can make my announcement. He begins by telling everyone his notes on the game. Thankfully, since we win, then he has more positive notes instead of critical ones. Maybe I shouldn't be thankful though, because that's going to make the news much more sour than if everyone is already in a mood.

"Before we leave," Coach begins. "I have an announcement to make. Well, actually I won't be making the announcement." He gestures to me. "Ramirez?"

Everyone turns their gaze to me, and suddenly, I feel as if I'm on a stage and there's one of those bright spotlights beaming down on me. Is this the moment where I can picture everyone in their underwear?

"Um." I stand up and join next to Coach. Here goes nothing. "I wanted to let everyone know that after today, I will no longer be playing for the Neptune Beach Seals."

All of a sudden, players are up in arms and they begin shouting over one another asking me why I'm leaving them, did I get fired, which...these players have played baseball in other capacities right? I guess you can get fired, but no one ever uses that terminology when you're playing on a sports team.

I try and interject my way to regain control of the conversation. "Don't worry, it's not because I got fired or released, however you want to call it. I've been called up to the major leagues."

"Wait, really?" Kyle chimes in.

"Yeah." I smile and nod. "I'm going to San Diego."

"Dude," another player begins, "that's awesome."

"I can't believe I played with someone who's going to be playing for a major league team!" someone else says.

Once everyone puts the pieces together and realize I'm leaving to play for a major league team, they all congratulate me. We share a group hug with one another and Coach officially dismisses us, to which some players give me a few parting wishes and pats on the back before they take off.

I start walking back to the dugout to begin cleaning up myself, when Kyle rushes to join me, out of breath from running.

"Why are you running?" I ask.

"I needed to make sure I caught you before you left!" He's panting between each word. "I can't have you leave without saying goodbye."

My eyebrows shoot up. "Oh."

He takes a seat for a second and inhales sharply before looking back up at me as I gather more of my equipment to toss in my bag.

"I wasn't going to leave immediately," I begin. "I have to wait until Leanne's done breaking down and we were going to leave to go back to my house."

"Well, I didn't know that! Also since when did you start dating?"

"Not long ago. I'm realizing that a lot has happened over a short amount of time."

He slowly nods. "Ah, okay. Anyway, I...before you go, I wanted to let you know...I..."

I blink back as he's trying to say something heartfelt. I'm touched that he's stumbling over his words. It means he's trying to conjure up an emotional message back to me, because if there's something I've picked up on when I started playing baseball with Kyle, is that the man is sunshine and rainbows, and when something affects him, you can't see it. He's young; fresh out of college, trying to figure out his place in the world whilst also trying to stay playing baseball. He didn't get drafted to a major league team and started out in the minors, but I think in due time, he would be ready to play for a major league team.

"I really loved getting to know you this past season," he says. "You are a really good player and you have been a good leader. I feel like I've learned a lot from you last season, and I..." His voice breaks.

"I'm going to miss you, man."

Man, this kid. He's starting to make me emotional. When I came here, I didn't think that I was going to make a lot of friends with my teammates. I thought of this as a job, and if I was going to eventually leave, then I couldn't make an effort to create meaningful relationships with my "colleagues." But this team was different. All the guys on the team have been welcoming, fun to be around, and lift each other up. And I'm happy that I've gotten to better know everyone on the team.

I pat him on the shoulder. "I'll miss you too, man." I want to have more to say, but I fear I'm just as overcome with emotion as he is.

"You've become kind of like a brother to me, which means a lot because I don't have a biological brother. I mean, I have a brother in law, but he's kind of a nerd and he plays Warhammer and spends too much time working on these little figurines and doesn't know anything about baseball, but that's neither here nor there. Point is, you've made an impact on me in a positive way, and I really appreciate all the advice you've given me to be a better baseball player."

I reach over to wrap my arm around his shoulder and pull him in toward me. "That means a lot to me, Ky. Thank you." I choke on that last bit of thanks. I've been playing baseball for a long time, having the opportunity to call a good number of teammates friends, but this might be the first time where a teammate came up to me and in a vulnerable state, breaks down at how much he's going to miss me and how big of an impact I've made on them. It's a moment I'll treasure forever, and almost makes me wish I didn't have to leave.

"Let me know anytime you want to come down to San Diego. I'd be happy to show you around and maybe if I'm lucky, then we may be on the field together again. On the same team or a different one."

"I'd love that." He smiles. He uses the back of his hand to wipe the snot that trickled down his nose. "Sorry, I'll let you go now. You should get to your girlfriend."

"Thanks, man. This isn't goodbye, alright?"

He nods. "It's see you on the field, right?"

I laugh. "Yeah, exactly."

Kyle walks up from the dugout, grabs a hold of his bag, and heads out. I don't feel ready to walk up yet. My legs feel heavy and like they're glued to the bench. I look out over the expanse of this field, which not long ago, was just overgrown grass that no one wanted to trim. The Neptune Beach community showed up in droves, with countless volunteers working sunrise to sunset to trim the excess grass, cut it, pour dirt, and make this a baseball field. The field I didn't think would come to life, would have such a big effect on me. It's a beautiful sight, and even if I was remorseful if I was coming back home at first, feeling like I was going backward, that's not the case now.

Leanne steps into the dugout and sits next to me. I don't move from looking straight ahead at the field as the sun is set and the lights are on, but I reach my hand over to interlock my fingers with hers.

"Taking it all in for one last time?"

I nod.

"Didn't think you were going to miss it so much, did you?"

I shake my head.

"Do you want to be alone?"

I don't shake my head to protest. I stay silent, because if I even utter a "no" I'm going to fall apart. I hope that my silence speaks enough volumes for Leanne to pick up on it. I shake my head and take in one big sniff.

She wraps her arm around my shoulder and rests her head on me. I lean my head against hers and we sit in silence as I take a final look at the field that's become my home again for the last time.

Chapter 29
Leanne

Corey remains fairly silent on the drive back home to his parent's house. I know he has a lot on his mind and the emotional final game he had today is only compounding those emotions.

I want to figure out some way to give him a proper sendoff, but I don't know what that looks like. I just know I want to host a party of some sort. The catering is easy for me to do. I can make enough food for the team, our families, and a few select extra friends from the bar. In total, that's about thirty and some change. That's easy to cater, and my parent's backyard is big enough for everyone to gather in.

I'd have to start planning this within a week and put all the details together while Corey is going down to San Diego for some paperwork and meeting the team. I can plan an entire goodbye party within that time, right? And then figure out a way to announce to everyone I'm moving down to San Diego to be with Corey as well?

It feels surreal that I've made this decision. I've started the transfer of ownership of the business over, started looking for jobs in San Diego, looking at roles related to cooking and even trying to apply as Director of Food and Beverage for a hotel.

Love alters your emotions in strange ways, but at the end of the day, I'm going to be with Corey, and I'm going to kiss Neptune Beach goodbye the same way he has to, and at the same time as he will.

I'm going to have to break my family's hearts the same way he will, and the hard part is, my family won't even see it coming.

We pull up to the driveway of Corey's parents' house, and Corey's mom asks if we're hungry for a late-night snack or even some hot chocolate. The one with the grandmother on it, obviously.

I quickly respond with an enthusiastic "sure" at the same time Corey unenthusiastically says he'll pass.

I worryingly shoot him a glance and he smiles, brushing his fingers over my knuckles. "Go ahead. I'm just going to take a quick shower and we can hang out. Besides, my parents will keep you company."

"Yes!" his mom chimes in. "I want to hear all about how you two started dating."

I chuckle. I guess it'll be good practice for when I need to tell my family. I think. "Okay, okay. Are you sure we can't make you some tea, or something? It might help with calming you down."

He shakes his head. His eyes are still slightly puffy, and his face is stuck in a frown. Even though I know the root cause of Corey's sadness, and I want to be happy I didn't do anything wrong, seeing him sad is making me want to drop everything and be next to him. But he needs to let me in first. I can't be hurting myself over his desire to be alone with his thoughts.

"I'll be okay." He nudges his pinky next to mine and interlaces them together. "Promise."

"Alright," I whisper. "Only because you made the effort to make it a pinky promise."

He laughs. "You won't trust me if I don't."

"You'd be correct."

We pull into the driveway and take turns heading out of the car, with Corey walking over to take his equipment bag out of the trunk. He closes it and leans against it to look down at me as I wait next to him. I'm still worried about him, as he's trying to shut himself out and solve his own problems without telling anyone about them. But I don't want to add fuel to the fire and have him think that he might not be making the right decision, because I want him to go.

"What's up?" I ask him.

"Not much." He shrugs. "I just didn't think I could have more than one dream, you know?" He stares down at me. "Getting the chance to be a role model for up-and-coming baseball players. Building a community back home when growing up I was always the person who just wanted to fit in. Falling in love with you and thinking about our future."

My mouth parts. I fixate on the "falling in love and future" part because my future is with Corey. I know that too. And this is a good time to tell him that there's something I've been thinking about to seal in that fate. "Corey..."

He grabs a hold of my hand. "Hmm?"

"I've been thinking about this since...since even before we made it official. But I made things official with the business and told Emma that I was moving to San Diego with you and that I would sell her the business."

He gasps. "Wait, Leanne, shouldn't we..."

"Talk about this?" I nod furiously. "Yes, but I want you to know that my dream isn't just my business anymore. Sure, it was for a long time, acting as a scapegoat to the people who didn't want to believe in me and the risks that I was taking, but, if all works out, I believe I'll find my way back to it again. Right now, my dream is to be with you, supporting you as you live out your dream."

"You're sure?" he asks. "You're willing to sell everything you've built so that you can move somewhere new, away from your hometown and your family, to be with me?"

"Yes." I nod. "I don't want us to figure things out apart from each other. I want us to wake up next to each other, decorate a home together, and obviously when we're both ready, then make those decisions about the future."

He scoops me up and tightly wraps his arms around my waist. He takes a sniff of my hair, murmuring apologies that my hair may now possibly be snot-infested.

"You're sure about this?" he asks once he breaks apart from me. "You're willing to start over again and leave your home and your family to live with someone you started dating a week ago?"

I burst out laughing. "Dating a week ago, maybe it sounds a little wild. But you forget I've known you for the better half of my life, and I think I've realized that you've always been an important person to me. Now we just fool around as a part of it too."

He bends down to give me a big kiss. "I love you."

"I love you too." I reach up to kiss him again. I press my lips against him once, then again, and soon enough, he's carrying me up in his arms and I open my mouth to flick my tongue against his. I grab a fistful of his once-sweaty hair and let out a moan as he continues to explore inside my mouth.

"We should probably head inside." I chuckle. "Before your parents catch us doing more than just making out on their driveway."

"Good idea." He nods, setting me down, and we walk up to enter the house through the garage.

"Do you want to stay the night?"

I stop short before walking into the house with him. "What?"

"What?" He chuckles. "Too forward?"

"No, of course not. God knows we've just been opening up our feelings to one another these past few days." I think I know most things that are in Corey Ramirez's inner workings, but I'd have to tell my parents I'm not coming home to sleep tonight, and I don't know what narrative I'm going to spin to them on where else I'll be overnight. Or if I'm just going to tell them over the phone I'm sleeping over at my boyfriend's house. My boyfriend, who is also my brother's best friend.

"I just...I'm worried about telling my parents like this."

"Just say you're sleeping over at Emma's or something," he counters. "They're not going to question that right? Or just say you're not coming home tonight and they shouldn't worry because you're an adult who can make your own decisions. Wild thought?"

I groan. The ounce of sarcasm laced in Corey's last response kind of irks me. While when he says it with that kind of sass, it can sound a little far-fetched. My parents care about me, which can be reason enough to worry when I say something vague like, "I'm not coming home tonight, but don't worry about me." What if I said that against my will, but they didn't care enough to ask?

"They just care about me okay?" I bite back. "And I'm trying to have a good relationship with them before I tell them I'm moving out and away from home for the first time!"

Corey jolts but narrows his eyes at me. "Well, I'm just saying, you decided you wanted to start dating. And then move. You're going to have to tell your parents at some point. Or else I'm going to get pretty annoyed if I have to keep my girlfriend a secret from her own family."

He doesn't say anything else back to me and turns to head upstairs to take a shower, I presume. I didn't want us to be angry with each other after I dropped the news to him, but doesn't he understand? He knows how my parents are. I just wish he gave a little more sympathy on how difficult this is going to be, dropping all these bombshells on them.

"Leanne?" Corey's mom calls out from the kitchen. "The hot chocolate is ready!"

"Okay!" I shout back. I sulk into the Ramirez's living room area, not bothering to turn on the lights. I need to stop being such a coward. I'm going to tell my parents Corey and I are dating. And eventually, when I tell them I'm moving, I'm going to tell them it's because I'm in love and need to act on it. I can't hide my feelings about it anymore.

I search for my mom's name in my contacts and press the call button. It rings once and my mom responds with a sweet, "Hello?"

"Hey, Mom." I know she knows it's me already, even though she didn't immediately answer with a "Hi, Leanne."

"Hi, Lele. Where are you at?"

"I'm um, I'm at my boyfriend's house."

"Boyfriend? Oh, you didn't tell us that you were dating. How long have you been with him? Do we know who he is?"

"Yes." I wipe a hand over my face. "Yeah, you do. It's Corey."

"Corey? Corey Ramirez?"

"Mhhhm."

"Oh," she responds. "That's wonderful, Leanne. As long as you're happy, we don't care who you're with.."

"Yeah," my voice cracks, "I am."

Quietly, Corey's mom comes to sit next to me. She sets down a cup of hot chocolate in a "Los Gatos University Fan" mug and smiles as I'm about to break down.

"Oh, Leanne. What's wrong?" my mom says.

"Nothing." I wipe my eyes with the back of my hand. "I...I just have a lot on my mind, that's all."

"Okay, well, you be safe. We'll talk to you in the morning."

"Yeah." I nod. "I'm sorry I didn't tell you sooner. There's a lot that's been going on the past few days."

"It's okay," she reassures me. "I'm sure you are going through a lot."

"Just...don't tell Lance yet. I want to tell him. I'm just bracing for how he's going to react."

"I think he'll be happy for both of you, but we won't say anything yet. You tell him when you're ready."

"Okay." I nod. "Thanks, Mom. Love you."

"Love you too, Leanne. Goodnight."

"Night." I press the end button and drop the phone onto the coffee table.

"Thank you," I whisper to Corey's mom, taking the mug by the handle and slurping up a little bit of that chocolatey goodness that powdered hot chocolate just can't seem to replicate.

"How are you feeling?"

I lean back into the couch, careful that I don't splash any of the hot chocolate out of the mug. "I'm okay. I needed to tell them at some point."

She laughs. "It is better that you told them first before they caught you in the act. Like what happened to someone I know."

"Oh." I look down into my mug. "Yeah, that happened, didn't it? I'm sorry. Corey and I wanted to keep it a secret for as long as we can because of..." I bite my cheek. They should know, right?

"If you're wondering if we know about Corey's call up to San Diego, we do. He made sure to tell us before the game today."

I sigh. "Okay, good. I think if he was going to tell anyone first besides me, it would be you. Not to say that he shouldn't have told me first...I was just there when it happened." I should probably stop blabbering before I make yet another lasting impression on someone I may consider one day as my in-laws.

"It's okay. We're just happy Corey told us. He is...not the best about sharing what he's feeling."

"Yeah, that much I can agree with."

"What do you think about it?"

"About Corey's move to San Diego?" I clarify.

She nods.

"I mean, I want him to be happy. He's wanted to play in the majors since he learned to hit a baseball for the first time." That's probably a stretch. He learned to hit a baseball at the age of four. He knew how to hit a baseball before learning how to read. I don't know at that time if he really comprehended a career and a future.

"Pretty much." His mom chuckles. "I still remember he wrote in a Kindergarten journal that he did want to be a baseball player when he grew up."

"Oh." Guess I wasn't very far off then.

"So you'd be okay if he moves down to San Diego?" she asks. "What are you planning on doing?"

"I'm...going to go with him."

Her eyes widen. "Oh. Well, that's great. Have you and Corey started looking at apartments down there?"

"No." I forget that those are things you need to think about. Adult things. Where are we going to live? What furniture are we going to buy? How much are we going to budget for things each month? We should probably be thinking about a budget, considering we're going to have to pay for everything on our own now.

"Well, you guys have time. Have you told your parents you're moving down with Corey yet?"

"No," I whisper.

"Are you afraid of how they'll react?"

I silently nod. They might give me a silent treatment at first, telling me they're happy for me, but deep down they're sad I left. It's a bit of an unspoken rule with the Fairbanks family: you never stray away from your family. They're the crux that holds your support system together. I won't be just a room away from them anymore, or a ten-minute drive. If I need help, I don't know if anyone will be available to hear those calls.

"They may be upset at first," Corey's mom says. "But they'll understand because they know you're doing it to be with Corey."

"I hope so." My parents have the kind of relationship I look up to, I want to hope mine will be as successful as theirs.

"Keep your head up, Leanne." Corey's mom gives me a pat on my shoulder. "Corey's about to embark on a pretty big change in his life, and I know that he's going to want you to be his support system through it."

"Yeah." I nod. I want to be that for him, but who's going to help me as my life changes too?

Chapter 30
Leanne

Once I hear the shower upstairs shut off, I excuse myself from Corey's mom, letting her know I'm going to wait upstairs for Corey to finish up his shower in his room.

"I wanted to ask," I begin as I'm standing up and grabbing ahold of my mug of cocoa. "I want to throw a farewell party for Corey at my parent's house, and was wondering if you would like to help? No pressure, you're more than welcome to just come and attend, and bring whoever you'd like, but I didn't want to start the planning process without letting you know first."

"Oh." She perks up. "Thank you for asking. Well, we would love to help if you would want us to. We'll invite some friends too. I'm sure they'd be happy to send Corey off. What are you thinking?"

"Nothing major." Considering I have to plan this in less than a week. "I'd make food, decorate the yard with San Diego related decor, have it be very casual. It's just a time to celebrate Corey before he leaves."

"Well, it sounds like a great time. Do you have a dessert planned out yet?"

I shake my head. "No, I don't." I also might know how to cook, but baking is not my forte. Maybe I can try and make cookies, but even something simple as those, I might fuck up. I won't take any chances.

"Well, let me bring a cake then. I have his grandma's tres leches recipe somewhere. I'm sure he'll love that."

I smile. "That sounds delicious, thank you."

"You're very welcome." She grins back. "I'm glad Corey's with someone who cares about him so much. We're hoping things will work out for a long time between the two of you."

"Oh," I respond. "Um, yeah, me too." I don't jump into the what-ifs with what the future brings, but something in my heart tells me I need to hang onto him for a long time.

"Have a good night, Leanne." Corey's mom stands up and walks back over to the kitchen to join Corey's dad, looking at something on his phone.

I walk upstairs and see Corey's closed bedroom door. I turn and see the bathroom empty, so I lightly knock three times on his bedroom door.

"Coming!" he answers.

He opens up the door, dressed in only his boxer briefs and hair slightly dripping wet.

His eyebrows shoot up. "Leanne," he begins.

"Can I come in?"

"Yeah, of course." He steps aside and I walk into his room. Much of it remains, as I assume, as it was when Corey was in high school. Plaid bed sheets, and posters of San Francisco baseball players and the stadium on the wall. Some players have now since retired, but are definitely legends in San Francisco's history. There are also team photos from when Corey played in high school and college, a desk in the corner that has a desktop computer on it, and a few stacks of cards of some sort.

I take a moment to look around the room and return my gaze back to him.

"Nice room," I note.

"Really?" he replies. "I haven't changed it much since I was in high school."

"Feels homey," I add on. "You might need to change the baseball posters, though. No shade to San Francisco, but I'm rooting for a new team now."

He looks down at me and a slight smile peeks through. "That so?"

"Yeah." I grin back. "My boyfriend got called up to a cool team in San Diego."

We stay silent, standing apart from one another, and I'm fighting the urge to make a peep about how delicious Corey looks right now. Thankfully, I don't have to hold my tongue anymore because Corey makes the move and pulls me into his body so my head can rest against his bare, hard chest.

"I'm sorry," he says after kissing the top of my head. "I shouldn't have lashed out at you about not telling your parents yet. I know you're going through a lot, with this big change and everything. I don't want to overwhelm you, but I also love you and I want to hold your hand and shower you with kisses without worrying about who sees."

"No." I shake my head. "You're right, though. I needed to tell my parents. So I did."

"Really?" His eyes widen.

"Yeah. It was time. I want them to know how much you mean to me."

"How did they respond?"

"They were happy. I mean, I had nothing to worry about." I omit the part where I also broke down and vaguely told my parents why I was so distraught. I'm going to figure that out when it comes. One step at a time, right?

"I figured. But, I get nervous now after thinking about it. They've known me for years; I feel like I have some kind of heightened expectations because they saw me grow up. They consider me like one of their own, which is really weird for me to say because now I'm dating their daughter."

"We're essentially siblings." I wink. "How taboo."

He rolls his eyes playfully at me. "Don't bring that up. Anyway, I'm happy they essentially approve. Does that mean..."

I pout. "No, he doesn't know it yet."

That one we're going to have to conjure up a game plan to tell him. Now that I've told my parents, I'm more relieved and I think Lance will have a similar reaction, but who knows? It's been going so good so far, am I due for a curveball?

"Ah. We'll figure out how to tell him."

"You haven't told him yet about the move either, have you?"

Corey's eyes flit down to the floor. "No."

"Dammit," I say. That one I'm kind of worried about.

"Yeah...we're really going to break his heart, aren't we?"

"We're breaking a lot of hearts," I counter. "I still need to conjure up a way to tell my parents."

"Do you think that they're going to tell you no?"

"God, I hope not," is the first thing that comes out of my mouth. That would be the last thing I want to happen. Trying to use convincing words to tell my parents I need to do this. It's been weighing down on me for some time now, and I'm nervous they're going to use the power of disappointment to tell me I'm not ready or constantly ask if this is what I want to do with the rest of my life. Drop everything for a boy. "Because

I'm not prepared to engage in an argument that my happiness depends on this."

"At least they know we're together."

"Yeah. I'm glad I told them."

He steps closer to me and holds my face in between his hands. As he examines me, his face tells me he's wistful, that we're ready to race through any hardships that come our way. And as anxious as I look, he wouldn't want to spend a day without me in it.

"Tell me what's on your mind," I plead. To validate everything racing through my head.

"I'm thinking about how beautiful you are," he begins. "How I never want to see you sad, but I know that you have a lot going on right now, so I'm trying to conjure up ways to make you happy. I'm thinking about our future in San Diego, and how I don't want to scare you yet, but I'm thinking about building our life together, and how I want to be with you forever."

I blush and blink my eyes back up at him. Whatever fears that were racing through my mind became overshadowed with "I love you, I love you, I love you," repeating in my mind over and over.

"Corey..." The rest of the words get stuck in my throat.

"Don't feel like you need to respond immediately to that," he responds. "But I just want you to know that there would be nothing more in the world that I'd want than to be with you forever. I won't get down on one knee yet, but you're it for me, Leanne Fairbanks."

"You're it for me too, Corey," I say confidently. "It's not a wild thing. It's what I feel too. And I'm ready to start this new journey together."

"Get over here and give your man some love," he says with a seductive voice.

I turn away from him and start to laugh. "I'm sorry, but that was so cringey."

He sighs. "Well, at least I can do a good job of making you laugh."

He steps closer and presses his lips to mine. I reach up and splay my fingers into his hair. He kisses like he's hungry, peppering me in small kisses at first but once I open my mouth, he explores deeper and begins flicking his tongue against mine. When I moan, he laughs into my mouth, and sucks at my bottom lip. He bends over me and grabs ahold of me under my ass, and scoops me up into his arms. When we're kissing, we're savoring each nerve that touches against one another. The faint smell of his aftershave pierces into my nostrils, coupled with that clean water smell.

"Strip for me," he says against my lips. "You're wearing too many clothes."

I concur, especially compared to how many he's wearing, which is still only a pair of boxer briefs.

"Help me?" My question topples the verge of a plea.

A rumble comes from him. "Where should I start?"

"Where do want to touch first?" I ask, lifting a brow.

"I want to touch you all over," Corey's voice deepens. "Where can I touch you that will make you scream my name?"

As his body remains still, he examines me up and down. He bites down on his lip and then reaches his hand forward to pull on the waistband of my leggings. I suck in a breath. A part of me was thinking Corey was going to begin by sliding his hand up my loose T-shirt and taking a squeeze of my breast. That's what he's gravitated to before.

"Everything good?"

"Mhhhm," I say. I keep my lips pressed to one another before I yelp in delight from what's going to come. Or who.

"So I can keep doing this?" He traces his fingers deeper down my pussy and rubs along my clit.

"Yeah," I breathe. "Keep doing that."

"You're soaked for me, baby," Corey whispers. "Keep thinking about me. How I'm going to put you to sleep and wake you up in the morning." He sticks a finger in and slides it over to make room for another. My legs go limp and as they bend, Corey grabs me by the waist and leads me down onto his bed.

I peer up at the posters of baseball players popular when we were teens hung on his wall.

"Do you think someone will hang a poster of you on their wall?"

He chuckles as he looks down at me. "I don't know if I'll be that cool."

"You underestimate just how cool you are then," I begin. "Because I am buying the first 'Corey Ramirez' poster that I see."

"And where are you going to put that?"

I smirk. "Maybe in the living room. Or if we have an office, right next to my desk. Just as a reminder of who my favorite baseball player is."

"I'll remind you who your favorite is." He grabs a hold of my leggings by the waist and pulls them down. "I'll make sure you never forget who makes you come, Leanne."

He bends over and I lose his face after he buries it in my pussy. He sucks at it and I forget how to breathe for a moment. I bend my head back into Corey's pillow and moan as he begins to stick his tongue in.

"That's it, baby girl," Corey says, taking a moment to come up for air.

"Corey," I begin. He climbs over me and rips off his boxer briefs. He slightly bends down and begins thrusting his dick into me. I can't contain the pleasure that builds inside my stomach. As he continues pushing himself into me, my heart rate picks up speed and I'm audibly panting as Corey and I keep our gazes trained on one another.

"God Leanne, you're so beautiful. So amazing. So...mine," he tells me. He slides his hand up to pinch at my nipple. I gasp when he slightly pulls at it.

"Mmmm, those perky tits," he continues. "I need to see them."

I quickly grab onto the hem of my shirt and pull it off my head. I toss it to the side and Corey sinisterly smiles down at them. He bends down, still pumping into me, and sucks onto my nipple.

"Oh," I cry out and arch my back. He keeps sucking until he bites onto it and I cry out again.

He groans after pumping into me once more and pants on top of me as I sink back down into his bed sheets.

"You like that, huh?"

I nod. I like anything that Corey wants to do to me, but that was a nice treat. "I just like being with you," I conclude.

"I like being with you too."

We go to clean up in Corey's bathroom, careful to ensure the coast is clear so his parents aren't prying us with questions. When we're done, I slide back into Corey's bed and he reaches to shut the light off.

"You're leaving to go to San Diego tomorrow?" I ask.

He nods. "I'll only be gone for two days. But after that, we can figure out a time to go back soon and see some apartments. I want you to have just as much of a say where we'll be living."

"Okay." I nod. "That sounds good."

He gives me another kiss as he slides under the covers. "I love you."

"I love you too. Goodnight."

"Night."

Chapter 31
Leanne

Keeping this party under wraps while Corey is finalizing the move to San Diego proves to be even harder than when we were trying to keep our feelings at bay for one another. Namely because when we were doing that, there was a point where we just said "Fuck it" and made our relationship official. I can't just be like "Fuck it" and tell Corey I've been planning a surprise going away party for him.

Or I can, but I want to make him cry. Mostly tears of joy, of course.

After I spent the night with Corey, I went back home and confronted my parents about our relationship face to face. I had to tell them that Corey's planning on moving. I wanted to use their backyard as the venue for his going away party, but I had to ensure they weren't going to tell anyone yet. Although, there was something more on their mind than Corey being called up to the big leagues.

"You two are still going to be dating even though he's moving? How is that going to work?"

I gently bite on my tongue. What am I supposed to say? I don't want to talk about my move yet. This is a good opportunity to feel out and see what my parents think about the whole situation.

"We'll figure it out," I conclude.

My mom blinks back at me. She shrugs, feigning nonchalance, before turning back to finish loading the dishwasher.

"Oookay," she says.

"What?" I retort.

"Nothing," she replies. "I'm just worried you might not like being in a long-distance relationship and want to give up. It's not easy being long distance."

"Well, hypothetically speaking, what if I'm going to eventually move in with him?"

She stands straight up and narrows her eyes my way. It's like she's shooting arrows straight through my corneas. I'm scared to blink and not gaze back at her. "You're thinking about moving?"

"No..." I hate how bad I am at lying. "That's why I'm saying it's a hypothetical."

"Why'd you want to leave Neptune Beach?"

"Because I would rather not be apart from my boyfriend for months on end!" I groan. I bend over the kitchen island and hold my head in my hands. Well, this conversation was going to be inevitable. I might as well just bite the bullet and confess. I better have a damn convincing enough argument that this is going to work.

"I wanted to spend more time marinating on how to tell you this, but since we're already talking about it, then I might as well say it. I've already been making plans to move with Corey next week and sell my share of *The Dragon's Belly* to Emma. She's already agreed to buy me out."

My mom gasps. "Leanne. You're serious about this."

"Yes." I nod. "I love Corey, and I want to do whatever it takes to be with him. Including moving away from the only town I've lived in."

She still doesn't show any hint of enthusiasm, so I explain further. "I want to work things out with him. I can't even tell you how much time I've spent racking my brain around all this. But at the end of the day, I thought to myself, I'd be more miserable living here while he makes a new life for himself in San Diego, even if I had everything secured, like my business, my room, my friends. If I'm not with him, it'd almost be as if I had nothing."

She comes around the island to stand next to me. Her face doesn't scream "disappointed," but more of a protective momma bear who's concerned about her child entering the outside world for the first time.

"Oh, Leanne," she says wistfully. "You know that I wish I never have to give you up. But the truth is, I can't hold onto you forever."

"Hold on. You're not mad?" I ask.

"Of course not. If anything, I'm just looking out for you. After what happened between you and Greg, I was so afraid that you'd get your heart broken again."

"I know. It took me a moment to learn to trust again, but Corey makes it a lot easier. He's..." Everything to me.

"He's your special guy?" She winks.

"Sure." I roll my eyes back at her. "He loves me, and I love him. And I know that I've dove into telling someone I was going to be with them forever before, but something in me feels different about Corey. He's ready to support me in whatever endeavor I want to take. And I think that I've reached a point now where I'm ready to be independent, beyond what I'm doing now. Not feeling like I rely on you and Dad to help me carry out my dreams, even though I appreciate everything you've given me."

My mom rubs my arm gently and shoots a sorrow-filled smile my way. "Thank you, Leanne. At the end of the day, we just want you to be happy. And to visit often, please. I still need to see my baby girl."

I start to sniff. God, it's not even a goodbye yet, but the thought of it is driving me to an emotional wreck. "I will. Of course, I will."

She pulls me in. "Oh, my girl. You're going to do amazing. And even if you don't claim a Neptune Beach address anymore, this will always be your home."

"Thanks, Mom," I whisper. "I'm really going to miss you guys."

"We're going to miss you both too. But you and Corey are going to have an amazing time in San Diego. Their beaches are pretty spectacular."

I nod. I love the beach here, but the temperatures are slightly cooler here than down there, so while the beaches here are very nice and peaceful, if you find the right beaches, the fog rolls in such a way that you can't bask in the sun.

"They are," I reply. And where Corey is playing is right in the heart of downtown, so we'll be near the water again. I don't know what I'd think if he joined a team that played in the middle of the country. I'd find my way of making it fun, but I have a special preference for ballparks located on the West Coast.

"Can you keep this a secret between us for a little bit?" I request. "I know Corey wants to wait until he gets back so we can tell Lance together."

"How are you going to invite them to the party then if you're not able to tell him what said party is for?"

That's a good point. Dammit, I didn't even think of a plan to mask what the party is to Lance. I have to figure out a way to get him to come over without teasing the reason why. He'll be convinced if I just tell him I'm making dinner, right?

"I just won't mention it to him," I say. "He comes over all the time anyway. He's not going to suspect a thing if I just say I'm making dinner." He doesn't have a partner or too many friends that he's trying to make plans with. That I know of.

"Okay." My mom nods. "You seem to have a game plan, so I'm just going to let you do your thing."

"Thanks." I, myself, don't know what that game plan is as of yet, but I can quickly adapt to the situation that's been handed to me. "I'm going to go upstairs and kind of start looking at things I need to pack." And set aside things I've held onto for years that I need to learn to say goodbye to.

Just as I am about to rush up the stairs, the front door's lock turns, and the door opens to an angry Lance, who slams the door shut immediately behind him.

"Lance," I begin.

He greets me with a "Can you believe this bullshit?" and sticks his phone out right in front of me.

"What am I looking at?" I grab the phone from him and examine the screen. It's a photo of Corey, dressed in a San Diego uniform, holding a bat and smiling. The photo caption below says, "Welcome" with his number and name.

Oh yeah. The social media post.

"Lance," I repeat his name again.

"Why wouldn't he tell me he was being scouted to play for another team? And he just decides to move to San Diego? Was he going to even say goodbye?"

"Lance," I try to say in a calming way. "I'm sure that he was going to tell you eventually."

"What, as soon as he's about to leave? I...I could have made a plan. We could've arranged a going away party. I think I can still talk to the guys at the Jolly Oyster to arrange..."

"Lance!" This was not the way I wanted to tell him, and probably not what Corey was envisioning either. But Corey isn't here, and I'm forced to put out the fire for both of us. "I've already talked to Mom about arranging a going away party here."

"Here?"

"Like in the backyard."

"But wait..." Lance eyes the photo again. "This photo was posted ten minutes ago. How did you..."

He narrows his eyes at me once the puzzle pieces are being put together in his mind. "What are you hiding from me, Leanne?"

I start blabbering nonsense as the nerves settle in. "I'm sorry, I was going to tell you, but Corey and I..."

"No!" he cuts me off. "None of that. What could you possibly be so afraid of that you wouldn't tell your brother of all people?"

"Corey and I are dating!" I shout back. "We're dating and we're planning on moving in together in San Diego, and I don't want to rush into saying things that won't come true, but I love him and I want to be with him forever and I'm really sorry that I didn't tell you before, but I didn't want to upset you or make you feel like I stole your best friend from you."

I await Lance's response, but his silence speaks for itself.

He takes a deep breath and closes his eyes as he exhales. "I would have been happy for you both, if I had found out in a way that doesn't involve you forcing to tell me after the fact because I found out some information on my own. Now, I just feel like the two closest people in my life betrayed me."

"*Lance*," I wail.

"I'm heading home. I hope you two enjoy your sendoff."

He shuts the front door behind him and I slump onto the bottom stair. It's true, we were going to break some hearts, and my brother's carries a stronger weight than I could've imagined.

Chapter 32
Corey

Hey – I know you're probably busy with the signing and everything…just wanted to let you know that Lance knows.

And he's not talking to me.

How'd he find out?

Fuck, the social media post.

Dammit this is all my fault I should have told him.

Don't worry, he will likely cool down in a bit. I hope. I do feel bad though, he kind of got bombarded with a lot of information all at once.

COREY

I'll talk to him when I get back. Sweeten him up. Buy him a beer.

LEANNE

Alright, I trust you.

Love you.

COREY

Love you too baby, I'll see you soon.

I take a moment to step away from the hustle and bustle and assess the situation at hand. Lance is pissed, rightfully so. I should have told him I was leaving Neptune Beach and not harped so much on the repercussions. Because that's not putting enough trust in my friend who will support me in whatever I do, and that makes me a shitty friend.

"Hey." Bruce comes up and sits next to me in the dugout. It's so casual. I forget it's because I'm his teammate, but I was watching him when he was a rookie in the MLB. First round draft pick and immediately goes straight to the Majors. Plays four seasons in Oakland, and then gets traded to San Diego. Six-time All-Star player. Arguably, one of the greatest third basemen in the MLB right now, with one of the best batting averages. I watched him hit home runs in high school, and now I'm wearing the same team jersey as him. I feel so small compared to him, but he sees us as equals.

"Hey," I reply.

"How's everything going so far?"

I chuckle. "Not going to lie, it's a little overwhelming. But in a good way."

We're doing photo shoots, acclimating with the team, legal and technical things I have to do but are the least exciting parts of this job, and quickly, we're thrust into the madness of actually practicing with the team. I'm not being put into the lineup until next week, but I'm seeing how other players fit so well working with one another, and starting to feel a rush of nerves that maybe I won't be as good as everyone's told I am.

That, plus now having to strategize a game plan to face Lance, who's shut us out for not telling him the truth about everything, is overwhelming me in the worst way. I'm supposed to be happy that I'm finally at this place and having this opportunity to play with some of baseball's greatest, but there's unfinished business at home I'm itching to settle.

"That's good. I mean, that you're not feeling so stressed out about it. It can be a lot to think about."

I shrug. "Well, I've got some other shit on my mind right now that's kind of taking up more space in my head."

"What, girl problems?"

I shake my head. "No." I'm actually doing just fine in that aspect. "My girl and I are doing great. It just so happens that her brother is one of my best friends, and things are a little rocky between us right now."

"Ah." He nods. "The good ol' dating your best friend's little sister."

"I know that I'm a bad friend right now," I explain. "I waited to tell him that we were dating, which I wanted to do because we didn't want to tell people unless we were sure of it. Which she told me that she wanted to move down with me before I came down here, so that's kind of the affirmation I was waiting on to start telling our friends and her family. But I've been holding onto telling him that I got called up and that I was going to move because I wasn't ready for him to feel sad that I was only home for so long before I'm leaving."

"Yeah." He nods. "I mean, you kind of had a good reason. Waiting to make sure that everything was going to fall into place before saying something that might change. And I mean, it's your best friend's little sister. He must be really protective of her."

"Yeah, he is." From what I know about Lance and what Leanne told me, he loves his family and would sacrifice anything for them. Which is why I love Lance, but this is also going to be a lesson for him that he needs to let go since I'm here to take care of Leanne.

"I think you all will be fine," he reassures me. "I think that even though he's upset that you didn't tell him, deep down, it might be because he doesn't want to think about how much he is going to miss you when you do leave."

"That's plausible." And even though I can and will tell him we're going to visit Neptune Beach as much as possible, it's not going to be every week. I'm not just a drive away anymore. I'm not meeting him every week at the Jolly Oyster, and I know that upsets him.

The coach calls all of us in, and we have one final meeting with each other before we're dismissed for the day. I coordinate with the team to come back in a week, once I've packed a few more items and made the move down with Leanne to San Diego. I have an early flight tomorrow back up while the team heads on the road for a game in Milwaukee. Once they get back, I'm up and running and will be on the roster for the next home series against Colorado. That means I have to, hopefully, amend things with Lance in a week, or that's going to make holidays feel really awkward.

I gather up my items and head back to the hotel I'm staying at just down the way from the stadium. As I'm exiting with the team, I turn to see a familiar face standing at the gate of the player's entrance. I nearly drop my bag when I see who's waiting for me.

"Lance?" I call out.

He pushes off the wall and walks up next to me.

"Hey," he mutters.

"What... How... You're in San Diego," is what I inevitably respond with. Does he have some magical powers that allow him to just arrive in another city in the blink of an eye?

"Yeah, I drove down last night. Couldn't sleep, so I just made the drive."

"That...that is not a short drive to make."

He shrugs. "Eight hours, give or take, without traffic. I mean, you're not really dealing all too much with LA traffic at four in the morning."

"Fair enough."

We stand in silence until I decide to ask, in a polite way, why the fuck he made the decision to drive down to San Diego on a whim. I'm certain Leanne has no idea he's here right now.

"What are you doing here, Lance?"

He groans. "Really? You're asking me that when you didn't tell me one, you had been called up to play in the Majors, and two, you're dating my sister?"

I hold my hands up. "Look, I know there are some things I haven't told you, but..."

"But what, Corey?" He furrows his brows. "You're my best friend, and I found out you got called up on social media. How do you think that makes me feel as someone who thinks they're your friend?"

I sigh. "I know it was shitty to withhold that from you, Lance."

"Then why did you do it?"

"Because I don't even know what my dream looks like anymore!" I yell back at him.

His face softens. "What? But, why? This is your dream, man. You've wanted to be a professional baseball player since we could practically hit a ball."

"I..." I can't believe I'm about to be saying this now, and Lance probably has no idea it's coming. "I love your sister, man. And the thought of us having to be apart was ruining me. In that moment, I had a different dream, and it was to be with her."

"But she told me she's moving down with you," Lance says.

"I know. And she did that on her own. If she had any reservations about it, I would have told her to wait. We'd figure things out as they come in Neptune Beach. I still could play for the Seals."

But Leanne said she wanted to be where I am, and if that meant finding a new dream, so be it. I'm lucky to be with someone who supports my career so much to make such a big sacrifice, and I'll do everything to make sure I help her find what her dream is in this new city.

I crane my neck to gesture over at the hotel I'm staying at across the street. "Do you want to come and talk over at the hotel I'm staying at? They have a rooftop bar." That's going to entice him.

Lance pauses for a moment, and god, if he says no, I think I would maybe lose my marbles in his face. Dude just doesn't drive down over four hundred miles from Neptune Beach without expecting something. An apology for sure, and maybe some final time with me before he won't get it anymore. And lucky for him, I'll give that to him, but only if he tells me that's actually what he wants.

"Yeah, fine," he says, pushing himself toward the crosswalk, "but you're buying me a beer."

***

"Leanne says she's sorry back," I tell Lance. We're sipping on beers and watching various sports games shown on the bar's many televisions. A few different baseball games, coupled with some preseason football games. Pretty soon, baseball season is coming to an end, and while I may be on the team if San Diego makes it to playoffs, which they have a good shot at, I'll have some time off to figure out what Leanne and I should be doing. Maybe we'll take a trip out of the country for a few weeks. Enjoy some time alone where all we'll do is eat, sleep, and each other.

"It's fine." Lance shrugs. "I mean, I get where you two were coming from. You two have made a lot of big decisions in a short amount of time.

And I wouldn't say I'm a believer in much of what is in the beyond, but I wouldn't want to jinx something when it comes to you two's relationship. As much as I felt betrayed you all wouldn't tell me immediately, I am really happy for both of you. If Leanne could fall in love with anyone, I'm sure as hell glad it's someone I can trust."

"Thanks, Lance. I won't get into the nitty-gritty of how I feel toward your sister, but I am deeply in love with her. I'd buy her a ring, like tonight."

"Woah, woah, woah." Lance almost chokes on his beer. "You two need to pass the living together test first before you can start spewing talks of buying her a ring. Just letting you know, her least favorite chores are vacuuming and doing the dishes, which is wild for someone who's a chef."

I narrow my eyes at him. "So, what chores does she like doing?"

"Weirdly, she loves doing laundry. Like the smell of clean clothes turns her on. She loves sticking her face in newly dried clothes."

The thought of Leanne taking one of my shirts and sniffing it against her nose makes me feel some type of way down there. Picturing her doing our laundry and the way my musk lingers on my clothes. It's a way of me telling her I'm always with her.

"Noted. Well, she can happily take over laundry duty. And I'll gladly take on whatever else."

Lance chuckles into his beer. "You all are so weird."

"You'll understand when you start dating," I tell him. The whole falling in love makes you feel a certain type of way. Where all the feelings in your body turn to mush and you feel like the world stops when you're in the presence of the person you love, but Lance doesn't relate. I don't even know the last time he's been in a committed relationship. He wasn't with anyone for too long in college, only one girl he was with for two years...but last I checked, Everly Chin was living in New York after being recruited to play for the women's hockey league. Why did the woman ever go to school in California when she was this big hockey star? Beats me. But she was too good of a player to leave that career behind.

"I don't have plans to date for a while," he mumbles. "Or ever again."

"Leanne said that, but look where she is now. The right person just has to come along."

"The right person came along," he said. When did he get another beer? "I'm just not making plans to chase after her."

I start laughing at him. Oh, now he wants to unearth his emotions. Is that why he was so mad at Leanne for deciding to move? Because she was doing the one thing he couldn't?

"You could be living in New York City, man," I start taunting him. He's going to be pissed as fuck, but I'm kind of enjoying getting a rise out of him. "They have engineering jobs in New York."

He rolls his eyes. "Too big of a city. Too many people."

"And yet, the one you still have feelings for lives there. Oh, and did you know? Your little brother has this huge crush on a guy who is also going to New York for law school. Something tells me you two are due for a trip soon. Leanne and I will stay over in the off-season. It'll be fun."

"What? How do you know Leon has a crush on a guy who's moving to New York for law school?"

I swat my hand away. "Eh, just a chance encounter with him and his friend on a trip to Alcatraz. Anyway, as much as you and I and our family and friends all love Neptune Beach, I think it's worth noting that someday, we'll find out that we need to spread our wings and fly."

"But...why leave something that you're so familiar with? Where you can walk into a bar where everyone knows your name?"

"Because...you have to follow where your heart leads you. And I know you're not going to admit that you might still be harboring feelings for...someone whose name begins with an E, but I think that if you feel a certain type of way and want to try and get her back, you should go for it."

Lance sighs and turns his head up to fixate on the television, ironically as a New York team is playing right now.

"Man, I hate when you make good points."

My face lights up. "Wait, does that mean..."

"No, I am not making plans to go to New York any time soon. But, maybe I can reconnect with those that I've had previous relationships with. In hopes they may want to talk again."

I smile at him. "Good for you, man. I hope things work out."

"Guess we'll see. Leanne's chapter closes and then mine opens up." Lance frowns at me. "I wish I could've had more time with you, man. I feel like we barely got much time to catch up, especially considering you spent much of your time back playing baseball."

"I know," I sigh. I do wish I had more time to settle down in Neptune Beach and build more memories, but leaving this time is different than when I left for college. I'm actually making it a point to come back now. I'm not going to shut myself out from family or friends because I think my life is beyond what Neptune Beach can provide me. I'm going to spend my free moments trying to create as many memories as I can so I don't forget what Neptune Beach has given me.

"But this isn't a goodbye forever," I reassure him. "Besides, something tells me we're going to be calling each other brother pretty soon."

"Ugh," he groans. "I mean, I did always consider you as a brother, but not like this. I swear to god, Ramirez, if you do anything bad to my sister..."

I raise my glass to him. "Don't worry, Fairbanks. Your sister means the world to me. I'll take care of her like she's precious cargo. And I don't want to see you when you get mad."

"Hell no you don't." Lance laughs back. We clink glasses with one another and savor the minutes we have with one another like the good old days.

Chapter 33
Leanne

Lance, driving down to San Diego on a whim, helped me buy some more time to prepare for this party that we were about to have. I texted Lance as he and Corey were slugging beers in Corey's hotel about my grand plans, and how I needed him to be my distractor while I got some more time to put the finishing touches on our parent's backyard and gather people in enough time so when Corey and Lance walk through that door, everyone will be in place to yell, "Surprise!"

Emma and I have been busy in the kitchen preparing food people will be enjoying. Enough food to feed probably an entire high school graduating class, but we'll be having maybe fifty people total at this party. But the average Seals baseball player can eat enough for at least three people, so even though I promoted we'll be having a buffet dinner, I know some people are going to challenge me on whether I know what a buffet is.

"It smells great in here," my mom says as she walks into the kitchen. I'm sweaty from standing over the stove creating my signature spicy vegetable lo mein, but I turn around for a moment to acknowledge her as she hands us a glass of iced Arnold Palmer.

"Here, I'm putting some drinks on the kitchen island. Make sure you're taking breaks. It's getting hot in here with all the cooking going on."

"Okay, Mom," I answer. "We will."

"Thank you!" She smiles back. "I'm going to be in the yard batching some cocktails. Where's Lance and Corey at right now?"

"Um, let me see." I scurry to the sink to rinse my hands off and check my phone. I pull up the "Find My" app and see that Lance and Corey just drove through Bakersfield. That gives us maybe a little under three hours to get everything done. We're on a good track cooking-wise, but we still need to stage and set all the food outside, get it into chafing dishes, and put our best smile forward to serve little bites to eager guests.

"They just passed Bakersfield."

"God, that drive is awful," Emma quips. "You're sure that you want to keep doing that drive once a month?"

I arch a brow at her. "Who said I was doing it once a month?"

"Me." Emma pouts. "I can't go more than a month without you visiting."

I sigh. Emma's truly my best friend. She's more than just my business partner. She's been through it with me from the moment I wanted to make The Dragon's Belly into my livelihood. She's seen me at my happiest, and she's also held me when I felt at my lowest. It was the hardest decision I've ever had to make — handing the business over to her. That business is my baby, but I don't have an idea of when I'm going to start it up again in San Diego. I don't want it to sit defunct and have to shutter it. I threw the idea out to Emma to ask if she would like to keep the food truck alive here, as the Seals are entering into playoffs and still want The Dragon's Belly there, and we've started to receive other inquiries to do popups in cities and even work music festivals.

"Em," I begin. I need to slap my face or something. Stay strong, Leanne. I can't start getting emotional now, as the party hasn't even started yet. Are people going to want me to make a speech? I haven't even thought of what I'm going to say, and now, I'm scared I'm not even going to get what I need to say out before breaking down and crying.

"I'm not going to ruin your mascara," she interrupts. "We can have our moment after everyone's left. Let's focus on making sure everything looks good for your and Corey's send off from Neptune Beach."

I nod. I need all the distractions thrown at me right now. Putting all the final touches on the decorations and food will help, but as the clock is ticking, I'm not going to have many more minutes left to savor.

As we're setting up bits and pieces of food on a tiered stand for guests to pick up as appetizers, I hear footsteps walk through the side gate.

"Hello!" Corey's mom and dad waltz in, carrying a domed container that holds the tres leches cake Corey's mom offered to make.

"Hi!" I wave. Shit. I still need to get ready. "Curious, what time is it?"

"It's a little past four," Corey's mom says. "I know the party isn't starting yet, but we wanted to come early and ask if you needed any help."

I purse my lips. Well, considering I still need to change out of my chef's shirt, touch up my makeup and, if I have enough time left, curl my hair, and I only have maybe a little more than twenty minutes left to do this and finish putting the final pieces on this appetizer tower.

Dammit, and I guess I also forgot to inflate the pool inflatables I bought to dress up the pool. They're all baseball and tropical-themed, and I completely forgot I bought them. I don't even know if anyone is going to swim. I guess Corey and I can go for a dip later if I can pry him from Lance's clingy fingers. He'll probably say something like, "You're getting to spend every day for the rest of your life with him! Let me have this!"

He can say that all he wants, but that's not going to stop me in my honeymoon phase and fight him for my man.

I sigh and admit that as much as I want to do a lot of the work myself to bring this party to life, I'm going to need to ask for some help.

"Dang. I didn't even realize how close we were to the party starting. I need to go get ready. Do you mind helping me out with putting the rest of these appetizers on the tower?"

"Of course," Corey's dad chimes in. He's mostly been quiet the few times I've been around him, and I don't know much about him other than he works for the city's electrical company.

"I don't think that I can make it look as pretty as you did," he jokes. "Is that okay?"

"Oh my gosh, of course it is. Don't even worry about how it looks. As long as it gets onto the tower. You're going to make it look amazing. I know it. I guarantee it."

I think Corey's mom can see my onset of panic, thanks to my blabbering, and lightly grabs onto my arm. "Don't worry, Leanne. Corey is going to love everything you've done. Hell, if you made him a nice dinner, he'd be thankful."

"Thanks." The reassurance is helpful. I know my boyfriend, and she's right. Whatever I do, Corey's going to love it. While this is to congratulate Corey, it's also to thank everyone who has helped us so much to build such a wonderful community while we've lived in Neptune Beach. And to say thanks for all the good memories.

"I gotta run and doll myself up. If you have any questions, then Emma's here to help." I run upstairs and change into a nice floral summer dress, and do a light beat of makeup when I hear a text tone coming from my phone.

LANCE

Hey, Corey and I are like, maybe half an hour away.

I don't want to say we were speeding, but we might've been fast.

LEANNE

Half an hour? That's barely when the party is going to start. I thought you all were going to be at least an hour out!

Didn't you go somewhere to eat?

LANCE

I tried to convince Corey, but he said he wanted to wait to eat whatever you cooked for him.

Curse you and your chef skills.

LEANNE

Ugh fine. Well try and stall him as much as possible. I'm rushing to get ready as we speak.

LANCE

Okay I'll try as much as possible. See you soon.

My getting ready routine quickens to almost double the speed, and I hastily put some dry shampoo in my hair and tease it a little bit to give it some volume. I spray some perfume and head downstairs as a few more guests have arrived and started mingling in the backyard near my appetizer tower, which looks well-stocked thanks to Corey's parents' help.

I greet some of Corey's teammates, who are enjoying a plate of small bites and a beer. Kyle, one of the teammates, who I also remember talking to in Ventura. He's what I think of as Corey's younger brother-slash-mentee because I remember how highly he talked of Corey when we chatted. And then, when Corey played his last game as a Seal, Kyle came up to him afterward and confessed how much of an impact Corey made on his life. It's nice that there was someone on the team who felt impacted by Corey.

"So, what are you going to do when Corey moves to San Diego?" he asks.

I raise an eyebrow. Oh, I guess not everyone knows what my pans are. I didn't post anything on social media proclaiming it. Looks like this is a good occasion to let people know. Hey everyone, this is my boyfriend. Did I mention that I'm also moving down with him next week?

"I'm actually moving down with him. So, this is as much of his going away party as it is mine. Surprise?"

"Wow," Kyle says. "Good for you. I'm happy that Corey's found someone that he enjoys spending time with, and that you two are taking this next step. You two are going to have a great time in San Diego. I'm already planning on visiting."

I laugh. "Well, we'd be happy to show you around, and take you to see a game or two."

"Oh, trust me," he says. "I'm going to see all games with Corey as I can. You have someone fighting you for the title of Corey Ramirez' biggest fan."

"Oh, come on." I lightly nudge him in the arm. "You know you can never beat me."

"Beat you at what?" a voice comes up from behind me. I sharply turn around when it dawns on me that I know this voice.

"Corey?" I squeak. "What are you doing here?"

"Um, well, Lance brought us here. Why are you looking at me funny? What's the team doing here? And my parents?"

I crane my neck up to the ceiling and clench my face that try as I might, I failed to surprise Corey with a nice going away party. Because while he looks surprised, he's not emotional like I had hoped.

"We'll just go ahead and let you two talk it out," Kyle says and beckons the teammates who were huddled around us to step away and let us have our space.

"What's all this?" Corey asks me.

"Um..." I bite my lip. "I may have thrown you a surprise going away party. Well, thrown us one. Because we're both moving. Surprise?"

Corey blinks, and slowly he starts looking around at the friends and family who are slowly walking in and waving at us while we're talking with each other.

"You threw me a going away party?"

"Yeah?" I shrug. "I wanted our friends and family to have one final moment to enjoy everyone's company and share in the love for Neptune Beach before we leave."

I wait for Corey to respond and I eye him continuously blinking, which quickly picks up in cadence until I see a lone tear stream down his face.

"Babe?" I grab a hold of his arm. "Are you okay?"

He silently pulls me into his chest and wraps his arms around my shoulders, taking in a big sniff.

"Thank you," he murmurs into my hair. "This is amazing."

I pull away from him for a moment to meet his stare. "I wanted to surprise you. Do the whole everyone gathers near the gate and yells 'Surprise!' kind of thing, but you came a lot earlier than I thought."

"Oh." He nods. "That's why you were kind of taken aback when you saw me. I should have known it wasn't because you were mad at me."

"Of course not," I reassure him. "I was just disappointed that things didn't go to plan, but I wasn't able to tell you, and I had to try and have Lance put you on kind of a wild goose chase to get back home, but I guess that he had a hard time trying to lead you astray."

"Yeeeeah, I was kind of just so ready to get back to my girl. Lance tried but I was starting to get annoyed, so he gave up. I feel bad that it was because you were trying to hold me for surprise. Sorry, babe."

"It's alright." I shrug. "You're here, and I missed you."

He bends down to plant a light kiss on my lips. "I missed you too, babe."

"But you had a fun surprise when Lance came, huh?"

Corey shakes his head. "That guy. When he wants something, he'll go get it, huh?"

I hold my hands up. "Hey, I had no idea he'd be driving all the way down to San Diego to tell you how he felt."

"I know. We had a good talk. And I did have to make it up to him after leaving him to think he's not an important person in my life for me to update life events to. I may have bought the guy a lot of beers to make up for it."

"Yeah. That guy does like his beer."

Lance saddles up to join in on our conversation. "Talking shit about me?"

"Psh, you?" Corey tsks. "No."

"Uh-huh." Lance nods, ironically while holding a beer. "As much as I hate to say it, you did a damn good job throwing a farewell party, Leanne. Well done."

"Thanks." I beam. "Why do you hate to say that?"

"Because I hate that this is a farewell party, duh. You weren't even here a year, man."

"I know," Corey begins. "I'm sorry. But you agreed when I got the call..."

"You couldn't say no," Lance finishes. "Yeah. And you just happened to have lured my sister to fall in love and join with your good looks and charismatic personality."

"What can I say," Corey says, pulling me into him. "She's won me over." He reaches down and plants a kiss.

"Ew," Lance butts in, and when we turn to see his expression, it looks like he's eaten something sour.

"Get a room," he teases, flashing a smile.

"I mean, that's not a bad idea. It'd be fine if we stepped away for a little bit?" Corey asks.

"No!" I elbow him. "We, aka the guests of honor, are not going to step away at our own party."

"Fine," Corey groans. "We should probably mingle then, right?"

"Yes," I tell him. "Go chat." I lightly push him away and make my own way to check on how the food is looking. Emma is doing a good job of replenishing food, because people are eating a lot. Good thing we bought enough food to accommodate a lot of baseball players' huge stomachs because people keep clamoring for more.

"You know, Miss Fairbanks, I have to say, I'm quite impressed."

I turn and see Greta McDonnell smiling at me while she eats a helping of soy-glazed salmon and signature lo mein. Who does she know that brought them here?

"Oh." I jolt. "Thank you so much. I'm glad that you like it." She's tried my cooking before, though. What's changed about this instance?

"I know that this isn't the first time I've had your cooking, but I am applauding you for coordinating such a fun, intimate gathering. You have a fun eye for design."

I raise a brow. "I do?"

She nods. "I mean, the food tables look nice, the way your parents' backyard has transformed with some fun seating and decor. Have you planned an event before?"

I shake my head. Wait. I've planned a wedding that didn't happen. Do we talk about that?

"I, uh, planned a part of a wedding, but it ended up not moving forward."

"Oh." Her face drops. "I'm sorry to hear about that."

"It's okay. Sometimes things don't work out, and that's okay."

She nods in agreement. "I can relate. Well, sometimes it takes two times in my case. They really mean it when they say the third time's the charm."

I chuckle. "Hey, it doesn't matter how you get to the one, as long as you're happy you've found them."

"Exactly. And I think that you've found someone you're happy with too now."

"Yeah." I take a quick look back to check on Corey, who's talking with some coaches and his parents have also joined the mix. They're all laughing amongst one another, and Corey's parents look like they're more comfortable talking with other guests. "I definitely have."

"Anyway," she continues. "I did want to apologize about the way I came off at the Seals donor event. I really respect your tenacity to try and promote your business. As a fellow woman in business, I do want to support those who radiate that entrepreneurial spirit and offer you a place on our preferred caterer list."

I gasp. This is it. This is my life full circle. What I wanted to work toward, finally manifesting itself. And...I'm leaving.

"I... Thank you for extending that offer to me. I would love to take you up on it."

Her face drops. "But I am assuming this is also your goodbye too?"

I nod. "Believe me. I love it here, but I love Corey and I'm going to move in with him as the next stage in our relationship."

"I understand." She flashes me a sad smile. "We will miss you here at Neptune Beach, but I know this isn't goodbye."

"No, it's not. My parents would never let me do that. And thankfully, we're just moving down to San Diego, even though it may be a bit of a drive to come up and visit every time."

"Well, congratulations to you two. And, if you do find yourself back here, I would still be open to a conversation about setting up a catering partnership."

Well, even if it's not my dream anymore, The Dragon's Belly is still a running business. And maybe I can convince Emma to take it on. She's tenacious, and she can take on another venture on top of the truck, right? I should probably ask her before volunteering to add this onto her plate for a business that isn't technically going to be mine anymore.

"Let me ask my former business partner-slash-best friend. She's the new owner of The Dragon's Belly, and I just want to ensure it's alright with her before I thrust her into something she can't handle."

Greta nods and wishes me a final congratulations before handing me her business card and telling her to keep in touch. I look at the card for a moment too long because Corey comes up to me and asks me why I'm looking so intently at this piece of paper.

"Greta McDonnell extended me the offer to be on their preferred catering list."

Corey beams. "Wow, babe. That's awesome! But..."

"But it's not my business anymore. And not my choice to make."

"Did you talk to Emma?"

I shake my head. "I'll be happy for whatever she decides to do, even if it feels like I'm too late to see something I've dreamt about manifest itself."

Corey blinks back at me. "Are you thinking of staying here for a little to try and have that happen? Because it's fine if you do, babe. We'll figure things out."

"No, no, no." I grip his arm. "It's not like that. I'm going. I can't imagine a moment where I'm not spent figuring things out with you. I just wish there was some best-of-both-worlds scenario."

"What if you did?"

I crane my neck up at him. "What?"

"Come up for like, big events. If you get on this preferred catering list, you'll have the chance to cook for big events. Emma can't do that by herself. You would get the chance to be like a catering coordinator or something to lead and help run logistics with timelines and whatever. It's not far to fly up here. And you'd have the chance to stay with your parents when you do."

"Corey..." This beautiful genius. Where did he come up with such a good idea? How did he even know about this?

"You know you want to do it, baby. And this means you'll still be tied to something that means so much to you. Talk to Emma about it. I think you'll work something out."

"Yeah." I grin. Emma wants to keep me as long as she can, and this is the perfect scenario where I don't have to fully say goodbye. I can even work on proposals from home and fly up for site visits. With one venue, it seems bearable. If we ramp up business, then I'll figure it out. But this way, I don't have to abandon my dreams completely.

"Thank you, babe." I wrap my arms around his waist and tilt my neck up to give him a kiss. "I can't believe I get the chance to stay tied to the business and Neptune Beach. You're a genius."

"You're welcome. I love you so much," he says, going down to give me a kiss again. "I just want you to be happy."

"Trust me," I tell him. "Thanks to you, I'm the happiest I've ever been."

Epilogue

A year and some change later in Honolulu, HI

Corey

This is nerve-wracking.

It shouldn't be. We're in Hawaii during the offseason, finally visiting my brother, his husband and their baby daughter. We should be relaxing, but I have other things on my mind.

This is Leanne's first time in Hawaii and it's going to be a trip that she'll never forget.

Leanne is a romantic at her core, and while she hasn't explicitly mentioned it, she wants to be proposed to in an outrageous way. Not just a "we're sitting on our couch and I decide to ask her to marry me." No, if she is going to be proposed to, it's going to be a production.

Not so great for me, because that means I have to coordinate with different parties to ensure that we're all aware of the plan before I execute it.

We're doing kind of the touristy things you do when in Hawaii, and one of those things is going to a luau. I am certain that many people propose at luaus, but for the case of making this the best damn proposal

I can, no one else can propose at this luau. I had to call the company and tell them that on this day, I am planning on proposing, so if there is any way they can slate me into their programming where we learn how to do the hula as my way to propose, please do it. My future rests on it. Well, not really. If I can't do it at the luau, there are plenty of other chances, but this ring has been almost burning a hole in my suitcase and soon, my pocket, and I can't live with this secret anymore.

I love Leanne. I knew that as soon as I reconnected with her as soon as I returned to Neptune Beach, she was the woman I couldn't stop thinking about, and I wanted to do something about it.

Guess I'm finally doing what I've been wanting.

We've been living together for a little over a year now since we both moved down from Neptune Beach to San Diego once I was called up to the Majors. I would say that I had a successful season in San Diego. A good first season, anyway. I'm not the All-Star, hitting home run game after game, and the player whose jersey everyone's wearing. I got a taste of what the Majors are like, and I have a long way to go, but, I'm excited to keep trying to make hits and plays and get to that player I aspire to be.

Leanne has been enjoying her time in San Diego. We live in a nice apartment downtown and spend our free time doing things like going to the zoo with our new membership, taking trips to the beach, or just doing nothing at all. We even got a cat. That was all Leanne's idea, and I just wanted to agree so I could do something that makes her happy, but I've grown to enjoy snuggling with our cat, Pumpkin.

She also figured out a routine to stay on with the Dragon's Belly to help them specifically with coordinating catering for private events. There's at least one event per month that requires her to drive up and be on-site to make sure everything goes to plan, but otherwise, she's been churning out proposals for everything dealing with deliveries for events and small-scale events that Emma handles. I'm happy she was offered to still stay on, and Leanne has been loving having control even though she lives farther away.

Before the luau, my brother thinks of this wild idea that we should go snorkeling.

"Come on," he argues. "It'll be so fun! You get to swim with dolphins."

"We have very different definitions of fun." Did I mention that I'm afraid of open water? Specifically, swimming in deep, open water? I know they'll give you a life vest so you can stay afloat, but what about the sharks? What if we get stuck on the boat?

"You don't know unless you try it, Corey," Bryce tries to reassure me. "You might like what you see under the sea. Like the song!"

"Whatever, Sebastian." I roll my eyes. "I'm already going to be a nervous wreck trying to plan this proposal at the luau and then you're going to throw this in my way?!"

"It only makes sense we do it on this day," Bryce says. "The snorkel boat is down the way from where the luau takes place. We don't have to get in the car and drive back here afterward can just bring our change of clothes and head to the luau right after!"

"Wait, I have to bring the ring on the boat?" I shriek. Thank god Leanne isn't here right now. She decided she wanted to go to some huge swap meet with my parents. Or else she'd be turning her head at why I sound like my voice is going to crack at any point from being so high.

"Uh yeah, unless you want to leave it in the car?"

"Hell no." I shake my head. "You do not want to know how much I paid for this thing to leave it in a car."

He holds his hands up. "Touche."

We're staring at each other for a moment before Bryce chimes in again. "Man, you're getting married."

I sigh. "Not yet. I need to ask first. And she needs to say yes."

Bryce rolls his eyes. "She's going to say yes, dumbass. That woman is in love with you."

"Yeah." I blush. "She is."

I grab the ring from inside a pocket in my suitcase I've been hiding it in. I open it again and peer at the diamond center, flanked by smaller diamonds around it to look like a flower. It's perfectly Leanne, and I know she's going to love it.

"Nervous?" Bryce asks.

"A bit. I mean, I don't doubt that she's going to say yes. But marriage is a big step. We're signing our lives away to one another."

"Well, yeah. But, if you envision spending the rest of your life with her, you're not thinking about the small details. You'll get through it together like you have for the past year. Do you have any idea what you want to do for a wedding?"

No. I barely came up with the idea to ask her to marry me not that long ago. I'm only deciding to do it in Hawaii because my parents and my brother will be present for it. With Bryce living in Hawaii, now with a baby, I don't know how often I'm going to see him, so I wanted to do it with loved ones we can celebrate with.

I wanted Leanne's family to join, but they couldn't coordinate all of them going. But little does Leanne know, we're staying in Neptune Beach for another few days when we go back stateside.

"I think I want to have it in Neptune Beach, but just because it means so much to us. Telling you in advance so you can plan accordingly. With Amelia and everything."

"Makes sense. And don't worry, we wouldn't miss it, wherever you decide to have it. Don't tell Mom and Dad, but we've bought tickets to spend Christmas in Neptune Beach already."

"Oh, nice. They'll be happy to see you. And you can take Amelia to the beach. But the beaches here are way nicer than in Neptune Beach."

"They're different," Bryce sympathizes. "They're both special in their own way."

"Yeah." I chuckle. That's a good way of spinning it.

"Alright, so I'm gonna book the snorkeling then. You'll be fine, and I think you may even love the water. Trust me."

"Whatever." My older brother is a bully disguised as a gay man, and I cannot be convinced otherwise. He'll soon see what mistake he's made when I have a very valid freakout on the boat tomorrow.

***

We get to the dock where the boat will be taking off, and the nerves come through in full force when I see how tiny the boat we're going on is.

"Oh shit," I whimper.

"Are you okay, babe?" Leanne asks. She puts a hand on my arm. "Are you scared of boats?"

"It's not boats," I explain. "It's the ocean."

"Corey, we live by the ocean," she counters. "We go to the beach all the time."

"Yeah, but our feet barely touch the water. And I'm still standing." We like to occasionally go to the beach, and I'll dip my feet in, but my feet are still planted in the sand. If I can't feel the floor beneath me, I'm going to freak out.

"You know how to swim, right, mijo?" my dad asks. "We used to put you two in swimming lessons."

"Yeah, I know how to swim. Pools are fine. Pools, you can eventually swim and touch the floor. And they're man-made."

"What do you have against the fishies?" Leanne chimes in.

"Nothing," I sigh. "I'm just scared of the deep ocean. Like how far does it go down? Are there sharks?"

"Okay, well, you can stay on the boat," my mom says. "And make sure you keep your life jacket on."

"Oh, I'm making sure this won't leave my chest," I explain. With the ring burning a hole in my bag.

We make it onto the boat, and everyone bounces out of their seat except for me. Bryce's husband, Noah, and baby Amelia are hanging out on the beach during the trip, and I lowkey wish I had joined them. But I decided to put my big boy swim trunks on.

The waves on the ocean mildly propel us so we're bouncing a little bit atop the waves. It's like an amusement park ride. Leanne beckons me to sit with her at the front of the boat, but I cling onto the pole more and tell her I'm just going to admire the waves from here.

She shrugs and practically skips to a small area at the bow that they've deemed safe for sitting. I would give her the Titanic moment that I think she deserves, but I think I might need to be the one who's coddled.

We stop for our first snorkel area, and our guide tells us what kind of aquatic life we can find here. No swimming with the dolphins yet, but it's coming at stop number two.

After Leanne jumps in and does some swimming around, she beckons me to join her.

"Come on, babe," she begs. "It's really cool under there."

"I'm fine," I reply.

"Just this once? For me?"

I groan. The for me trick works this time, but I can't guarantee it's going to work again. "Fine."

I slowly step off the boat and let myself down into the water. I shudder a little bit when the cold touches my skin, but as I swim to join Leanne, I start to warm up a little.

Leanne shows me again how to put the snorkel on, and recommends to swim at the surface because then I can breathe using the air above us. I bend my head down and peer around at the small fish swimming below me and the coral that hangs out on the ground. Okay, I think I might have been psyching myself up for something that's not even that bad. This is actually really cool.

Leanne bobs her head up and I join her. "Cool, huh?"

"Yeah, I'll admit. It's pretty awesome."

"See? Not so bad. They wouldn't call this a beginner tour if you were going to be risking your life."

"Sure." I nod. "You're right."

I feel better enough that I decide I'm going to swim around a little more. Leanne's right, it is cool to see what life is underwater, and I smile to myself when I further explore what's down there.

That's where I make the mistake.

I knew at some point, I was going to get too cocky and then think that nothing is going to bother me, because as I swim farther away from the boat, excitedly following the path of fish, I come up for air and realize I'm alone.

I've deviated too far from the boat and my family, and I'm scared.

"Fuck," I whisper to myself.

"Corey!" Bryce calls out. "We're heading out soon!"

My legs suddenly feel like they're not able to move, but I frantically start flailing my arms and legs to swim back to the boat in hopes of subsiding the absolute panic I'm feeling. I feel like I'm Michael Phelps all of a sudden and quickly swim back to the boat, running up the steps and planting my ass back down on the seat, hyperventilating.

"Babe, are you okay?" Leanne asks.

"The ocean is way too big," I answer. "God, that was so scary. I'm staying right here."

"Here," Leanne says, reaching over to grab my bag, "Let me get you some water."

"Wait." My fears subside once I realize what Leanne's doing. "Babe, it's okay...I..."

But it's too late. Leanne's silent when she touches a small box in my bag.

"I didn't see anything!" she immediately answers. "I'm sorry, I didn't know...did I ruin something?"

She starts crying and I don't know if it's from excitement or fear, but I rush over to her and grab a hold of her arms as she's still touching the bag.

"No, no, babe, you didn't ruin anything." I guess there's no use hiding it. This wasn't the plan at all, but I guess our relationship hasn't gone to any specific plan either.

I ask the captain to give us a moment before we move so I can do something. He nods and I take the bag from Leanne and pull out the small box that grazed her fingers.

"I, um, had this great plan to do this while we were learning how to hula at the luau, but this has also been making me a nervous wreck ever since this trip started.

"Leanne Elizabeth Fairbanks, you make me so happy. I love every minute I spend with you, and want to make you mine forever, officially."

I get down on one knee on the slippery boat floor. Leanne gasps when I pull the box open and ask her the magic phrase: "Will you marry me?"

She nods and I slide the ring on her finger, take her in my arms and give her the biggest kiss to the crowd of my family whooping and hollering.

"I love you," I say, pressing my forehead to her.

"I love you too," she says back.

And that's all it took for me to forget we were in a boat in the middle of the ocean. And for me to tell Leanne to keep the ring off until we get back onto solid ground, or that ring may join the fishies as she's swimming around.

About the author

Brittany Arreguin (she/her) is a Mixed-Chinese American author from the San Francisco Bay Area. By day, she works in the hospitality industry coordinating events and during her free time, she loves to read romance novels and work on her next novel. She lives with her husband and two cats, and enjoys devouring Asian soups of all types.

a

amazon.com/author/brittanyarreguin

instagram.com/brittanyarreguinwrites

Acknowledgements

I can't believe that I am writing the acknowledgements on my third book, and I am so thankful for everyone who has been with me on this journey. This book, truly, may be my favorite book I have written, just because this book hits so close to home for me.

To Mario, my wonderful life partner, thank you for supporting me throughout this year since I have debuted my novel. You give me the motivation I don't think I deserve, and cheer me up when I have come so close to wanting to hang up my pen and quit. Your excitement over my work, the times that you tell random strangers that "your wife is an author" make me want to hide but I also deep down, love that someone supports me as much as you do. I love you so much and I am so excited for the future for us.

Also, shoutout to my amazing husband for helping me with my questions regarding Corey's Mexican heritage and family dynamic. I don't want to say I based this love story off of my own, but I won't not say that either, *wink wink*.

To everyone who made Fielded Dreams possible:

Madison, thank you for creating such a beautiful cover. I have been a fan of your work for a long time, and I think you captured the Fielded Dreams story so beautifully in its cover.

Cassidy, thank you for being an amazing editor and helping the book sound a lot better than my original rambles. You put me in place and teach me so much about my writing, and I always love working with you and cheering on your work.

Jessica Joyce, thank you for being an amazing author in the Bay Area. Your vocalness as an A's fan and your writing inspired me to write Fielded Dreams, because I just thought you would love a romance stemmed from a sport team so dear to us both. I'll read everything you write.

The Oakland Ballers, thank you for your work again in keeping baseball rooted in Oakland. Here's to another season of baseball in the Town.

Grandpa, thank you for instilling the love of baseball into me after all these years. You are greatly missed, and I hope you're smiling down on us, who still love baseball long since you passed twenty one years ago.

Thank you to the readers who have found my work and told me how much they love it and how it has affected their life. I never thought I would ever have fans, and the fact that I do blows me away. I hope that I can continue to create books that make you happy. Here's to the next one! x